# COLTON
# COUNTDOWN

---

## Tara Taylor Quinn

HARLEQUIN

ROMANTIC
SUSPENSE

Special thanks and acknowledgment are given to
Tara Taylor Quinn for her contribution to
The Coltons of Colorado miniseries.

Recycling programs
for this product may
not exist in your area.

ISBN-13: 978-1-335-75977-1

Colton Countdown

Copyright © 2022 by Harlequin Enterprises ULC

For questions and comments about the quality of this book, please contact us at CustomerService@Harlequin.com.

Harlequin Enterprises ULC
22 Adelaide St. West, 41st Floor
Toronto, Ontario M5H 4E3, Canada
www.Harlequin.com

**Printed in U.S.A.**

Having written over ninety novels, **Tara Taylor Quinn** is a *USA TODAY* bestselling author with more than seven million copies sold. She is known for delivering intense, emotional fiction. Tara is a past president of Romance Writers of America and a seven-time RITA® Award finalist. She has also appeared on TV across the country, including *CBS Sunday Morning*. She supports the National Domestic Violence Hotline. If you need help, please contact 1-800-799-7233.

### Books by Tara Taylor Quinn

### Harlequin Romantic Suspense

#### *The Coltons of Colorado*

*Colton Countdown*

#### *Where Secrets are Safe*

*Her Detective's Secret Intent*
*Shielded in the Shadows*
*Falling for His Suspect*

#### *The Coltons of Grave Gulch*

*Colton's Killer Pursuit*

#### *Colton 911: Grand Rapids*

*Colton 911: Family Defender*

#### *The Coltons of Mustang Valley*

*Colton's Lethal Reunion*

Visit the Author Profile page at Harlequin.com for more titles.

# Chapter 1

Ezra Colton's chin hit his chest and he jerked awake. Every muscle tensed, he quickly assessed his immediate danger level to be zero and relaxed back into the quite comfy-for-his-big-shoulders chair, in his great-aunt's lovely, homey room. Glancing across at the woman who'd been mostly dozing in a matching chair during the entirety of his afternoon visit, he noticed she was also awake and staring at him.

His smile was immediate, and he tried to shrug off her lack of response. His siblings, his mom, had all warned him that his aunt's memory loss had drastically worsened since he'd last been home. Still, fingers tapping on bare knees beneath the army-green shorts he'd pulled out of his duffel that morning, he couldn't accept that she didn't know him. At least a little bit.

"It's pretty hot outside," he offered, looking her right

in the eye. "People are grumbling a bit, but after being in Afghanistan, I'm fine with the heat. You remember that time I went tubing in the river without Mom and Dad's permission and ripped my swim trunks on that tree limb? I came straight to you. You had me change into some of Uncle's old shorts, and you fixed those trunks for me. And then told me to go home and tell my parents what I'd done."

Not a snippet of response. Of any kind of recognition, even.

But she was still looking straight at him. So he kept chatting until she dozed off again. Figured he needed to get his lumbering butt up and active. A month of leave could make a guy soft, and no way he was letting his men down. His sergeant stripes were way more than uniform decoration, and he'd die before dishonoring them.

Still…a few more minutes to relax… That was what leave was for, right?

What did it say about him that he was more relaxed hanging out in a room at the Sunshine Senior Home than with most of the siblings who'd all, for once, gathered in the same town at the same time for his big brother Caleb's wedding?

The home—at least, the wing where Aunt Alice's room was located—might be filled with memory-care patients, but there was order to the day, to the rooms and the patients who wandered in them. You knew what to expect and how to deal with it.

Unlike the chaos and drama that attached to his huge, well-known family like bees on honey. And sometimes stung like bees, too.

But…did sitting there make him a coward? He ran

a hand across the top of his close-cropped hair. Stood, stretching muscles that, while difficult to fit into some shirts, served him well, and glanced again at his great-aunt. When she was sleeping, she looked…as he remembered her. Like herself. The vacant stare when she was awake…

His mom had been right. He hadn't been prepared.

He should just go. It wasn't like she'd know—or remember that he'd been there. Still, she was Aunt Alice. He couldn't just walk out on her.

With a hand on the back of her chair, he bent to kiss her cheek like he'd done every time he'd left her since he was a little kid, moving slowly so he didn't startle her. And then, with a hard bump in the butt from behind, nearly fell over.

"What the…?" Swinging around, his first instinct to defend and protect, he had an arm half raised in front of him as he shielded his aunt with his body and had to drop his gaze to meet that of his attacker.

Big brown eyes gazed soulfully up at him from a mutt's tilted, light brown head. Before he could even drop his arm, a very young voice, in a place filled with old voices, called out, "Charlie!"

And two dark-haired urchins appeared in the doorway. "Charlie!" The girls, in identical sundresses and sandals, didn't even seem to notice him as they hurried straight to the errant dog. "We're really sorry, sir." The child with braids and holding a book spoke up. The other one, wearing her long straight hair down, patted Charlie on the head.

"He doesn't like it when someone claps at him, and he ran off," the bookless one of the two of them—and, he noted, the one without freckles as well—added to the first's apology.

With virtually zip experience around children—his little niece, Iris, didn't count because she was only a few months old, still just sleeping, eating and being held, and because with his career mostly out of the country, he'd only seen her, sleeping both times, in the few days he'd been home—Ezra was mesmerized by the pair, clearly sisters and most likely twins, until a slight movement caught the corner of his eye—and his attention.

Charlie had a paw on the edge of Aunt Alice's chair, and her hand moved to cover it. His gaze rose slowly from that gesture to his aunt's face, and he could hardly believe the small smile he saw there. He'd been there a couple of hours with no sign of life from the woman other than a blank stare, but Charlie had a response out of her in less than two minutes.

Bookless was reaching for the dog's collar.

"I'm a triplet," he blurted, grabbing her attention before she pulled the animal away. Even if the girls weren't twins, they were dressed alike as though someone wanted them to be. "And I have three sets of twins for brothers and sisters," he added, as though someone was adding up multiple birth values.

"We're twins," Bookless told him, her little fingers resting on her dog's neck. And not holding the collar. "We were born at the same time," she added.

"I'm Claire and she's Neve," the girl with braids told him. Her adorable freckles made him want to smile at her. And he might have if she hadn't worn such a serious expression. "We aren't supposed to be in here."

"We can't help it, Claire," Neve said, shrugging. "We had to get Charlie. Claire was reading to Mrs.

Sally and Mr. Bo, and I've heard the story a gazillion times—" she rolled her eyes "—but I like the part where Flow—that's the smaller horse who everyone thinks can't win—gets ahead of everyone else because she's trying harder—and I guess I forgot to hold Charlie's collar tight enough right when Mrs. Sally clapped for Flow and, well, what's a triplet?"

"It's three instead of two, Neve," Claire said. "We're two. Triplets is three. But—" she peered up at him, nose scrunched "—what's three twins?"

"Three sets of twins, right, mister?" Neve said. "And that's…" Letting go of Charlie, she held up the fingers on one hand, pointing with her other to individual fingers as she tried to count to two, three times.

"One, two, one, two, one, two," Claire butted in then, holding up a finger each time she named a one or a two, and then looking at the total of held-up fingers when she was done. "You have six twin brothers and sisters?"

"That's right." He nodded, noticing that Aunt Alice's hand was moving atop the paw still resting on her chair, as though Charlie knew that the lost old woman needed him.

"Six kids being born at once?" Neve burst out, her voice rising markedly by the end of the question.

"Just two at once," he said. "Remember, that's twins. Two born at once. They were born three different times, years apart."

"Is triplets years apart, too?" Claire asked.

"Nope," he told her, suddenly enjoying the moment of diversion more than he had anything else since getting off the plane in Denver. "It's three born at the same time."

"You have two more of you born at once?" Neve asked, giggling.

Thinking of Dom and Oliver, he couldn't in any way see his brothers as two more of him. He and his fellow triplets were very different guys. But he ended with, "Yep," because the girls seemed so delighted by the thought.

"Two against one," Claire said. "That's what sometimes happens if someone wants to play with Neve but not me. Is that what happened to you?"

"I always say you can play, Claire. You just sometimes want to read."

Not sure if he was still required to answer the question Claire had posed, but certain that he didn't want to do so, he asked her, "Are you the younger or older twin?"

"I'm younger," Claire said, her gaze serious.

"I'm her big sister by two minutes!" Neve chimed in, standing next to her sister to gaze up at him. "But I'm a little person. You sure are big," she said. "Almost like a giant."

"Are your other triplets as big as you?" Claire, full of questions, apparently, asked.

"My older triplet—" he used her word for him and his brothers "—is named Dom, and he's taller than me by one inch. And the younger one, his name's Oliver, is my same height, but he's a little skinnier than I am." Lean, Oliver was lean.

"Oliver?" Neve asked, her nose scrunching up as the lilt in her voice rose. And then she giggled. "He's a cat! And him and Jenny are together forever, just like Claire and me."

When Ezra stood there, his brain racing trying to figure out the reference, Claire said, "Did you ever watch *Oliver & Company*, mister?"

The Disney movie. Right. Had he ever seen it?

"You're like a sandwich." Neve popped back into the conversation, once again sparing him from Claire's question. "Smooshed in the middle of two more!" she pronounced, clearly pleased with herself. "A giant sandwich."

He followed the conversation, and also noticed something pretty cool going on apart from the girls. Aunt Alice's hand rose to Charlie's head, her fingers moving slightly. Wanting to prolong her enjoyment, and unable to come up with any interesting reply to a giant sandwich, he motioned toward the book that Claire had been hugging to her chest since they'd come in. "So your book's about a horse named Flow?"

She held it up, showing him the cover. *Flow Goes to the Races.* The title was in bold purple-and-pink lettering.

"I have a brother and sister, one of the pairs of the twins I told you about, who run a ranch, the Gemini, and they have horseback riding. Have you been there?"

The question gained him identical shakes of two little heads, in tandem. And while Neve stepped back beside Charlie's head again, Claire pointed to Aunt Alice. "You want me to read it to her?"

"Sure, if you want to," he said, as another movement caught his eye. This one from the doorway—a woman hovered there, just off to the side, mostly out of sight.

For the first time since the kids had appeared in his great-aunt's room, he wondered why two young girls were roaming freely through the halls of the memory-care unit.

And had a feeling he was about to find out.

And perhaps get chewed out as well, for engaging with them.

Figuring he'd much rather have it be him than them, he invited Claire to start reading and backed slowly toward the door.

She'd been made. Dealing with all the feels, Theresa Fitzgerald stepped farther back from the door, but not so far she couldn't still hear her daughter's sweet, so serious voice as she read her beloved story to the memory-care patient. She'd never have believed it was possible to love anyone as much as she loved her twins.

And she most certainly hadn't expected to be caught eavesdropping—by one of the gorgeous Coltons, no less. Embarrassment joined the flood, but there was so much more. Her girls…the ease in their tones, the innocent, unfiltered chattiness…

As she came down the hallway, the sounds had stopped her in her tracks.

She hadn't heard them talking like this since their father died…

Mark.

A year later, and she still lived with the gaping hole his death had left in their lives.

But the girls… She'd had to see who'd managed to elicit natural engagement with them…who'd had the ability to draw them out of whatever darkness had held them captive. Even if just for a moment…

"Are you…?" The man broke off, his gaze going to the badge she wore pinned just above her left breast. "Oh…you manage this place? I sincerely apologize here," he continued on, his blue eyes meeting hers with none of the complexity or veils she'd have assumed a Colton man would wear naturally. "I know I should have sent these girls out immediately, the second they came into the room to retrieve their runaway dog, but…" He glanced at her badge again. "Senior Care Manager?" he asked.

To which she nodded, intending to say more, but he said, "Then you know Alice," nodding at the scene playing out in the room. "Maybe you see this all the time, you know, if the dog is a regular or something, and Alice always responds this way. But from what my mom told me, my aunt is almost always little more than a breathing statue, showing no reaction or awareness at all, and she's smiling. Kind of petting him. I'm afraid I purposely kept the girls chatting so that the dog could stay a moment and…" He glanced down at his feet, showing her the top of his head, covered with shortly cropped light brown hair, before looking up at her once again.

The quick look shot a flame through her…one she hadn't felt since Mark got sick…shocking her so much she barely heard his next sentence: "Please apologize to whoever is in charge of them. I swear they weren't harmed…"

"I know they weren't. I've been standing here listening." She had to fess up. It was just her way. "Enjoying the conversation."

Claire's voice carried over to them, the words filled with the emotion of the story and yet a very distinct pause at the end of each sentence, too, as the little girl read, rather than recited, the book Theresa knew she had completely memorized. Neve, bless her energetic little heart, stood right there, listening, her little fingers on Charlie's collar, as though she hadn't done exactly the same, hearing exactly the same, far too many times to count over the past months.

"They bring Charlie to visit specific residents every Tuesday afternoon," she said, when there was so much more important information to glean in the minute or two she had. What had he done to draw them out?

Why him? What quality did he possess that had performed this small miracle for her daughters?

"And I'm sorry for eavesdropping, Mr. Colton."

"You know me?" the man asked, frowning. "I'm sorry, but I don't remember us ever meeting. Did we know each other in school?"

She shook her head. "No. Your mom talks about all of you, has shown me, and others, pictures of all of you…" But nothing had prepared her for this Colton in the flesh. If her girls hadn't been on the other side of that door, she'd have turned tail and run.

Or walked away as quickly as proper protocol and manners would allow.

"And…I know you're Ezra because you told the girls your triplet brothers are Dom and Oliver." There, could that be enough baring of her soul, please?

He was sorry. She was sorry.

And there they stood, with Claire pronouncing every single word, slowly and distinctly.

"I've not had much experience with kids, but they're a delight." Ezra Colton warmed her mother's heart that time. The woman heart, the mother's heart—what was the man trying to do to her?

"Thank you."

He looked at her. Back into the room. "They're yours?"

She'd taken for granted he'd known that. When he'd had no way of knowing. "They are," she told him. And then, with her heart so discombobulated, more came pouring out. "And I don't know what kind of magic you came bearing, but what you're seeing, well, not the reading, that's how it is every week, every visit. But the way the girls were talking to you, so open and friendly... It's just kind of sent me into a state of flux here."

He shook his head. Probably thinking her a blubbering person incapable of maintaining responsibility for an entire care home.

Not wanting to hear what he was thinking, she hurried forward with, "They've been... They haven't been comfortable around strangers since their dad died."

*And you want to know my slightly-larger-since-I-gave-birth pant size, too?*

"Their dad...your husband?"

Looking at the girls, not him, she nodded, embarrassed. "I can't believe I just laid that on you... I'm just..." Her chin trembled. That meant tears were imminent. Stiffening her shoulders, she continued, "I'm just glad to see them happy."

They were talking softly, standing so that Ezra Colton was the only one immediately visible to those in the room. She blamed her wayward tongue—and emotions—on the false intimacy their little tête-à-tête created.

"I'm...sorry. I had no idea." Ezra's soft tones seemed to carry a rare brand of tenderness, coming from such a muscled, imposing figure. "I've lost comrades, who were family to me. And—" he glanced toward the girls, who were nearing the end of their story "—like them, I lost my father at a young age."

She knew the story, of course. She'd been too young

to remember much more than hearing Ben Colton's name in the news, but pretty much everyone who'd been in Blue Larkspur for any length of time knew the story. And eventually heard how the revered justice had been taking bribes and sending wrongfully convicted individuals to prison. She'd even heard it said by an old-timer at the home that the car accident that took Ben's life had been a blessing…

She'd never figured a wife and children would find the loss of their loved one a good thing, though. No matter the wrong choices he'd made, Ben Colton had loved his wife and kids. Or so she'd heard.

"How old were you when he died?" she asked.

"Just turning sixteen."

Which made him, what, thirty-six? "You were ten years older than my girls are," she said aloud. "They were five when Mark died, but he'd been sick for a while before that."

They'd been through a lot, her twins, strong, sweet, and compassionate beyond their age.

Too much. She would not have any more of their childhood robbed from them—no matter what Mark's parents said or tried to do to her.

Claire's voice faded away. Neve slid her fingers under Charlie's collar. Ezra's great-aunt was dozing off, and he straightened, moving back into the room.

As always, Flow, against all odds, had won the race.

Stepping away from the wall, Theresa rounded the corner into the room, showing herself to her recalcitrant daughters with a smile, not a frown, and silently promised them that they were going to be winners, too.

Just like Flow.

# *Chapter 2*

$A$s soon as the twins saw their mother, they immediately made a beeline in her direction, Charlie and Flow book in tow. They were leaving. Shocked at the sudden onset of disappointment the realization begot within him, most particularly since he much preferred order to the chaos of kids, Ezra blurted out without forethought, "There's a big Colton summer barbecue coming up this weekend, on Saturday, at the Gemini Ranch. You all could come as my guests, and the girls could see the horses."

After one look at the shock on Theresa's face, followed by a frown, he saw his misstep. The twins jumped up and down and said, "Yay! Can we, Mom?" First Neve and then Claire, followed by a chorus of "Can we?" He'd never been a man to speak without thought. What had the visit to Sunshine Senior Home done to him?

"I'm sorry," he quickly backtracked. He'd never meant to put her in a precarious position, period, and most particularly not with her daughters. Possibly forcing her to disappoint them. "I should have checked with you first, asked whether or not you were working," he stumbled, words over thoughts, hoping he'd given her an easy out. She could say she had to work.

Who could argue with that?

Glancing from her daughters' expectant faces back to him, she smiled. And Ezra had to take a physical step back. The woman…the way her gaze, her grief, and probably recovery from grief, too, seemed to resonate with him… It was like he'd known her his whole life but just hadn't met her until now.

"If you're serious, then thank you. We'd very much like to be your guests. Can we bring anything?"

Had he just asked her out on a date?

Had she just accepted an invitation to go out with him?

Or were they just treating two young kids, who'd already lost a lot, to an outing that would bring great joy to them?

He had no answer to any of the three questions.

But as he arranged to pick her up Saturday afternoon, and actually thought about showing up to a Colton family function with a gorgeous widow and her two fatherless daughters in tow, he knew his family would assume he was on a date.

He didn't hate the idea as much as he'd assumed he would have, either.

Theresa listened to her girls chatter on about Ezra Colton as they walked back to her office, holding on to

Charlie while she shut down for the day. They walked with her and the leashed dog out to the parking lot and climbed into their booster seats and belts in the back seat, while she got Charlie settled in the passenger seat beside her. The twins were calling him Mr. Giant, though Theresa told them he was Mr. Colton, and they wanted to know if someone as big as him could ride a horse without hurting it.

She wondered if the man had some kind of potency potion. As much as the girls were talking about him, she'd been in her own thoughts thinking about the man. She'd never met any of the Coltons other than their mom, Isa, face-to-face—

Never met any men of the family, period.

The experience had her way hotter—in that way a woman got when she was near a guy who did it for her—than she had any business being. Hotter than she'd been since Mark had gotten sick.

She'd loved her husband. And even when he'd made her promise that she'd love again, she'd half wondered if she'd ever be able to feel sexual feelings for any other man.

Well, there were no more doubts on that score.

And now she had a date with him.

Of sorts.

Maybe.

She was less than a block from the senior home when she had a feeling that she was being followed. Not wanting to alarm the girls, she tried her best to act natural, while constantly checking both side and rearview mirrors for sign of a twenty-year-old, overlarge, four-door blue pickup truck. In mint condition.

Just because she couldn't see it towering behind her

didn't mean it wasn't there, though. Lurking at corners, waiting to see her pass, moving on to another intersection where her progress could be tracked.

Mark's parents, who'd never even met the children before his death, were determined to have rights to their grandchildren, to indoctrinate them, by any means necessary. Mark had been estranged from the doomsday preppers—children during the Cold War who still, decades later, felt that a nuclear blast was imminent—since before he'd met Theresa. He'd told her about the guns they'd been stockpiling since he was young, about the apocalyptic bunker they'd built out in the middle of nowhere in preparation for the nuclear attack they were sure was coming from somewhere. But after he'd died, they'd contacted her for visitation, talking about their grandparental rights to know their flesh and blood.

About Claire and Neve's right to know their father's family.

So many years had passed since Mark had first told her about their tendencies.

And they'd been shocked by their son's death, even though Mark had kept them at a distance while he was alive. Grieving as only parents could.

She'd insisted on mediation first. To make sure outside sources found them suitable to visit with the girls. And had eventually allowed a couple of playdates. Their first visit had been like a dream come true. Eric and Jennifer Fitzgerald had been overwhelmed with emotion—and devotion—for Mark's children. Had mourned their son's death. And been so utterly grateful to her.

To think she'd let them take the girls for even one afternoon playdate... She shuddered.

The night after that one and only unsupervised visit,

little Claire had come to her, asking about their plans if the blast came that night, wondering if she'd be safe to sleep in her bed through the night or could the end happen before morning. Neve had come home talking about the gases that were going to kill people and Claire had asked, the next time they'd filled up their car with gasoline, if they were all going to die...

No truck in sight at the next intersection, but having to keep her gaze on the road meant that she couldn't peruse every parking lot of every strip mall and store they passed. The truck could be lurking in any of them.

The Fitzgeralds had told her point-blank that they weren't going away.

Would they wait for just the right moment and T-bone her front end with just enough force to disable her, maybe denting her door shut, but leaving the girls unharmed behind her so that they could snatch them and run?

They'd been...upset...when she told them they couldn't see the twins again. She hadn't expected the threats that had followed. Nor had she ever in a million years thought that that old blue pickup would show up outside the elementary school. But the week before, it had been there. Had she not beat them to the pickup lane, would they have taken Claire and Neve and run with them?

Theresa shook her head.

She'd actually tried to talk to the Fitzgeralds, to get them to see that they were scaring the girls, but when they'd grown belligerent with her, calling her a horrible mother who wasn't preparing her children properly...

She'd had to cut them off. There'd been no other choice.

And they weren't respecting her wishes. Seeing them parked outside the girls' school...

Still, maybe she was being a bit paranoid, she acknowledged silently as she pulled onto their street and into the driveway of their little three-bedroom house that needed some work—including a new coat of paint. There was no sign of a big blue pickup anywhere around. The couple had said they'd been at the school, at a completely safe distance, just to get a glimpse of the twins. They loved them and missed them so much.

She'd had no concrete reason to call the police, in spite of her threat to get a restraining order taken out on them. Keeping weapons in a private bunker for personal safety in the event of a doomsday event was perfectly legal.

Their threats, to that point, had all been veiled enough that they could just seem like the result of grief and lonely desperation. And the mediator who'd interviewed the Fitzgeralds separately and together had found them to be sane and rational. They were both retired, but had held regular jobs, paid their bills on time.

Maybe she wasn't being followed at all.

Maybe she was feeling guilty—having the hots for a man who wasn't Mark. Feeling like she was being unfaithful to Mark's memory, and to any regard his parents held for her because their son had loved and married her—the fact that they'd never met her before his death had been his choice, not theirs.

Maybe she was overreacting to the entire day, she allowed. She watched the girls race each other to the door to see who could get inside first, never minding that neither of them could enter the premises until she was there with the key.

"Charlie, my boy, what did you get us into?" she asked the dog as, holding his leash, she waited for him to jump down from the car. "Of all the rooms to seek solace in, you had to choose the one bearing a gorgeous man?"

She'd just unlocked the door, hadn't even had a chance to follow the girls inside, when her phone rang.

Ezra Colton? Calling to cancel?

Or…just to further their acquaintance?

Heart pounding, she pulled the phone out of her pocket, checking the screen, wondering if she'd actually answer or not.

If she didn't, would he leave a message?

Did she want him to?

Her heart rate sped up even more when she read the number. Sped up and pounded harder, too.

She'd deleted the contact.

But knew the number.

It belonged to Eric Fitzgerald.

Theresa didn't pick up.

Ezra found his mom in the kitchen Wednesday morning. He'd looked for her when he'd come in the night before, but she'd either been out or already in bed. Isa out at night, without telling her visiting son where she'd be, brought questions to mind.

She'd been looking more than just polite, dancing with chief of police Theodore Lawson at his big brother Caleb's wedding. The eighty-one-year-old lawman might have some age on him, but Ezra had heard Naomi—his TV producer baby sister—call the chief a silver fox, and he couldn't deny the tall, charismatic man had the kind of aura that attracted attention from anyone around him.

Pouring himself a cup of coffee and landing his butt

on one of the white square bar stools at the kitchen island, Ezra didn't ask any of the questions he wanted to ask his mother about her personal life. He didn't want to scare her off from having one.

Pushing aside the tablet she'd been focused on, her finger moving with precision and flair as she chose virtual tools and colors to design on-screen, she smiled at him. Told him there was leftover breakfast casserole in the refrigerator.

He'd had it a couple of times already, appreciative of her effort, if not as fond of the result, and went for it again, while she continued to watch him, her mature, beautiful face beaming.

He could crash with siblings, or even get a hotel room when he came to town—which wasn't often—but Isa wanted him there. And so there he was.

The wedding and all…

"I met Theresa Fitzgerald yesterday," he said. "She seems quite fond of you."

"She's a sweet woman," his mother responded with a long look at him that put him a bit on edge. But she continued with, "She's been through some rough times… and those two little ones of hers. We've talked a few times about raising twins."

"You'd be the supreme authority on that one," he said and smiled at her. "If anyone could give tips, you could."

Isa shrugged. "I just told her to honor their individuality," she said, as though her contribution had been nothing, but Ezra figured there'd been more than that.

"I met the girls, too," he said.

She frowned, briefly, and then nodded. "Right, it was Tuesday. They're always there with the dog on Tuesday."

"Have they come in to see Aunt Alice before, then?"

Just because it had been a first for him, one that was still holding center court in his head, didn't mean the unexpected encounter had been all that much out of the ordinary for Theresa or her daughters.

"No. Didn't seem much point, since Aunt Alice is so unresponsive. Better that the residents who get true joy out of the visits be given the time slots."

He glanced up, midchew, swallowed and blurted, "But she did enjoy it, Mom! She smiled. Put her hand on Charlie's head. I saw her fingers moving like she was trying to pet him. She continued that way for most of the time little Claire read her story…"

Maybe the occasion had been momentous after all. And he wasn't merely losing his perspective on reality.

"Seriously?" Isa sat forward, her gaze intent. "She smiled?"

He nodded, thinking he should have pulled out a phone and snagged a picture. Wishing he'd had the mental wherewithal to do so.

The girls, and then their mother…their instant effect on him…was bothersome.

"And she reached her hand to touch him," he told her. "It wasn't like Charlie headbutted her for attention. He just had a paw on her chair and she touched that first."

Isa's teary but clearly happy smile was worth the monthlong visit home to a town he'd been happy to escape.

Knowing she was being overly cautious but bothered by Eric Fitzgerald's number showing up on her phone, Theresa took Wednesday as a work-from-home day. Her employer allowed her two days a week at home, but she mostly preferred to be on campus.

The girls grumbled about missing day camp. They wanted to swim.

She didn't want them in any other public space where their grandparents could just be hanging out, hoping for a glimpse of them.

Because she didn't believe that was all her in-laws had been doing. If they'd had the chance, they'd have taken her daughters. She'd bet money on it.

She just had no proof of anything criminal to report.

Nothing but hearsay—which wouldn't be enough for any kind of subpoena or warrant, and…

At five after twelve, normally the day-camp attendees' lunch break in the park, her phone rang.

Jennifer Fitzgerald.

She'd left a message.

Wanted to know if the girls were okay. Requested at least a text as reassurance that Claire and Neve weren't sick.

And Theresa knew…they'd been watching the park.

Looking for their chance.

Knew it and had no way to prove it. The only way she could get protection would be if they actually did more than talk and watch.

And then it would be too late.

# *Chapter 3*

With only a few days shaved off his month of leave, Ezra went against better judgment and headed back to the Sunshine Senior Home. He'd been fond of Aunt Alice while growing up. Had found at her house solace from the cacophony in a home with eleven siblings, many close in age.

He liked order. Aunt Alice had been orderly.

She'd also been unimpressed by Ben Colton's stature in the community or his wealth. She'd liked her niece's husband for the love he gave to his family.

And after the scandal, that hadn't changed. Ben had done very wrong things. The man had used his ill-gotten gains to pay for the best of the best for all of them.

Ezra had never needed the best things, though. He'd needed his father to be the hero he'd once thought him. Aunt Alice had helped him see, in part, that Ben hadn't been all bad. After Ben's arrest, the shame he'd brought to his wife and dozen kids, Ben had still cared for his family. On some level, that mattered.

In Alice's current state—even if she hadn't been sleeping soundly in bed that afternoon—she wasn't able to remember who Ezra was, let alone the lessons she'd taught him.

Or the familial love she'd bestowed upon him at a critical age.

Which was why Aunt Alice hadn't been his sole reason for visiting the home today. When he didn't see Theresa around, he found her office.

The door was locked. And an aide, seeing him standing there, offered the information that Mrs. Fitzgerald was working from home that day.

Since he'd been spotted lurking, he figured the only decent thing to do would be to stop by Theresa's place, to let her know he'd been looking. Just so she didn't hear about it through the grapevine and figure she had to seek him out to see what he'd wanted.

A stretch…but with just enough logic to have his rental Jeep pulling into her drive a few minutes after three. He had a legitimate reason to talk to her.

A phone call would have worked.

If he'd had her number.

He'd been so bowled over by his encounter with her and her girls that he'd failed to ask for basic information. Her address had been a matter of public record.

She hadn't invited him to call her.

She hadn't invited him to knock on her front door, either. The place needed paint. Though Ben's crimes hadn't left the family penniless, Ezra had painted a house or two to earn money the summer before his senior year in high school. If wealth had been the cause for his father's walk to the dark side, Ezra had figured he wanted no part of it.

He had a month to kill at home. Maybe, just like the work had helped him deal with being around family so much that summer, he could do a little painting over the next month, too. And help out a widowed mother in the process.

Lord knew, not a lot of people had helped out his widowed mother back in the day.

There was no hesitation in his knock on the door of the modest home. He had information, an activity invitation of sorts, and was eager to share it. He'd asked his younger brother for a favor—and the smirk Jasper had sent him, the slightly snarky comment about Ezra asking favors on a woman's behalf, had been well worth the chance to be the bearer of good news.

"Ezra?" The surprise in Theresa's voice as she pulled open the door was obvious. He didn't know her well enough to be able to tell if there was pleasure mixed in there as well. "I just had a call from Bonnie that you'd been by to see me."

The aide. He'd made the right choice, following up with her at home. Better that than have her wonder why he'd stopped to see her.

"I guess, in light of the fact that we have a barbecue to get to on Saturday, we should have exchanged phone numbers."

She came outside, pulling the door mostly closed behind her. Her hair was up in the same messy kind of bun she'd worn the day before. He noticed right away that he hadn't imagined the auburn glints in the dark strands.

"I apologize for the shorts and T-shirt," she told him.

"Since I'm working from home, and the girls wanted to go down to the river for lunch…" She shrugged.

Did she think he was on a business visit? He'd thought mention of the barbecue had made his intentions clear…

"Should I apologize for my shorts and sandals, then?" he shot back at her. Same basic attire he'd had on the day before. Different-color shorts and shirt.

And he'd changed his skivvies, too. Not that she'd have any cause for the information.

"I'm just not used to…a Colton, here? I…"

"I'm an enlisted army man," he told her. "Straight out of high school. You've got your master's degree in health management. I saw from the letters behind your name on your office door. I'm guessing that if anyone should feel lesser here, it would be me."

He had no idea who her parents had been or what kind of family she'd grown up in, but he'd bet everything he had that her father hadn't been headed for spending the rest of his life in prison before dying in a car crash.

"You're driving a luxury Jeep that could easily buy my old van four times over."

"It's a rental. And I don't vacation much."

They could go on. He grew up in a big house—was staying there with his mom.

"Just to be clear," he said, "I've already told my mother that I don't want any Colton money, which is really just whatever she's made in her graphic design business and from her investments. I'm never going to be a rich man. Wealth doesn't equal health and happiness, in my book."

The compassion that filled her expression about sent him to his knees.

What the hell…?

Before she could speak, and split him wide-open, he said, "I came by to tell you—and the girls—that I've made arrangements for them to have horseback rides on Saturday. It'll probably be best that they wear jeans, to protect their legs from saddle burn and horse-hair, and boots."

Somehow, he came off sounding all lord of the manor. Not him at all.

To defend against any pity she might have been about to bestow upon him.

He wasn't that guy, either. But... "My brother Jasper stopped by Mom's this morning, and I cleared it with him," he allowed. It wasn't his manor he was lording over.

"I don't want to impose," she said then, her eyes squinting somewhat in the afternoon sun. The brightness also gave them a glow he was pretty sure he was never going to forget.

The kindness that seemed to emanate naturally from the woman...

To a man who spent his life fighting enemies—always expecting bad guys to be lurking around every corner—she was...nice.

For a brief moment.

"You aren't imposing. The horses are going to need exercise. Jasper was actually glad for the chance to get new bodies up on them. I guess several of the buildings at the ranch experienced storm damage a while ago, and they have to close for repairs."

A fact that could have been financially difficult for Jasper and Aubrey, except that Naomi was going to be renting the ranch out for filming, so it had all worked out.

Sometimes, being from a big, dynamic family had its benefits.

"Well, then, the girls will be thrilled!" Theresa said. "And I'll let you tell them about it yourself, if you'd like."

He'd like to. And was suddenly loath to walk inside that home, too. To get in too deep. "It's hot out. Why don't we all go for ice cream? Unless it's too close to dinner?" There'd been strict rules in the Colton household—at least, according to his memory—about snacking too close to mealtime. Maybe because he'd always been the one trying to snag cookies before he had to contend with vegetables and other such things.

Her hesitation that time was unmistakable. She actually stepped back, and there was no sign of a smile, or even any welcome on her face.

She was a widow whose husband had been gone only a year. He totally got it.

"Just as friends," he quickly assured her. "I'm in town for a month, and then it's off to another assignment God knows where. I'm not making moves here. I just... felt good around you and your daughters yesterday and would like to ease your way for a second or two, if I can." He'd get to the painting offer later. A military man knew how to pick his battles. "Seriously, you'd be taking pity on me," he added, thinking about how he'd just eschewed the idea that she'd do so. And then he told her in all truthfulness, "You and Claire and Neve are much easier to be around than the pack of Coltons waiting to take their turns at grilling me and then giving their opinions as to my life choices..."

He loved them all. Would give his life for any of them.

And hated that they always tried to get up in his business. Like they knew better than him what was best.

The fact that their concern very likely stemmed from worry did ease the burden a bit.

But Coltons versus ice cream? The choice was a no-brainer.

Luckily, Theresa seemed to see the value in the choice as well. With one last glance at Ezra, she called the girls, and within minutes they were all bundled into his rented Jeep, car seats installed and seat belts fastened, and heading out to a little family-owned place he knew of not far from town that had been serving homemade ice cream since before he was born.

To anyone on the outside looking in, they probably looked like a real family.

A happy one.

Shaking his head at the thought, Ezra turned his mind to more important matters.

With a quick glance in the rearview mirror, he asked, "What flavor of ice cream is your favorite?"

And tried not to notice the sexy bare knees within hand's reach on the passenger seat beside him.

The girls just wanted chocolate; she could have told Ezra that. Didn't matter what kind of fancy, one-of-a-kind flavors the place made; they'd just want chocolate.

It was all she really wanted, too, but at his suggestion, she ordered a chocolate brownie concoction that he'd said was to die for, and...he was right. Ambrosia in the mouth. So much so that she hated to swallow a single bite.

Or maybe his smile was part of the reason she wanted that ice cream cone to last forever.

That and the easy way he had of talking to the twins. Like they were equals, not little girls, and yet seeming to stay on topic for a six-year-old.

Mostly, she noticed, he didn't look at them or speak to them as if he felt sorry for them. Or was in any way trying to compensate for their loss.

A change from everyone else who'd been around the girls over the past year.

Out of town, in a vehicle no one would recognize, at a place no one would ever expect her to be, she actually started to relax, to let herself believe, just for a moment, that she was on a real date and she could one day have the happy family they must appear to be to all those around them at the outside picnic tables and going in and out of the shop.

Right up until Claire said, "Grandpa said that we should wear our breathing helmets all the time when we're sitting outside around other people. 'Cause the explosion will happen when lots of people are gathered together. Is this lots of people, do you think?"

Neve shook her head. "No, Claire, this isn't that kind of lots of people. Is it, Mom? That kind is bunches and bunches like you could build a really, really tall people tower, one that could almost reach the sky, huh?"

"Remember, I told you, there isn't going to be an explosion," Theresa said with a twist in her gut, careful to look only at her girls—so they'd have her full attention and be better able to trust her words. But also because she suddenly wanted to look anyplace but at Ezra Colton.

So much for the real date.

Or ice cream lasting forever.

"But Grandpa said you're wrong about that," Claire

told her, solemn as ever as she licked her ice cream, a chocolate ring surrounding the edges of her lips.

Theresa didn't want any more ice cream. She wanted to snatch her girls and run. Far. Fast. Forever.

"When did Grandpa tell you that?" she had to ask—airing family problems in front of Ezra be damned. She'd explained about the explosion being a figment of their grandparents' imagination after she'd banned the Fitzgeralds from seeing her girls.

"You know," Neve said. "The other day ago when we were on our swing set."

In their gated backyard? The couple had been on her property?

"You were swishing the toilet," Claire piped up. "They said not to bother you and they'd come back another day."

The only time she'd had the twins out of sight had been when she'd been cleaning the bathroom. Otherwise, she'd had them in view from one window to the next as she'd cleaned the house. That had been Saturday.

Her in-laws could have taken the pair from their own backyard.

The fact that they hadn't didn't mean as much as she'd like to hope. They were planners. Investigating their options. Collecting information that they'd process well, allowing for every eventuality, before making their move.

Horror-struck, she could hardly pretend to enjoy the rest of the outing. She had to get home. The couple had been on her premises. Could that rank as rating a call to the police?

Would anyone listen to her fears?

Or merely find her as irrationally out of touch as she considered the older Fitzgeralds?

They'd merely say they'd been by to visit her, that the girls had been outside, they'd asked for her, the girls had said she was busy, they'd said they'd come back…

She heard the mental play-by-play with a sinking feeling of helplessness and dread.

Tried to keep up with the chatter going on between Ezra and her daughters.

And had never felt more alone in her life.

# Chapter 4

The girls wanted to show Ezra their swing set. There was nowhere else he had to be.

Nowhere else he wanted to be, either. He'd never hung out with a woman with kids before and was finding the experience enlightening.

Children, their innocence, their lack of conversation filters, brought life to a different level.

He wasn't opposed to hanging out on the level for a second or two.

His sister Rachel had recently become a mother. Isa's first grandchild. Ezra had just met little Iris for the first time recently. Maybe that was why he was suddenly noticing a part of life he'd heretofore ignored.

With one hand on each of the two little backs, he pushed both girls in tandem on their swings. Then he watched them take turns sliding down the slide in all kinds of contortions, meant, he was sure, to impress him.

Truth was, the two feisty little beings did impress him. As did their mother, who was a lot quieter than she'd been at the beginning of their outing.

He was pretty sure he knew why, and wasn't leaving until he had a chance to make sure she and the girls were okay.

Whether she sensed his intention or not, Ezra didn't know, but when the twins tired of outdoor play and asked if they could go watch *Frozen*, she didn't even pretend that she might follow right behind them. Unlocking the door for them, she stayed outside on the stoop with Ezra.

Leaning a hand against the small porch support, he said, "I have to ask."

"I don't have to answer."

"No. But I spend my life fighting bad guys to protect my country and all of her citizens," he said, deadly serious. "That includes you and your daughters. What explosion? What helmets?"

She said nothing.

And she didn't leave, either, when she could so easily have escaped into her home.

"I thought, at first, that it was just some kind of game the girls played with their grandparents, but your reaction... When you heard they'd been in your backyard, you went white. And haven't been the same since."

That time she nodded.

"Are they your parents or their father's?"

"I never knew my parents."

Filled with a ton of new questions, all about her,

Ezra waited. And knew that that conversation wasn't any of his business.

Obviously Theresa felt the same as she continued, "Mark was estranged from his folks." A small peek into what he knew was going to be something bad.

He needed to know how bad.

And even with that, the way she said the man's name… Mark…the familiarity and warmth, stung him. With jealousy. He was jealous of a dead man.

But welcomed the needed reminder that Theresa was a grieving widow.

"They're extremists," she said. "Irrationally obsessed with the belief that there's going to be a nuclear attack that's going to wipe out anyone who isn't prepared. Mark walked away, refusing to have anything more to do with them when they started talking about giving some guy tens of thousands of dollars to build them a bunker somewhere. He said they hoarded everything from medical supplies and food, to guns and ammunition. But that was nearly fifteen years ago."

He straightened, every hackle he owned standing on end, as she continued. "After Mark died, they contacted me, expressing deep grief at their loss of him before they could make amends. Asking to see the girls."

Appealing to her compassionate, motherly heart. He gritted his teeth. Remained silent.

"At first I refused, but then they started talking about grandparents' rights. In Colorado—and elsewhere, I've discovered—grandparents have the right to visitation if their son or daughter who parented the child has died."

"No way the courts would give irrational theorists visitation rights." The words tore through him, and out. He wished he could have been a sounding board back then, even though he had been on the other side of the world and hadn't known her.

To offer advice, or use his connections to get her help, if need be.

There was no room in either of their lives, or time, for him to be getting emotionally involved, he reminded himself. Not with her, her children, or her situation.

"They seemed to be over all of that. They were so rational on the phone, and in letters…"

It took all Ezra had not to grab her and the girls up and take them to his mom's house.

"I didn't want to take a chance on the court ruling in their favor, so I suggested that instead of forcing them to file for rights, I'd agree to visitation willingly, as long as we all went through professional mediation first. Which we did." She glanced behind her, and then back up at him. "They appeared to the mediator and social services specialist to be caring, rational people. So I introduced them to the girls. We met for lunch, that kind of thing. Eventually I let them take the girls for a playdate, following the guidelines we'd all established. They couldn't take the girls for more than two hours, they had to have cell phone access at all times, and they couldn't leave the Blue Larkspur city limits."

That sounded reasonable to him.

"So they had a right to be here on Saturday? Looking for you?"

Had he so grossly overreacted?

He wanted to believe he had, but his gut—and Theresa's reaction to her daughters' news—told him different.

She shook her head, and he asked, "When did things start going wrong?"

"After the first playdate. Claire was afraid to go to bed in case the blast came while she was asleep." She hugged herself with both arms, her brow creased beneath the few loose strands of long dark hair that had escaped from her off-center bun.

"I tried to talk to them, to explain they were hurting the girls, but they got belligerent, told me I was going to send the twins to their death, too, along with Mark. I ended up telling them they couldn't see the twins anymore. They said they'd sue for rights, and I threatened to get a restraining order against them, testifying about their bunker filled with guns and ammunition. I was so upset I just blurted that out, going only from what Mark had said, but it seemed to work." Her brown eyes wide and imploring, she seemed to be asking him for something.

He wasn't sure what, but knew he wanted to give it to her, whatever it was. Knew, too, that he was in no position to allow this woman to rely on him for more than a few fun outings.

Not only was he army all the way, and leaving as soon as he got his next assignment, but he most definitely wasn't a family man. Any of his siblings could vouch for that one. While most of them had stayed local after their father's duplicity was exposed, devoting their lives to making up to the community for their father's sins, Ezra had split.

Along with Dom and Oliver.

"And then on Friday, I saw them parked down from the girls' school. And now I hear they were here, at my house, on Saturday?" She shook her head. "They're making me as paranoid as they are…building up this whole conspiracy theory that they're watching everything we do, investigating the best place and time to take the girls and hide them away in their bunker for the rest of their lives, indoctrinating them until they won't be able to think straight, either."

Maybe she was a little bit right about being paranoid. Her theory, while understandable, was a bit far-fetched. And yet he understood it, too, which meant he couldn't completely discount it.

"Have they tried to get in touch with you directly?"

She nodded. "They called yesterday and then again earlier today. They left a message."

He asked to hear the message.

She played it for him.

The expression of concern seemed completely appropriate, given that their son had died and they were clinging to what was left of him. He told her so.

She nodded again. "I know. I was telling myself to calm down, but now I hear that Eric told the girls I was wrong about there being no imminent nuclear blast?"

Yeah, he didn't like that, either. But the Fitzgeralds had left the kids alone as soon as they knew Theresa was busy. Maybe they'd come to the front door, to try to work something out with her, and, after their knock went unanswered, they heard the twins in the back and hoped to find Theresa there?

"Have they threatened to take your daughters?" he asked. Families, as much as a pain in the butt as they could be sometimes, were also sacred. Grandparents wanting to be a part of their grandkids' lives was understandable.

"No. Just to go to court for visitation rights until I threatened to counter the motion with the request for a restraining order. That's how Mark got rid of them in the past. They never bothered him again after that. He said that they'd feared losing their bunker and their stash more than they'd loved him."

"That's somewhat comforting," Ezra said slowly. "Did you get the feeling, when you made the threat, that it still carried the same weight?"

"I did until recently." She shook her head, and he waited for the bun to topple. It didn't. And neither would she, he realized. "I'm probably just overreacting."

He mostly agreed with her. "Probably," he offered. "But just to be safe, do you mind if I put a word in with the chief of police?"

"You know the chief of police?" she asked, then shook her head one more time. "Of course you do."

Ezra let the comment go. "Do I have your permission to speak to him?"

"Of course. Yes!" And then, after a glance that seemed almost shy, she said, "Thank you."

And suddenly there he was, standing there wanting to kiss her.

Backing away, he confirmed the time he'd pick her up on Saturday and told her he'd see her later.

No kissing. As far as anything intimately personal went, Theresa was off-limits.

As soon as he'd switched back the car seats and was headed down the street, he put in a call to Chief Lawson, the man who'd been dancing so closely with his mother at his brother's wedding. He didn't mention Isa, though. And was grateful when the top lawman said he'd see what he could find out about Eric and Jennifer Fitzgerald.

Talking with Ezra had helped. Theresa stretched out in the tub in the bathroom attached to her bedroom, let-

ting the bubbles soothe her as she listened to a popular
New Age album and watched the candlelight flicker
against the walls.

She and the girls had had a fun night—baking cookies and using the new markers she'd bought them to
draw on the whiteboard she'd mounted in the playroom
the previous weekend, with one of their favorite ani-
mated films playing in the background. It had been
the most just plain fun she'd had with them since Mark
had died.

It wasn't because of spending time with Ezra earlier
in the day personally. He hadn't done anything anyone
else couldn't have done—just talking to another adult
about her concerns regarding the Fitzgeralds had helped
her step outside the situation and see how large it had
loomed in her imagination.

Consuming her.

Instead of being a victim, she was drinking a glass of
white wine and remembering how to relax. Pampering
herself in the attempt. She hadn't done that since Mark's
death, either.

She wasn't going to think about that. Or the past year's
worth of struggle. She was there to grab a few minutes
of good feels and...

Her phone rang.

And her stomach sank.

Grabbing the cell off the counter, wet hand and all, she
wouldn't let the dread seep through her veins. Wouldn't...

It wasn't the Fitzgeralds.

It was Ezra Colton.

She answered before she could stop herself. And except for her head and the hand holding her phone, she

promptly slid down to hide her nakedness beneath the bubbles.

"Is it too late to call?" he asked, leaving her wondering if she'd sounded sleepy.

As long as she hadn't come across as aroused, she didn't care. "No. The girls go to bed at eight, and I was just settling down for a few minutes to myself…"

"I won't keep you, then," he said. "I just wanted to let you know that Chief Lawson is going to check into the Fitzgeralds for you. If nothing else, this will put them on police radar."

Okay, now the relief was because of him personally. Him and his Colton contacts. "Thank you."

"I also talked to an old buddy of mine and was wondering how you'd feel about having your house painted."

Jolting up so fast water sluiced around her, over the sides of the tub, splashing onto the floor, Theresa sat there barely holding the phone. Mouth gaping.

The house needed several repairs, but the paint… It was the most crucial. If she didn't get it done, there were going to be structural issues. And it was the most expensive thing, so the farthest down on her budget, too.

How did you tell a man that you couldn't afford to keep up your modest little home?

Like a strong woman, that was how. "I can't afford to have my house painted."

She worked hard, but with Mark's lingering illness, there'd been so many medical bills. Things insurance didn't cover. And his modest life insurance policy hadn't done so, either. Another year and she'd be out of debt. Just one more year…

"I'm offering to do it for free," he told her. "I painted houses when I was in high school—it was my way of working my way out of the mess of crap my father had landed us in—and I just ran into this buddy I painted with. I mentioned to him that I might have a job he could help with, and he said he'd like to get back up on a ladder, too. Give us a chance to catch up."

"I cannot let you paint my house for free."

"You just said you can't afford to pay for it."

"I can't."

"So I'm hoping you'll reconsider and let us do it for free. I've got three weeks left in town, and I'm going friggin' bonkers just hanging around Mom's place, a sitting duck for whichever Colton wants to stop in and save me from myself."

"I'd think your family would be proud of you—the job you do."

A dangerous job. One she didn't want to think about.

"Maybe. They'd be happier, though, if I came home and painted houses."

After holding her breath for a second, Theresa slowly let it out. Reminded herself of her recent foray into letting her imagination run away with her. But then she asked, "Is there a chance you'd consider that?"

"Not one in hell," he said. "But since I've committed to being here, and I'm already buzzing with claustrophobia, I'd appreciate it if you'd let me help you out. It's what the Coltons do, helping others, so no one will give me a hard time about being busy."

"And your friend? He has nothing better to do, either? Or does he have a family he needs to escape, too?"

"Nope. He's a cop with a wife, two kids and a full schedule, but he wanted us to get together on Friday, and I told him painting was the only way."

"I don't…"

"He was actually kind of happy about the idea," he said. "For some of the same reasons. No grief, and an excuse to hang out…"

"Well…then…" She couldn't believe she was actually considering it. The thought of having the huge worry off her mind was so tempting, and…

"I'm taking that as a yes," Ezra said. "I'll come by tomorrow to get started. Don't call if you change your mind," he added, and while there was no laughter in his tone, she could tell he was teasing her.

"You're a good man, Ezra Colton," she said softly, suddenly more aware of her nudity than she'd been in years.

"Nah, I'm just not a vacationing type of guy, so hovering on the desperate spectrum."

She believed that, too, but his words didn't negate her opinion of him at all. To the contrary, every time he opened his mouth, she was moved more.

He talked about paint finishes, and then brands, asked about colors, and hung up as though he was no more than her hired help.

Who was working for free.

As she sat there in the cooling water, staring at her phone, she had to strictly remind herself that no matter how wonderful Ezra might seem in the moment—how wonderful he might be, period—he wasn't wonderful for *her*. Not only was he only in town—a town he clearly didn't want to be in—for just a month, but his job was super dangerous. She'd already lost her heart to one man who'd died.

She couldn't go through it again.

Nor could she risk her girls getting too fond of him and having their hearts broken.

Period.

He was going to be around. The kids would be outside playing at least some of the time. She and Ezra were
bound to run into each other—more than just an afternoon at a barbecue as she'd originally thought.

She'd have a talk with them in the morning. Make
certain that they understood Ezra was only a visitor in
their lives; he was not even going to be around long
enough to be a friend. They had to get that Ezra needed
and wanted it that way.

And Theresa had to accept that while her body had
chosen that particular inopportune time to come back
to life, Ezra was not the man to engage with in that
way. She'd promised Mark that she'd seek out happiness again.

Giving any part of herself to a career soldier who
lived for dangerous assignments was not an option.

# Chapter 5

Up at the crack of dawn on Thursday, Ezra did some cardio and was at the paint store when it opened. As small as Theresa's house was, and with help, he'd have it done before the barbecue. He'd hoped to get to her place before she left—for no real good reason—but no one was home when he arrived.

Considering their conversation the day before, and the fact that he hadn't yet heard back from Lawson, he called her cell just to make certain everything was okay. He heard that the twins were at day camp—an indoor pool and gymnastics day—with strict instructions to counselors that Claire and Neve were not to go outside for any reason. Just a precaution. Probably unnecessary, but one of which he wholly approved.

And then he told her, "I'll be at your place all day, up on a ladder for most of it, and will keep an eye out in the area." Enemy surveillance was what he did. He hoped there was no threat.

But when it came to irrational theorists, trust was just plain stupid. Unrequited love, even in grandparental form, was an aggravator.

He was probably just a soldier with too much time on his hands and looking for trouble where it didn't exist—but looking didn't hurt anyone.

As it turned out, the day passed uneventfully, if you didn't consider the peacefulness, the completely unexpected relaxation that slowly settled upon Ezra as he first scraped where necessary, and then rolled and brushed, rolled and brushed. How weird was it that he actually had fun moving his rented ladder around the outside of Theresa's house?

The physical exertion helped, too. He'd learned long ago that the best way to keep himself mentally alert and healthy was to exercise his body, expending energy before it built like nerve bombs inside him.

And though he might have hoped to see Theresa and the girls at the end of the day, he had to take off before they showed up.

After a quick shower, pulling on jeans and a gray T-shirt, he called her again, on his way to meet his fellow triplets for a bit of letting loose at The Corner Pocket, before Oliver left the next day. And he ended up sitting in his car for a couple of minutes after he'd pulled in, looking at the riverfront and listening to Neve tell him about hanging on rings that day and having bumps in her arms just like him—muscles, he realized. Theresa apologized for her six-year-old's insistence that she had to tell him something and took the phone back the second Neve was done, leaving him no chance to respond to the remark.

Rescuing him was more like it. What did you say to something like that?

But he was smiling as he walked into the English-feeling pub, turning right to head straight for the billiards, finding his brothers—Dom with somewhat shaggy blond hair, and Oliver with his slicked-back blond hair and lean runner's look. Both wore jeans and stood at their favorite pool table in the back, balls racked, three beers already on a small high-top close by.

"Uh-oh." Dom was wearing a knowing grin as he nodded.

Seriously? "What?" Ezra's tone had a bit of an edge. He was going to take Colton crap from his own triplet sibling now?

"Nothing, just know that look."

"What look?"

"The 'a woman I know is making me smile' look." He glanced at Oliver, who gave a bit of a cynical shrug.

"Whatever, dude, you break." Ezra took a long cool swallow of beer and decided to whip Dom's butt at the table. Winning was always a toss-up between the three of them, but Dom had just given Ezra a reason to want it more.

After an hour of daring each other, taking foolish, behind-the-back shots, acting like they thought they were pros, Ezra had met his goal, thrice over.

Clearly, Dom had his head still too filled with thoughts of Sami, his newfound life love, to fully concentrate and had come in last all three times.

Ezra, who was starving by that point, told him he had to buy food. Dom obliged, bringing a huge tray of unhealthy and delicious bar munchies back to the table. Cue sticks resting up against their small high-top, with balls already racked and ready on the table, they leaned butts to stools and dug in. Except that Oliver was keeping up appearances with a wing in his hand, rather than gorging himself as usual.

"What's up?" Ezra asked, as Dom looked at the wing and raised an eyebrow.

With a shrug, and an odd look of…feeling…Oliver took a bite, and then another, put the wing down and said, "I had dinner before I came."

"Let me guess—at the Atria," Dom said.

To which Ezra frowned, looking between the two of them. "What gives?" he asked.

"A certain waitress is working in her family's restaurant," Dom said, then ate half a potato skin in one bite.

Ezra's gaze shot to his clearly-cynical-about-women financial wizard brother. "Seriously?"

"It's nothing," Oliver said, swigging from his beer like he did it all day, every day. And that was the end of that.

"You notice Mom dancing with Chief Lawson at the wedding?" Dom asked then, obviously reading, as Ezra had, their brother's lack of amusement regarding the waitress.

"I noticed."

"I actually called the chief yesterday," Ezra told them, though he maintained Theresa's privacy on the issue. "Had him check into something private, unrelated to any of us, that I kind of walked into at the Sunshine Senior Home the other day."

"I don't want him pressuring Mom," Dom said. "I'm keeping my eye on things."

"She didn't look unhappy," Ezra admitted, but he was glad to know that Dom, who lived in Denver, would be around.

"She needs to sell that house," Oliver piped up, helping himself to a jalapeño popper. "It's too big."

Ezra nodded. "I just talked to her about it this morning. She's hanging on to it because it's where we all grew up, but there's no way we're all twelve going to be staying with her at the same time, not with some of us having places here in town. It just doesn't make sense for her to be rambling alone in all that space so much of the time."

"Agreed." Dom said the word. All three of them were nodding in unison. "I hear you kind of walked into something else at the Sunshine Senior Home," Dom continued then. "Or should I say some*one*?"

Ezra shook his head. He wasn't getting into that.

"Who?" Oliver, looking between the two of them, appeared completely interested all of a sudden, until Dom filled him in on Ezra inviting a widow and her twin daughters to the Colton barbecue on Saturday. "Taking up with a widow with kids? That's not like you, man," Oliver said then, holding his beer in both hands, his expression concerned. "You can't just have a quick fling with a family. What happens to them when you leave in a few weeks?"

Dom was clearly waiting for an answer as well— which was probably why his brother had brought up Theresa to begin with.

"Cool it, guys." He gave them each a stern, I'm-not-fooling-around look. "Theresa's still grieving her ex-husband and isn't interested in dating. She made that very clear. The barbecue is a chance for the girls to be at the ranch and ride horses, that's all. Just something nice."

And when they heard, as they surely would from some family member or another, that he was painting the widow's house? "Anyway, did you hear about Naomi filming some reality TV thing at the Gemini this summer?" he asked to change the subject. "Can you believe the baby is really a TV producer?"

"Here's to the Coltons making good," Oliver said, raising his beer mug.

Dom and Ezra clinked heartily, ate a bit more and got back to the real feature of the evening. Finding out which one of them most had his eye on the ball that evening.

Ezra needed it to be him.

He had to know that Theresa Fitzgerald, her daughters and their problems were only ships passing in the night. They were not personally meaningful to him and absorbing his focus.

Theresa waited until the kids' bedtime to have a "talk." She'd been thinking about it on and off all day, wondering if, like with the Fitzgeralds, she was over-reacting to Ezra Colton's effect on the girls. Seeing more than was there about the potential for heartache that an association with Ezra Colton would bring her girls. He was only in town for another three weeks or so. How attached could they really get in that time?

But when Neve had started to cry earlier that evening when Theresa had been ready to hang up without giving the six-year-old a chance to tell Ezra about her newly discovered arm bumps, and Claire had corrected her that they were *muscles*, with a bit of an attitude, after looking sad that she hadn't had a chance to talk to Ezra, either, Theresa knew an Ezra conversation had to happen.

The only way she could allow any further interaction with the man at all—including Saturday's scheduled barbecue and horseback riding—was if the twins understood, clearly, that they were not making a new friend for life.

"Remember when we went on vacation right before Daddy got sick?" she asked them as, snuggled in their double bed in the room they shared, they both lay, heads on their pillows, looking up at her.

"Yeah, we went to Disney World, and I peed my pants," Neve said, giggling. They'd had to wait in line for a couple of hours, and though Theresa and Mark had continually questioned the girls regarding their bathroom needs, they'd both shaken their heads every time they were asked. That was, until right before they boarded the boat that would take them on a ride through a tunnel into a world of fantasy, song and color. Neve said she had to go. But when told that they'd have to get out of line, she'd insisted she could hold it.

And, of course, the excitement of seeing the magnificent, larger-than-life moving figures, and hearing the music, the boat ride, had been too much for her...

The memory of the girls enjoying the ride, even with the peeing, was sweet. But not where she could hang out at that moment.

"You remember the princess you had lunch with?"

"She was so pretty!" Neve said.

"I liked her hair," Claire added, nodding, her young eyes bearing a bit of her sister's sparkle.

"Remember how she was ours just for a little while

and then we had to go away and we'd never see her
again?"

"Yeah, and remember her lips? They were so red,
even when she drinked," Neve continued.

Okay, this probably wasn't the best analogy.

"Our time with the princess is like our time with Mr.
Colton," she pressed on.

"Mr. Giant's not a princess!" Neve giggled.

"Shhh, Neve, you should call him Mr. Colton 'less
you make a mistake and say that in front of him, right,
Mom?" Claire, her hair still in braids and brown eyes
big, was looking at Theresa for support.

"Right, but it's not going to matter what we call him
for long, because he can't be our friend forever. He's
just like the princess having lunch with us, and then
he will be gone."

"You said he was the one who made the front part
of the house so pretty, Mom," Claire replied. "And he's
taking us horseback riding. That's way more than lunch
with the princess was."

"Yeah, horseback riding," Neve repeated, nodding.
Her loose, long dark strands lay like a halo around her
on the pillow, and Theresa had to hold back tears.

God, she loved them so much.

"You're right," she acknowledged, refusing to give
up. "It's more than just eating one lunch with someone,
but the going-away-forever part is exactly the same as
what happened with the princess. Mr. Colton is only in
Blue Larkspur for a vacation, like the time we were in
Disney World, and then he has a home and a job that
he will go back to."

She didn't actually know about the home part. Isa
had said Ezra traveled all the time. From one assign-

ment to the next. She'd never mentioned Ezra having a home base. But surely he at least had permanent barracks someplace where he kept whatever personal stuff he had. Or an apartment.

For all she knew, he could have a girlfriend tucked away there, too.

"He's going away like Daddy did?" Neve asked, frowning.

Life shouldn't be so complicated—not at six.

"Sort of," she told them. "He will still be living, like the princess is, but he'll be too far away for us to likely ever see him."

"Why?" Neve asked.

"Because his job is far away, and he's very good at it."

"People have to work their jobs to earn money," Claire announced to the room in general.

"That's right."

"Why can't his job be here?" Neve asked then, no hint of levity in her tone this time.

"Because he works for our country, Neve, and has to go where the president sends him. He keeps the whole United States safe, like our policemen here keep us safe." She was winging it, and not doing a very good job. Had no idea if the girls would get the concept of a much bigger world, of which Blue Larkspur was a part.

Not sure she wanted them to, at this age.

"Is the president nice to him?" Claire wanted to know.

"Very," she said, but then had to be clearer because she and Mark had determined, when he'd gotten sick, that they'd always be honest with their girls. "The president doesn't actually know Mr. Colton to talk to him, but he sends the thousands of people who do jobs like Mr. Colton all over the world."

Neve yawned, and Theresa took that as her cue to kiss the girls' cheeks one more time, tell them she loved them, wish them sweet dreams and head for the door.

"Mom?"

Claire's voice called her back.

"Yeah?"

"Can we talk to Mr. Colton the whole time he's here on vacation?"

"We'll see. Now, go to sleep. We have to be up early in the morning." Disappointed in her total cop-out response, she flipped the switch in the hall, plunging herself into near darkness, heading toward her room.

A flash of light caught her eye through the door of the playroom, from the street outside the window. Heart pounding, she moved along the wall to get a better look, and she relaxed when she noticed the police car passing through the neighborhood.

If she wasn't careful, she was going to be jumping at her own shadow like some kind of helpless woman.

And helpless she was not.

She couldn't afford to be.

On her way to a full-out pull-on-your-big-girl-panties talk, her mental tirade was interrupted by the sound of a text coming through on her phone. She bet it was from Eric and Jennifer; she hadn't thanked them for the box of the twins' favorite cookies that had been waiting for them when they got home. Sent via a respected and well-known shipping courier, not delivered in person.

Jennifer trying to be a grandma without disrespecting Theresa's wishes.

The text was from Ezra, wanting to know if she'd be

up in an hour or so. He was with his brothers but would like to speak with her that night if he could.

No way she'd be going to sleep after that—not that she'd intended to go to bed anytime soon, at any rate. She'd brought work home with her—accounts to go over—and was too het up to sleep.

She texted back a simple Yes and then pretended that she wasn't feeling a new burst of energy coursing through her as she watched the clock, waiting for the hour to pass.

He probably just had a question about the house, the paint job he'd be working on again the following day. Maybe he'd found some dry rot and she'd have a bigger problem on her hands than getting through a couple of weeks without throwing herself at a visiting soldier.

Maybe he had another function he wanted her to attend. With just her. Like a date.

Her stomach flipped at the thought. And then flopped.

She prepared herself.

If Ezra asked her out again, she had no choice but to tell him no.

# Chapter 6

"I'm sorry to be calling so late," Ezra said as soon as Theresa picked up the phone. Sitting in his car in the parking lot of The Corner Pocket, he'd dialed her as soon as he'd seen the taillights of both of his brothers' cars turn out of sight. "Oliver's leaving tomorrow to head back to Malaysia…" he started in, then stopped, Oliver's words ringing in his mind. *What happens to them when you leave in a few weeks?*

A question followed by his own… Even if he wasn't leaving for good, or she was willing to be hooked up with a career soldier, he worked a dangerous job. How could he ever ask a woman who'd already buried one love prematurely, or those precious little ones who'd suffered far too much in their young lives, to chance their hearts with a man who faced the possibility of death as a regular part of his job?

His personal business was no concern of hers...

"No, no, it's fine." Theresa's tone sounded stilted—because it was coming over the car's audio system? Or because she wasn't "fine" with him calling so late?

Which brought him back to business.

"I heard from Chief Lawson," he jumped right in. "He didn't find any immediate cause for worry. There are no police reports on the Fitzgeralds, period, anywhere in the state. Not even a speeding ticket for either one of them. If they own a bunker, that's not something that would show up, but a surprising number of government officials have them, too. He found nothing at all that could lead to any sign of criminal behavior. But he didn't like what I told him you'd said, and so, just to be safe, he's putting extra patrol around your home, the day camp and the nursing home."

It was overkill, and he knew it. He also knew that he was probably getting special treatment because he was Isa's son. He didn't care why. He'd use whatever influence he had if it meant keeping a widow and her two daughters safe. Any widow.

"I had a package at the house today."

He started his Jeep and put it in Reverse with one hand, ready to back up and get to her house. "You didn't open it yet, did you? Why didn't you call sooner? That's the kind of thing that warrants..." He'd made it out of the parking spot, and with the Jeep in Drive, foot on the gas, he shot forward.

"I opened it," she interrupted. "It was just Jennifer's homemade chocolate chip cookies. Mark used to talk about them. And every time they saw the girls, both with me and that one time alone, she sent some home."

He still didn't like it. He turned toward her part of town—the opposite direction of home.

"Have they already consumed some?" Maybe he spent too much time living on guard, ready to go up against the worst of the worst…

"No."

"I'd like to pick them up, if you don't mind. Take them to have them analyzed. Just to be sure. We can do it on the down-low. No one needs to know…"

"I can leave them for you in the morning," she said. "I don't want them here, anyway."

Right. The morning. It wasn't like forensics would be called in that night, or even that the job would be top priority, if he collected them that night. They'd sit until early the next day, no matter what.

Slowing, he turned his vehicle toward his mother's house. "I'll get them to the chief first thing," he assured her.

"I don't know how to thank you…"

"For what? Making a few-minute phone call and taking a ten-minute drive out of my way to deliver a box?" She might make more of it. He knew better. He couldn't have either of them making more of his interest than was there. "Look, for what it's worth…the one thing my siblings and I have in common, other than our name and growing up in the same household, is a need to make up for what our father did to people in this county and beyond. Before my dad got greedy, to keep his huge family with all of the creature comforts and monetary security he'd wanted to provide, he was a good guy. I was in the second batch of births and remember him back then. He ruined his own legacy, but we're determined to right as many wrongs as we can.

To help where he hurt. We started The Truth Foundation ten years ago, to exonerate everyone he wrongfully imprisoned and to help others in similar straits. We're the new Colton legacy..."

What the hell? Him, part of the legacy? Where had that come from him? Ezra had skipped town at eighteen by joining the army and had never looked back. Oliver and Dom...pretty much the same.

"The painting...and the riding... I'm not one who takes charity," she said, her voice soft. "We're doing nothing in return."

Slowing, he took a detour down by the river. Parked and looked out over the moonlit water. "Aunt Alice is my great-aunt, but I was closer to her than most of my other relatives. She was on Mom's side, not a Colton, and she was where I went to escape being a Colton. You're doing things for me in return every single day that you're at work, making sure that my aunt has loving care, offered with patience and respect, at a time when she can't possibly look out for or speak up for herself. If anyone's in debt, it's me, not you."

All true. And maybe too personal, which he sought quickly to correct. "I wasn't kidding about the painting being something I enjoy, which also gets me out of sitting at my mom's, the unwilling recipient of nosy drop-in visits all day long. Most people have to pay for their vacation entertainment."

And if painting as entertainment made him a dull guy, all the better.

The activity was actually serving a much more important purpose for him. Up on a ladder at her house all day, he'd be able to guard the place easily. No subterfuge necessary.

He'd already decided to slow his pace. And to find other jobs he could do, if necessary, to keep him at Theresa's all day until the Fitzgerald situation calmed down.

And if it didn't calm down before he left?

Ezra shook his head. He'd learned long ago to take his battles one at a time. He didn't borrow trouble.

"And, actually, there is one thing you can do," he said then, already congratulating himself on his flash of insight. "You can put Aunt Alice on Charlie's list, for as many visits as he can make. Did you see the way she was petting him?"

"I noticed the slight smile on her face most," Theresa said. "I haven't seen that expression out of her since she came to us."

"Family took care of her as long as they could."

"Rest assured, she's on Charlie's list from now on."

Which left them nothing else to discuss. "So, I'll see you in the morning." He didn't want to hang up.

"We'll probably be gone by the time you get here," she told him. "I'll leave the cookies on the bench in the garage."

Unless she was leaving before dawn, he'd be there before she left. Figuring the Fitzgeralds for nighttime sleepers, since their known activities had all happened during the day, he'd assigned himself daily painting shifts, dawn until dusk. He was hoping that, since the grandparents apparently wanted to get the girls without alarming them—their motivation being to save the twins from whatever blast they thought was imminent—they wouldn't break into Theresa's home to kidnap them.

"By the way," she said, when he'd braced for the

goodbye that had to come next, "I saw a patrol car passing by outside when I put the girls to bed. So…thank you. What you're doing might be small to you, but it's making a huge difference to me. I just want you to know your efforts are appreciated."

His male part went to immediate attention, misunderstanding her appreciation for something much more personal. At first, he felt like a skunk, until he realized that her tone of voice had changed.

"I'm glad," he told her, equally soft. And personal. And then hung up before he ruined everything.

Ezra, in painter's pants and a T-shirt that left the remarkable muscles in his upper arms in plain view, was already up on a ladder at the garage side of her house when Theresa pulled out the next morning. She hadn't even known he was there but noticed him at the same time as the girls did.

"It's Mr. Giant!" Neve yelled, drowning out Claire's more restrained, but equally enthusiastic, "Mr. Colton's here!"

The eagerness in their tones was sufficient to keep Theresa from stopping the old vehicle for a quick good morning.

She waved instead, as did the kids, and tried not to make anything of the man's smile and lifting of his paintbrush as she drove away. She walked the twins into day camp—another mandatory indoor day for them—and arrived at work. Same thing in reverse that night, except that he was in his truck, just getting ready to drive away, as they got home.

He waved, she waved, the girls excitedly gesturing, and off he went. The timing of that one was almost meant to be—as though she was supposed to see him there—and she sent up a silent prayer to whatever angels were watching over them. Thinking of him that way, as a gift sent from above to help her and her daughters out of a tight spot, felt...wiser.

Safer.

And so, on Saturday afternoon, when Ezra's Jeep pulled into the drive to collect them not five minutes after they'd returned home from a morning spent at gymnastics and then shopping, she scurried the excited girls along with the thought that the angels watching over them had arranged an afternoon of horseback riding, too.

The butterflies in her stomach were a little harder to explain.

Reminding her daughters that Ezra wasn't a permanent friend, but rather a fleeting companion, she checked their jeans and matching princess T-shirts. She'd handed out the new tops that morning as a reminder of their only lunch with the princess. She'd spared a quick glance down to ensure that her tie-dyed cotton sundress and matching red sandals bore no morning stains, and led her small family out of their home, locking the door behind her, and supervising as Ezra quickly loaded the car seats.

The friend reminder might or might not have worked on her daughters. But the second she climbed into the passenger seat next to Ezra, smelled his musky scent and saw those arms only partially contained in a short-sleeved polo shirt above faded jeans, she started to quiver from the inside out. More so when he leaned in to quietly let her know he'd dropped off the cookies, but that it could take a while to get results from the analysis. The man was too good to be true.

So angels, fate, whatever, had an ironic sense of humor, she mused. And ended up with the thought as a mantra as they arrived at the Gemini after ten minutes of nonstop six-year-old chatter on the ride over. Nine of the twelve Colton siblings—Gavin wasn't in town, Oliver was in Malaysia and Caleb was on his honeymoon—had gathered for the barbecue. From the adult conversation that flowed with almost as much abandon and cacophony as Claire and Neve's, she was able to ascertain that Ezra's presence at the event was a near miracle.

"You haven't attended this function since you were eighteen?" She leaned over to whisper to him as they walked through too many adults for her to remember all at once, toward the tables and grills set up behind the massive lodge.

Cheers went up as someone threw a ringer at a game of horseshoes, and she heard a large splash right before Neve cried out, "Look, Mom, a pool!"

"Crap, I didn't think to tell you to bring their suits," Ezra said, a frown on his face. Wondering how he handled being disappointed in himself, she almost didn't have the wherewithal to comment.

But that same look drew words from within her. "Are you kidding?" she said, wanting only to let the man know that rather than being a disappointment of any kind, he was a miracle worker. "The girls swim all the time at day camp. You're giving them a chance to be close to horses. To actually sit on one, which neither of them have ever done, by the way. Their outfits are perfect for what their little hearts desire today."

It was all the chance they had for any kind of private conversation before they were swarmed by another gaggle of Colton siblings and some significant others, too. Some in bathing attire with cover-ups. Others in shorts.

And then she saw Isa Colton, who had been a great support during Mark's passing.

"You finally get to meet my crew," Isa said with a smile as Theresa and Ezra approached the table behind which Isa was standing, arranging covered dishes. The woman came around the table, dressed elegantly in white close-fitting pants and a colorful, formfitting top that showed how lovely her hourglass figure remained, even at seventy-two. The lovely blonde didn't try to hide her age. She just looked fantastic in it. "Though I have to say," Isa continued before Theresa could respond, "Ezra is the last person I'd have expected to bring you to us…" She was grinning, gazing so adoringly up at her son that Theresa almost felt envious.

To be loved to that extent, that someone didn't care you'd missed eighteen years of parties, because they were so happy you'd come to one…

Isa took over the girls then, taking them first to see baby Iris, who was sleeping, and then showing them a kids' hut on the other side of the large grassy area where the picnic tables had been set up.

An hour later, Theresa still hadn't had her girls back at her side or had a chance to speak with either one of them. Nor had she had a chance for any private conversation with Ezra. The first made her a tad bit uncomfortable. The latter she knew was for the best.

"You think we should take Claire and Neve to ride before or after we eat?" The man in her thoughts spoke into her ear, leaning from just behind her. They'd just finished listening to Naomi talking about her plans for the show she'd be filming at the ranch soon, and Theresa figured they had about five seconds or so before someone else came up to join them.

"That's entirely your call," she said, and then took the rare private chance to tell him, "You can go play horseshoes or cornhole or whatever with your family. You don't have to stand here and babysit me."

She needed him to go. Give her a breather. She loved having him there, too much. Loved listening to him banter with his siblings almost as much as she loved the serious answers he gave to a couple of sincere questions Dom had asked about Ezra's last assignment in Afghanistan.

A very strongly needed reminder to her that Ezra Colton had a real life.

And how very far away it was from anything she could live with.

"Are you kidding?" he asked, leaning toward her again, as though anyone else could hear him in the chaos going on around them. "You're my excuse not to have to whup their butts or pretend that I'm not letting them win."

The bravado was only more of what she'd been hearing from the brothers and sisters for the past hour, but in Ezra's case, she had a feeling he was speaking the truth. At least somewhat.

Mostly, she had a feeling the man really did prefer standing with her rather than hanging out with his siblings en masse. He'd seemed to relax when Dom had joined them for a few minutes, but the man had been so clearly besotted with Sami—a landscaper who Theresa had thoroughly enjoyed speaking with—and had been eager to show her around.

Get her alone was more like it, though Theresa kept that thought to herself.

"I had no idea the girls would be the only kids here besides the baby," she said, as they had another minute with no one approaching. "Everyone is spoiling them so much I'll never be able to get them to sleep tonight. I was expecting a slew of kids running around."

"Nope, Iris is it," he said with a shrug. "Who'd have thought—twelve kids, the oldest two being thirty-nine, and only one grandchild." Who was still sleeping. Or maybe sleeping again. It wasn't like she'd been privy to the baby's activities all afternoon. The girls had come out of the kids' hut with a couple of horses painted with watercolors, running to show them to her, and then had been called over to play cornhole. One on each team. They were laughing, hollering encouragements and having the time of their lives.

And they hadn't even been on the horses yet...

"It looks like Dom could be providing a grandchild in the not-so-distant future," she said, happy for her daughters, and worried, too. Disney World was halfway across the country. Gemini Ranch was right there in town.

"I'd never have thought Dom would ever settle down or want a family, but it does appear like he's on his way there," Ezra allowed, frowning as he looked over the grounds at clusters of siblings and others they'd invited. "Caleb's married now, too. And Aubrey, Rachel and Gideon have all found happiness..."

"You don't like the people they're with?" she asked.

"Yeah!" He glanced at her then. "I do, actually."

And she felt stupid for thinking she knew him well enough to read his expressions. "Sorry… I just thought you sounded…not happy about it…"

His shrug brought her attention to those massive shoulders, but only until she saw the troubled look in the blue eyes trained completely on her.

A woman could happily melt right there…

"I don't like the change," he said then. "Or maybe, better put, I don't like that things can change so drastically in such a short time." The words seemed to make him more uneasy.

And Theresa went into immediate nurturing mode. It was what she did best. What she was born to do. "And yet you know that they can," she said softly. "Your experience with your dad taught you that."

A tragic course of events that, at sixteen, could mar a man for life. Ezra clearly liked order. His military haircut might be mandatory, but everything else about the man was in place as well.

Even the way he seemed to need a solid explainable reason for every single thing that he did.

Something that drew her to him in a very dangerous way.

"Just as it taught you that it doesn't take away your own ability to make choices for yourself," she added. "If Dom didn't want to give up undercover work, I'm guessing he wouldn't be doing it."

"True, that…"

Whatever else Ezra had been about to say was interrupted as another attractive, dark-haired woman joined them. Ezra introduced her as Morgan. Twin to the Caleb who just got married. An attorney like her twin, in partnership with him at their own firm. They were the firstborn Colton heirs.

And had made the news a number of times as they ran The Truth Foundation, an organization they initially spearheaded to help free the innocents their father had wrongfully put away. Last she'd heard, they'd taken care of almost all of them.

Morgan's welcome of Theresa sounded sincere. She praised Claire and Neve. Was polite, kind, and seemed to be heading somewhere, a purpose for coming over to them with no one else around. But when the pleasant-ries were done, she just turned to Ezra and said, "So, how were things at The Corner Pocket the other night?"

His night out with Dom and Oliver. The night he'd texted Theresa, and then called late…

"Same as usual. I beat the crap out of them. They said I cheated."

"They let you win. You know that, right?"

"Ha! That's what they want you to think." Ezra didn't seem the least bit concerned one way or the other.

"I'm guessing Roman comped your beers," she said then. Roman DiMera, owner of The Corner Pocket. Theresa knew who he was, of course. The man owned the entire waterfront building that housed the pub, but lived in a little apartment above his eatery and bar. But she'd never met him personally, let alone had him offer to comp as much as a French fry.

"No clue," Ezra told her. "I wasn't buying." She asked a big-sister question confirming that they'd had two apiece, to stay within legal driving limits, and walked off when Isa called out to her, leaving Theresa to won-der why on earth she'd brought up the bar at all.

Figured it was probably just Morgan's way of engaging her recalcitrant soldier brother in conversation, but she took the whole episode as a needed reminder that she was way outside her league at a Colton barbecue.

But so it went for most of the afternoon. Introductions. Kindness. Great food. Conversations that gave her insights into Ezra.

The Colton siblings enthusiastically taking turns entertaining the six-year-old twins their brother had invited into their midst.

And she and Ezra, side by side.

It took all of Theresa's great well of strength to keep herself from falling for the moment.

# Chapter 7

Who'd have thought that seeing the glow on the faces of two little kids could bring such pleasure? Glancing up at Claire and Neve as Jasper and Aubrey helped the girls into their saddles and then asked if they were ready, Ezra felt the jolt like lightning shooting through him.

As though he had some ownership in the joy and happiness of anyone's kid.

He was so not a family man. All it took was an outing with all of the Coltons, a reminder of a lifetime of cacophony, and he knew that, unlike Dom, he wasn't open to a major life change.

He was a normal guy who noticed an incredible woman when he met her, though. From the way Theresa held court with his siblings, engaging with them so naturally, keeping track of who was who, to the way her long dark hair—free from the bun for once—

flowed around her upper body…she'd snagged his attention.

In a huge way.

And the beauty was, he could enjoy the moment, without having to fret about any of the rest of it. Theresa wasn't at all interested in, or probably even capable of, falling for any guy. Not while she was still a young widow grieving for the husband she'd lost.

Having her at his side for the entire afternoon, someone whose conversation was an immediate draw, not a potential threat, with a body that tantalized in a hands-off kind of way… The combination distracted him from his constant need to put up walls where his family was concerned. Not once, in all the hours they were at the Gemini, did he think about lands far away.

Or long for escape.

In the Jeep on the way home, while the girls took turns reading from a new horse book Aubrey had given them from the kids' hut, Ezra couldn't remember ever being so relaxed—and so alive at the same time.

As he glanced at Theresa, a curious desire to unburden himself came over him. He fought it. Made it most of the way home. But when he turned a couple of blocks from Theresa's place, he glanced at her again and said, "You thought you didn't have any way to pay me back for what you perceive to be huge favors on my part, and I just have to tell you, the favors you do might not seem like much to you, but back there, the afternoon we just spent… I owe you."

She frowned. But wasn't looking at him. He was turning the corner onto her street and she was staring down the road.

Following her gaze, he understood immediately. The

mint-condition old blue truck would have stood out on any street. In front of her house...

Slowing, with a quick glance in the rearview mirror to ensure that the girls were still engrossed in their story, with Claire correcting Neve on a sentence she was sounding out, he asked, "You want me to turn around?"

His instincts insisted that was what he should do. Immediately.

Theresa shook her head. "They have an end goal that I can't allow, but they aren't violent people," she said softly. Always the nurturer.

He admired the hell out of her. And wanted to shake her, too.

Years of training had taught him how best to save innocent lives. When danger was posed, you went into defensive mode first, made a plan, then attacked.

And the call wasn't his. She'd made her wishes clear. If he did anything but deliver her and her daughters to their home, he technically became a kidnapper.

And law aside, Theresa's life and the lives of her children were hers to run. Not his.

Besides, she knew the enemy. He did not. Making her intel better than his.

Driving around the offending vehicle to pull in the driveway, he took a quick but detailed glance at the older man and woman sitting inside. Noting...nothing but a couple of grandparent-age people waiting outside a house.

They definitely weren't hiding their presence. In that truck, they'd be noticed pretty much anywhere they went.

Had Lawson's extra patrol already checked them out?

Or had the couple just arrived a minute or two ahead of them?

Before Ezra had even turned off the engine, Mark's parents had exited their vehicle and were walking up toward the back passenger-side door of Ezra's rented vehicle. If they so much as touched...

"Grandma's here!" Neve said, bursting out of her door before Ezra could figure out how to stop her.

A feat he'd have failed at, no matter what, because Theresa was already exiting his vehicle as well, heading immediately toward the Fitzgeralds.

Hearing the click of a seat belt behind him, Ezra turned around to look at Claire, who'd been seated behind him.

"Grandpa says scary things," she told him.

"I heard."

"Do you know about the blast, Mr. Colton? Grandma and Grandpa say it's coming, and Mom says it's not."

Keeping an eye on the two females who'd already exited his vehicle, while also giving Claire his attention, Ezra noted Neve hugging her grandmother, and Theresa standing right there, with a hand on her daughter's shoulder the entire time, while he tried to figure out how to answer the frightened and confused, hurting child relying on him for...promises he couldn't keep?

"I can promise you that I believe that the blast is not coming," he told her. He gave his life up every single day to ensure that threats of the kind Claire now feared did not hit American soil. "You know what's worse than the blast?" he asked her then.

Wide-eyed, she shook her head. "Being afraid to have fun because something bad might happen." He heard the words, and then had to quickly qualify, "Not to be confused with doing something you know is wrong, but doing it anyway just to have fun. That kind of fun you should be afraid of. You should always make good, safe choices, but if you're afraid of things that could happen that you can't stop, then you won't ever be happy or have fun."

"Like when Daddy got sick." The serious little voice broke his heart in one sentence. And climbed inside it, too.

"Yes. Just like that."

"Is the blast like Daddy's sickness? It happens to some people only and they didn't do anything to make it there?"

Theresa! Panicking at his lack of response, he glanced her way. Saw her arm around Neve while they stood there in what appeared to be serious but nonthreatened conversation.

And knew, for better or worse, he was on his own.

"No. Because sickness does come from time to time. The blast doesn't." And the rest of the answer occurred to him. "It never has, Claire. Not even once in all the thousands of years since the world has been here, there's never been anything like the huge blast that can ruin the whole world your grandparents talk about."

Wide-eyed, she stared at him. "You sure?"

"Positive."

Claire nodded. Gathered her new book to her chest and, without looking his way again, climbed down out of his vehicle and walked around the Jeep to stand on the other side of her mother.

Feeling as though he'd just come out of battle, and not sure he'd won, Ezra followed right on Claire's heels.

"Who is this man who's carting my son's kids around?"

Eric Fitzgerald didn't present as a nonviolent kind of guy as he glared from Ezra to Theresa. Landing on her with obvious accusation.

"He's Mr. Giant!" Neve popped in, before either adult had time to respond. "You know, like the princess at Disney World, only he's not a princess, but a soldier man who goes far away to keep everyone safe."

"Soldier!" Jennifer said, shooting a mistrusting look at Ezra before turning to her husband, as though he had to do something about Ezra's profession immediately.

"What are you doing exposing our granddaughters to a man who kills for a living?" Eric practically spit the words. "One whose job will take him to God knows where, and, if you two hook up, could take them, too, into God knows what. No way Mark would want them palling around with such a dangerous man!"

The guy was clearly unstable in his thinking, but hadn't made any moves toward Theresa or Ezra, in any physical sense. When she sent him a pleading look, directing his attention with a nod toward Claire's distressed expression and holding out her house key, he stepped forward, noting the irony in the older couple being so singly focused on their own conversation that they didn't seem to notice him ushering the twins away.

Taking one of each of the girls' hands, reminding them that they'd told him they'd show him the wall of horse drawings in their playroom before he did his best to make the exit seem natural.

He'd been going to help them choose where on that horse wall to put their watercolor paintings from that afternoon, so though Ezra wanted the kids away from their grandparents immediately, he took them around the Jeep, putting the vehicle between them and the

Fitzgeralds, but made himself stop at the truck to retrieve the paintings first, then spoke loudly enough to
at least distract from the tirade emitting from the other
side of the truck.

"I had a lot of fun today," he told the girls, leaning
down as he walked to be more easily heard. "What part
did you like best?"

Neve, as usual, was the first to answer. Horseback
riding was first, of course. And cornhole came in second. For third she wanted to know if she could go back
and try the swimming pool sometime. She didn't give
her twin a chance to answer, but Ezra was fairly certain Claire's attention wasn't on the question anyway.
The little girl had reached up her free hand to hold on
to Ezra's arm above their clasped hands.

He said hello to Charlie, who greeted him at the door
as though he'd known him forever, and put the dog out
back for his business as Claire instructed. Then he followed the two dark-haired urchins down the hall to
their playroom.

And while he tended to the girls, thumbtacking their
paintings to spots on the wall too high for them to reach,
not seeing much at all of the house for the glances he
kept sending out the window, keeping Theresa in sight,
he knew that he was never going to forget this little
family.

Or his brief time being a part of them.

She couldn't reason with them. Theresa tried again.
Failed again. And warned the Fitzgeralds that if they
came anywhere near her home, her place of business,
the girls' school, day camp or anywhere else any of the

three of them might be, or called or texted her again, she was going to file for a restraining order against them.

Let them try to take her to court for visitation rights. She'd have a child psychologist interview Claire if need be, to prove that Eric and Jennifer Fitzgerald were not a healthy influence on her children.

And if they didn't leave her property immediately, she was going to call the police.

The last threat was a new one. And one she wouldn't have made if not for Ezra's intervention. He'd alerted the chief of police regarding her family struggles, and the chief had found the situation worthy of extra patrol. Her worry was understandable, actionable, even if in the end it turned out not to be warranted.

As her former in-laws turned and silently walked away, Theresa swallowed back tears. She'd wanted to love them. For her girls to have a loving relationship with them. Shaking, she wished so hard that life had been different. That Mark had been able to grow up with emotionally and mentally healthy parents. And that he hadn't been struck down with a terminal illness.

She'd had her time to say goodbye to Mark. And as she turned to go into her house, stopping first to retrieve the car seats from Ezra's Jeep, she thought of the promise she'd made Mark that she'd find happiness again. She was ready to be happy.

To give her girls back as much of their carefree childhood as she could.

And she felt helpless. It wasn't like you could just order up a pound of happiness on the internet, pay for same-day shipping and have it simply show up.

Just as no amount of hoping had helped Mark get

well, she couldn't positive-think his parents into people they were not.

Feeling defeated, worried, like she had to find some way to scale an impossibly high mountain in order to give her two precious angels the emotional and physical security that had been robbed from them, she entered her house to hear Claire say, "Thank you, Mr. Colton. The paintings look beautiful up there. Are you for sure you have to go far away and be a soldier?"

Fear struck through her. Her talk with the girls... She should have known there wouldn't be anything she could say that would be strong enough to prevent them from falling for the man.

How could she have expected two innocent six-year-olds to guard their hearts when she hadn't been completely successful in doing so herself?

Ezra Colton was a sergeant in the army. He'd be on active duty again in less than a month. And might be killed at any time.

She could not take on that possibility of loss for herself. She most definitely couldn't subject her girls to it.

With the resolve a viable source inside her, she headed back to the girls' playroom, only to hear Ezra say, "Why don't you two draw pictures of the horses you each rode today, while I go talk to your mom for a minute?"

He knew she was there.

She quickly backed into the kitchen.

She'd been quiet entering the house. Had greeted Charlie with the scratch on his chest that he liked best to keep him calm.

Knowing what she did of Ezra Colton, she figured he'd probably been watching her the whole time she'd been outside. Had seen the Fitzgeralds' truck drive away. The man didn't seem to miss anything.

At least, not with her or her twins.

Much like Mark had been with them…

Ezra had his phone in hand as he came into the kitchen—the only place in her small home where they could speak without being heard in the playroom. "I'll call Chief Lawson," he said.

"No!" The word came out far more sharply than she'd intended, and she softened her tone. "At least… Just… no." The girls, the problems, were hers. "I'll call the police myself," she told him. "To make an official report of the unannounced visit." And to make sure she knew exactly what to do, straight from law enforcement, if she saw or heard from the Fitzgeralds again. "I don't think they're going to bother us anymore." She told him what she actually believed.

There'd been resignation about their withdrawal from the fight that afternoon. A sense of knowing that they'd gone too far and had lost their chance.

Probably because they'd been through it all before with their son.

And they'd never contacted or been near him again.

"They didn't seem ready to just walk away," he told her, and the way his words immediately ramped up her anxiety had her walls shooting up higher than they'd ever been around him. "You don't have to go through this alone, Theresa. Let me help. We can explain to the girls enough about conspiracy theories to help them understand that people just sometimes get caught up in stuff, like thinking cartoon characters are real and…"

She'd thought of comparing Ezra's time with them to eating lunch with a princess, but she hadn't thought about easing her daughters' fears by likening their grand-parents' beliefs to cartoon characters. He was good.

And as soon as her heart started to reach out toward him in gratitude, she knew it had to stop. Him in her home. Interacting with her girls.

Touching her heart…

"Stop." She hadn't actually meant to say the word aloud, but knew when she did that it was the right thing. "Just stop, Ezra. You aren't their father. You aren't even going to be in town much longer…"

He didn't so much stiffen as just stand up straighter, but she knew her words had done what she'd set out to do.

"I apologize," he told her. "You're right. And it's probably just better if we don't see each other again."

Her nod was the right thing to do, too.

"I'll be back to finish the painting and, to that end, would like to work tomorrow as well. Carlos, my friend, was here yesterday, but I'll be alone tomorrow. Can you make sure the girls don't see me?"

He was even good, decent, about ending things. In that moment, the truth pissed her off. "You don't need to finish painting."

Even if they weren't there, she couldn't handle know-ing he was at her house. Still taking care of them.

He didn't need to be spending his vacation working free of charge for a virtual stranger.

"I already bought the paint. And would appreciate the activity."

"Fine." She quickly added, "And…thank you. I'll take the girls to the river for the day. We'll leave early, and I'll keep them out until you text to let me know you're leaving. And if you need Monday to finish, we can do the same. Communicate with each other so the girls aren't here to see you. Same for Tuesday, if it takes that long."

She had no idea how she was going to tell them that Ezra had left without saying goodbye, but she knew it had to happen.

The long look they shared then might have said things that she couldn't afford to acknowledge. And maybe she'd only imagined that it had.

"You've got this," he said as he pulled his keys from his pocket. "Just, please, call the police."

She nodded.

He gave her a smile filled with warmth. Friendship.

Then turned around and walked away.

Out of her house.

Out of her life.

Theresa quickly brushed away the tears that fell.

# Chapter 8

Thank God for rotting eaves and fascia board. The need to replace them—with paid help from another high school friend—in order to paint them kept Ezra busy Sunday and Monday. With all signs of wood and sawing removed before he left the premises.

Theresa had enough to worry about without thinking she owed anyone anything else.

And he could leave town knowing that he'd done all he could to help her and her kids.

As long as the Fitzgerald situation was resolved. Though how he'd measure that result, he wasn't sure. There'd been no sign of the older couple at Theresa's house. His surveillance skills were top-notch. And he'd had a few calls from Chief Lawson as well.

He knew Theresa had called the police to report Saturday's incident. And he knew that there'd been no sign of, or reported trouble about, the Fitzgeralds since that time.

Did that mean the situation was resolved? As Theresa expected?

Or was the couple just lying in wait? Formulating a plan, as Theresa had once intimated?

Finishing up at her house on Tuesday, he wasn't ready to just pack it in and call the job done. Doing so on a personal basis—he'd handled that one just fine.

But leaving a woman in potential danger?

Not his style.

He pondered the matter as, still in his new white painter's pants and a white T-shirt and tennis shoes, he turned into Sunshine Senior Home on Tuesday afternoon, his gaze automatically searching for, and not finding, the mint-condition old blue pickup truck. He saw Theresa's old vehicle, though. Parked right where it had been the last time he'd been there.

He was at the home to see his aunt—having promised himself he'd see her at least once a week, and it had been a week—and if he saw Theresa, he would let her know that the work at her home was done.

He could text her the message. Their brief communications to arrange their departures and arrivals at her home so that they didn't coincide over the past couple of days had worked fine.

He just couldn't bring himself to admit to her that his work was complete.

The painting was done.

His job, self-appointed as it was, protecting her from the bad guys, didn't feel done.

And the twins... He knew Claire and Neve would be

on the premises. It was Tuesday. They were there with Charlie every Tuesday. He shouldn't go in.

His phone rang while he sat there. His oldest brother, Caleb, back from his honeymoon, and all business. He was calling all of the siblings to let them know that Ronald Spence, the last man to be let out of jail due to their father's illegal dealmaking, had been seen multiple times at his old haunts, and Dominic's suspicion that the man was back to his old smuggling business was looking likely.

"It appears that he's working right here in Blue Larkspur," Caleb said, "or pretty close to it. I'm hoping you, in particular, with your skills and time on your hands, can keep a watch out for anything suspicious."

"Of course," Ezra told his sibling. He was always on the lookout for suspicious activity. No matter where he was or for what reason. His belief that evil lurked in the world around him was just part of who he was.

The reminder had him out of the Jeep and heading toward the senior-home entrance as soon as Caleb hung up. Either he needed another job to do at Theresa's house, and he had one or two to suggest, or he had to be straight with her and let her know that he had a bad feeling about her in-laws and would be obliged if she'd let him continue his surveillance for a little bit longer.

He'd learned to trust his gut, and it was upheaving on this one.

He'd avoid all contact with the girls. Neve could always be heard from halfway down the hall, at least, and if they got close to Alice's room, he'd slip into the bathroom before they saw him.

Plan in place, he was barely in the door of the spacious, warm and somewhat elegant reception area before he saw Theresa. He'd known her office was there, but hadn't expected to get lucky and have her sitting at her massive desk with the door open.

She stood, giving him a full view of the black jacket and short skirt covering her delicious-looking curves. Professional dress had never been a particular turn-on for him before. Nor had auburn highlights in messy buns, but his body was sending a new memo.

At thirty-six.

He didn't have time to reject the message, but with his shirt hanging over his fly, he could ignore it. Refuse to listen.

Discipline himself so the body didn't have a say.

"Ezra, can I see you for a moment?" she asked, politely, all business. The warm gaze peering at him from those expressive dark eyes seemed to carry a much more personal note.

Since he was there to speak with her as much as see his aunt, he took the invitation as an omen that his gut had been correct in terms of needing more time to watch over her safety from the Fitzgeralds.

Which honed his nerve endings to the edge, and gave him need for a plan, too.

In her office, with the door open, but with no one else in the lobby, she stood just inches from him, her face turned up toward his, and said, "I owe you an apology for my waspishness on Saturday." Eyes wide, filled with concern, and that constant hint of reaching out with her heart, she didn't blink as she continued, "Seeing Mark's parents again unnerved me. And with you there, and them attacking my right to have you there... I overreacted, and I'm sorry."

"I'm sorry, too." The words came. He didn't approve of having uttered them.

"What could you possibly have to be sorry for?"

The conversation wasn't supposed to be on the course it seemed to be following. It was supposed to be serious, but only in terms of the threat she might be facing, and his ability to help alleviate it to some extent.

"For letting you ditch me so easily," he told her. Theresa compelled his honesty. "I took the route of least resistance, and while I'm here to see my aunt, I also came to see you. To talk about…"

Frantic dog barking erupted, cutting him off.

"Charlie!" Theresa cried out as, together, they hurried in the direction of the memory-care unit from which the barking was emitting.

Swiping a card rather than having to type a code on the keypad as Ezra would have had to do, she was on the unit and heading toward Charlie's anxious-sounding alerts coming from behind a closed resident door. Moving past Theresa, Ezra ran the length of the hall, skirting a couple of people in wheelchairs set along the wall, heading straight for the back exit.

Charlie locked in a room…

The back door was set to an alarm—he'd noted all details the week before, when he'd been taking stock of security measures for his aunt's safety. An alarm hadn't gone off.

The door was closed. But a quick glance at the sensor had his blood raging. A kitchen magnet covered the sensor, triggering the alarm to think the door was closed even if it wasn't. The door was set to prevent confused residents from wandering out alone, unattended, not to keep people from leaving the building in case of emergency. With the slide of a security bar and a hard shove, he had the door open.

And saw a flash of metal through the trees along the road behind the home. The Fitzgeralds' truck? He hoped to God he was wrong.

Pulling out his phone, he was connecting to the police by the time his gaze fell to a bush just outside the door.

Claire's new horse book.

The so-serious little six-year-old had let them know she'd been outside that door.


She saw Charlie. Mrs. Wright, the room's occupant. Not her daughters. Gaze darting frantically around the room, Theresa didn't see Claire or Neve anywhere!

Her heart practically clogged her throat as she tried to speak to the elderly resident who was hard of hearing, and she couldn't get Charlie to stop barking, so she ran for the private bath attached to the room, hoping the girls had disobeyed orders not to use the patient facilities.

The small room, including shower, was empty. Blood pounded through her so rapidly she couldn't feel. Could hardly think. Ran out of the room, desperately searching, and saw Ezra coming toward her, his phone in his hand.

And a look of deep sorrow...

"*Noooo!* No." She toned her wail down to a command. "No," she said, shaking her head. Charlie, quiet all of a sudden, stood beside her. Ezra strode to the room where the dog had been shut in.

"Did you see anyone come in here?" Ezra asked the

woman sitting in a chair by the window, but Theresa shook her head.

"She can't hear, and doesn't comprehend enough to…" She broke off, panic rising so high within her she started to see stars.

"You need to put the building on lockdown." Ezra's voice called her back from an abyss. Commanded her action. "When I was here last week, I read that there are protocols for that, in case a memory-care patient goes missing…"

"Yes," she cut him off. "Yes." Pulling a phone from her pocket, she pushed speed dial to tap into the building's rarely used intercom system, ordering all personnel to instigate an immediate lockdown. No one was to leave the building. She barely had the wherewithal to remember to assure everyone that there was no immediate danger.

That told staff that they were dealing with a possible resident escape, one or two people in a troubled situation, as opposed to a multiple life-threatening situation.

Except…multiple lives… Oh, God. The Fitzgeralds might not be violent, but if they'd actually kidnapped her girls…

"The police are on their way," he said next, striding purposefully toward the window. As though troops would be coming through it at any moment. But what about her girls?

She ran for the door. Intending to search every room, every closet, under every bed until she found Claire and Neve…

"I've already searched the rooms on this unit," Ezra said. "Can you check security tapes? I know cameras aren't in individual rooms, but they'd show us hallway activity, right? And outside?"

Yes. Absolutely. "Of course," she said, tearing out of the room, down the hall, past employees—who, under lockdown protocol, were standing at their assigned doorways—off the unit and over to her office, not sure if Ezra was even behind her.

It didn't surprise her when she pulled up the live feed on her computer and his face lowered right next to hers in front of the screen. For a brief second, it comforted her.

Until the blue truck flashed up on her screen from the top right camera image. Then all she knew was stone-cold fear.

"They've taken them to prepare them for the nuclear blast." The wealth of terror, and of certainty, in Theresa's tone grabbed at Ezra's gut. "Oh my God, what are they going to do with them?"

He didn't have that answer. And couldn't think as emotion poured through him. Her emotion. His.

Until another glance at the blue truck galvanized the man he was into action. "They aren't going to do anything to them," he told her with a bit of his own certainty. "Their goal is to save them, right?"

The fact that some unstable family members had been known to take the lives of their loved ones with the thought that they were saving them hit him hard.

He didn't share it.

"Their goal is to hide them away in their bunker that's underground God knows where and train them to live like animals, with survival the only thing on their minds..." Panic filled her words, raising her tone as she spoke, and he could see her falling in on herself, literally bending her head, her back.

"Hey." With a hand at her chin, and another at her back, her lifted her head until she was looking him in the eye. "They need you right now. They need you to not give up believing that they'll be okay. They need you to find them. Because I can guarantee you, they're believing you will." The words flowed naturally, a sergeant talking to the troops that became family to him.

And when she nodded, he felt more like the sergeant he knew himself to be. Capable of remaining calm. Aware. And outthinking the enemy.

The front door opened and Chief Lawson walked into the lobby outside Theresa's office door, followed by suited and then uniformed men. A glance out the window showed Ezra the entire road up to the home filled with police cars. Theresa saw the number of law enforcement filling her lobby and turned to Ezra, her gaze begging him for something.

Without another thought, he stepped forward, spoke to the man who'd danced with his mother at his brother's wedding. Spoke as though he and Chief Lawson actually really knew each other. As though he had a right to demand help. To speak and be heard in a professional sense.

And within minutes, a BOLO was out on the Fitzgeralds' blue truck, and an Amber Alert was being issued for Claire and Neve. Theresa looked shell-shocked by the speed with which everything was happening. Ezra wanted it all to happen faster.

Officers, detectives, janitors and other personnel who weren't preventing residents from leaving their rooms went over every inch of the place, making certain the girls weren't there, and then while some law enforcement started taking personnel and resident statements, others checked out means of entry and exit.

Ezra stayed with Theresa. He wasn't going to slow things down by getting in the way, but he did tell the chief, who relayed the message over his radio, that the point of exit was at the rear of the memory-care unit and the point of entry, Ezra believed, was the window in Mrs. Wright's room.

"She likes fresh air," Theresa said slowly, as though in a daze, standing in the middle of a circle of officers. Ezra, from right behind her, felt her shudder. "I never thought an open window in a senior home would be cause for a security breach. None of the residents on that particular wing are capable of getting the screens out, let alone climbing out of a window. We keep the more agile memory-care patients on a different hall because they need different stimulation and different types of caregiving…"

She was rambling. He was grateful no one interrupted. Those who had immediate jobs to do were doing them. And she was distracting herself, whether she knew it or not.

He'd seen the jimmied screen the second he'd entered the resident's room.

He'd seen Aunt Alice, too, sleeping in her chair as he'd stridden past her partially opened door. Resident families would be notified of the breach. His family.

He had to get to work. To figure out where the Fitzgeralds were going and stop them from getting there without endangering the girls.

And he couldn't walk away from their mother, couldn't leave her there trying to be a rock and floundering. She'd already lost one man who gave her strength. Had already lost too much. And not that he was a man in her life, but she'd turned to *him* in her time of greatest need.

His immediate response, the emotional one that drove his actions, shocked the hell out of him. As did the livid anger burning through him every time he thought of Claire leaving her book outside that door—a very smart and desperate cry for help—an action generated by fear for her life.

And also a sign that she held hope that she'd be rescued.

He cared—in a way he didn't understand and with a force he didn't recognize. Something he could ponder some other day when he was out in a desert hole spending hours waiting for the enemy to fall into a trap. Or working out in the gym during mandatory downtime.

He had two weeks until then. And if the girls weren't found before then…if they were in captivity for fourteen days… He shook his head. Fourteen days of being held in a bunker for what their grandparents perceived to be their own good…

No. He'd die before he'd let that happen.

Die to save his own from suffering. That was what he'd signed up for at eighteen, and he'd never looked back.

The girls weren't his to call his own. Their mother wasn't really even something as official as a friend.

Didn't matter how he felt.

He wasn't on the job. Didn't have an assignment. But he was going to move hell if need be to use his skills and bring those little girls home.

The powerful emotions prompting the actions would have to come under scrutiny at a later time. Every minute those girls were out there was another moment they might remember in the future. Another moment they could be emotionally or mentally scarred.

Lord knew Claire was already carrying heavy burdens of fear regarding the damned blast actually happening that was more a figment of someone's imagination than any real and valid threat. Because the threat was guarded against. Things were in place. Had been for many years. Things he hadn't been able to explain to a six-year-old.

As he waited for Theodore Lawson to get off a call, Ezra put a hand on Theresa's back, at the base of her neck. More like a heating pad for relaxation than anything else.

An attempt to help her hold on.

While his mind spun.

Lawson was taking too long.

"The police have everything handled here," he told her, not wanting to leave her, but not being able to just stand there any longer. "And there are things I can be doing, things my family can be doing…"

"Do them." She looked him straight in the eye. No questions asked.

He nodded and headed out to his Jeep.

## Chapter 9

The second Ezra left the lobby of the senior home, Theresa started to shake. Her mind jumbled, bringing her images of Claire crying, Neve yelling, the girls hugging each other on the back seat of a truck. Without car seats.

Did they have seat belts on?

She saw them in an underground cave of mud with such pitch-blackness at night that Claire would wet the bed. Would there be beds there?

Oh, God, would the girls feel sun on their skin? Be warm enough?

Would they sleep with guns beside them?

*Stop it!* She stomped her foot and noticed several of the officers moving to and fro throughout the lobby stopping to glance at her.

Just when she thought one might lead her away, Ezra

was back in her line of vision. "I'm assuming I can use your office to set up in?"

"What?" *Set up in.* She replayed the words. Or they replayed themselves. He was…staying?

"Yes!" she said then, too quickly, adding, "Of course."

Where was her calm? Her coping abilities? She'd nursed the father of her children through a debilitating end. Had worked, too, so they'd have money to pay his bills and still provide for the girls. She'd seen things she'd never expected to see. Had buried the man she'd expected to spend the rest of her life with.

She was not going to fall apart when their daughters needed her.

And…she didn't have to do it alone, either.

As she stood in the lobby, the only unmoving being, it seemed, just existing there like a statue surrounded by urgency, she saw Ezra in her office. Behind her desk. Typing on her keyboard.

And then he came out again. "I need your password."

Something she never gave anyone. "Cleave1!" she said without hesitation. "Capital *C*." Giving him access to a part of her she never gave to anyone. Ever. Not even Mark had known her passwords.

Weird, probably. But…

Was she really going to stand there and think about password habits? While everyone else moved with greatest energy to find her children?

"Claire and Neve combined in a word of promise. I will cleave to them forever. Exclamation because they are the most magical part of my life. And 1 because they both are my firstborn," she said, following Ezra into her office.

Giving no indication as to whether he'd heard or

not, Ezra sat at her desk, his fingers flying on the keyboard, his gaze intent on the screen. He picked up his phone, pushed one button, waited a brief second and said, "Okay, now what?"

He typed, his eyes narrowing on the screen. And then, "Got it," and hung up.

"There are things my siblings and I can do faster," he said as he typed and moved the cursor with her mouse. "Dom's an FBI agent," he said. "I've got clips from surveillance cameras, and Dom's tracking phones for GPS coordinates," he said as he continued to move the mouse on the pad.

And suddenly, Theresa was behind him. Focused. With a resurgence of the toughness that had seen her through bad days, she studied images as they appeared. And when Ezra turned the seat so she could sit with him, she did so without hesitation, right there on one of his thighs.

There was nothing sexy about the move.

But it affected her more than she'd ever thought possible for a simple physical contact. It was like he wasn't just at her back, he was a part of it. In that moment, he was a part of her. Warmth to warmth. The panic, the fear…he shared it.

And in the sharing, there was strength.

The second he pulled Theresa onto his knee, Ezra knew he'd made a mistake. He'd pulled Naomi down to his knee tons of times when they'd been younger and he'd been teaching her things on the computer.

Theresa was most definitely not his little sister.

And he had no business treating her as though they

were…something together. But he didn't have time to worry about any of it, either.

She stayed seated. He kept working. Aware of her. Of wanting her there. For more than just that moment. But not focused on any of that. More desert-hole stuff. The times in foreign deserts when he contemplated life.

At that moment all he was contemplating were the images he was scrolling through on the screen as they downloaded through his brother's equipment. He wasn't getting the actual footage, but still shots from them. Some program Dom had access to that put the video in still frames.

And…there it was.

"It's the truck!" Theresa called out, and then lowered her voice to say, "Can you make it bigger? See if the girls are there?"

He tried, but neither of them could see the back seat of the truck from the view they had. They couldn't even make out occupants of the front seat.

But it was something. He made note of the photo designation—camera location and time. And continued scrolling.

Theresa sat still as could be, her gaze glued on the screen. She didn't chat. Didn't ask the questions that had to be racing through her mind. He didn't have any answers to them.

And then…he felt the muscles of her butt clench against his thigh. There it was again. The same distinctive blue truck. Ezra took one look at the camera's location—and the time the Fitzgeralds had been there.

"I gotta go," he said then, practically pushing Theresa off his lap as he stood up. Except that he didn't have to push. She was right there with him. Grabbing her purse.

"Where are we going?"

He didn't take ride-alongs. In the desert, on the battlefield, no one ever wanted to ride along.

"I'll be in touch soon," he told her. "I just have to go check something out."

"No way, Colton," she said, sounding as fierce as his mother ever had. And having raised twelve kids, seven of whom were boys, Isa had a lot of practice at putting her foot down. "I won't be left behind."

He had a lot of practice at standing his ground, too. And didn't budge. He had no idea where his hunch would lead him. How dangerous it could be if he got lucky and there was a showdown with the Fitzgeralds to get the girls home in time for dinner.

Or how disappointing if it didn't pan out. He also didn't have time to fight her.

Unable to look at her, he grabbed his keys and headed for the door.

"Please, Ezra. They're my children. All I have. I can't just sit here…"

He paused, but didn't turn around. That last line… hit him where it counted. He'd had the same thought not half an hour before, and Claire and Neve weren't even remotely his.

With a glance back over his shoulder, he motioned for her to come with him and continued his determined stride out to the Jeep.

He was racing against time and couldn't afford to lose the race.

Most particularly not with the twins' mother sitting in the vehicle beside him.

\* \* \*

She didn't know where they going. Didn't ask. Didn't even question her unwavering faith in putting her life in the hands of a man she'd known only a week.

Or stop to consider that perhaps she'd be of better service to the trained police force working to find her daughters. Ezra called Chief Lawson once they were on the road. Let him know that he'd had to get Theresa out of there for a few minutes. Told him to call if they needed her for anything.

And then it was just the two of them.

She didn't make the mistake of asking a second question. The first one had nearly gotten her sidelined.

"I'm not a magician." Ezra's comment was so odd, she stared at him. Trying to figure out what had prompted the words so she could reassure him. Got nowhere.

"I know."

"This could be a wild-goose chase."

And she got it. He was afraid he was setting her up for disappointment.

"If I was in on the details, I'd be more apt to realize that, and not build up unreasonable expectations," she told him. But in truth, she was just glad to be doing something to try to help save her babies rather than sitting around, letting worrisome scenarios take over her brain.

And doing it with him. Ezra made her feel more alive, more capable, than she could ever remember feeling. Even before Mark got sick.

"The area between the one camera and the second… I know it. There's a road that heads across state, away from any towns, and that road is not far from that second camera…"

"You think that's where they're headed."

His shrug drew her attention to his massive shoulders, to his strength, and yet she sensed a vulnerability about him. He wasn't sure.

How could he be?

She drew a deep breath.

"I know a shortcut to that road. Dom and Oliver and I used to drag race out there. There's a gas station about an hour from where we saw that last camera image."

It had been time-stamped half an hour before they'd been in the Jeep.

"Do we have time to make it before they do?"

"Probably not."

"But we're going to try."

"Yes."

"Good."

For the moment, it was enough.

They didn't make it. Ezra was actually hopeful—an occurrence that wasn't normal for him—as he pulled into the vacant lot at the little country station, that they'd arrived in time. Most people driving the long road into nowhere knew that the little family-owned place was the last stop until past the state line. Most stopped.

Pulling the Jeep around back, so that there was no chance either the girls or the Fitzgeralds would see it and recognize it, he suggested that he and Theresa head in to talk to the guy behind the counter. A younger guy Ezra didn't think he'd seen before. If the blue truck pulled onto the lot, he could be out the back door and in the Jeep to head them off before they knew they'd been made.

"Sorry, man, you just missed them," the guy said as

Ezra described the truck. He'd explained that he was trying to catch up with in-laws. He hadn't said whose. "They was here maybe twenty minutes ago."

"You're sure it was the same truck?" he asked, certain that there weren't two of them in the state in the condition Eric Fitzgerald kept his vehicle. "They had our daughters with them. You wouldn't be able to miss them…"

"Twins," the man cut him off, nodding. "Yep. They bought 'em each an ice cream sandwich," he said, as though that solved all the world's problems.

"And they were headed toward the state line?" He pointed into no-man's-land, refusing to let dread, or fear for Theresa and her girls, sink in. Slow his thinking processes or inhibit problem-solving skills.

*"Noooo."* Frowning, the young man shook his head as he drew out the word. "They headed back the way they'd come."

"They were going back to town?" Theresa asked.

The guy shrugged. "Maybe. Unless they took that turnoff that leads to McClintock and Benson and them other small towns up that way. One of them girls had to pee is why they came down here, I think. No places to stop on that other road."

Which made it not likely to be on police radar. Or have surveillance cameras.

A good choice of travel for someone wanting to stay off the grid.

"Thank you." Ezra dropped a twenty on the counter and, taking Theresa's hand in his, hurried from the store.

"The girls don't like ice cream sandwiches." They'd been in the car a minute—just long enough for Ezra to report in to his brother Dominic, the FBI agent, that they were headed on a road to small towns upstate.

"Mark liked them," she continued. Made sense, then, that Jennifer would think to buy for her grandchildren the same treat she'd bought for their father. "He bought a box of them once, had the girls try them. They ate the ice cream and gave him the chocolate-cake part. After that it was tradition. He never seemed to mind eating the sandwich without the filling."

"You miss him." The quiet response came from the muscled, powerful man at her side. Filled with an understanding, a gentleness, that while in direct contrast to the look of the man, and to his job, still felt...right.

She thought about his statement. About the past year on her own. "I do," she said. There would always be a part of her that would be tied to the gentle man she'd known and married. "And yet if he were here now... I feel horrible for saying it, but I'm not even sure we'd work anymore. I've changed."

The thought slipped out, sounding blasphemous. It was also the truth. And if she hoped to get her daughters back safely, she had to make no mistakes.

Lying to herself, or anyone else, was definitely a mistake.

The ringing of his phone prevented any response he might have made. She cared little about their conversation when Ezra answered his phone with a push of a button on the steering wheel and said, "Yeah, Dom, what's going on?"

"I got myself officially on the case—kidnapping being within FBI jurisdiction—and should only be reporting to family or their designated spokesperson." The voice came over the Jeep's audio system.

Ezra looked at Theresa. "That choice is yours to make," he said, and then added, "You need to know I won't stop looking. I'll just stop talking to my brother."

"No." Dominic's voice came firmly over the line. "You don't stop talking to me. You tell me everything you know when you know it. I just stop giving you official updates on what I know."

"You aren't giving them to him. You're giving them to me." Theresa spoke up. "And, for the record, Ezra Colton is my official spokesperson." Her entire being warmed at the pronouncement. It was nothing. Getting around red tape was all.

But felt like so much more.

He glanced her way, a brow raised, as though asking her to be sure.

She nodded.

"There you have it, bro. Now, what do you know, for God's sake?"

"Authorities have been notified in every burg along the road you mentioned, cars have been dispatched, but so far, nothing."

"I'm heading that way anyway."

"I expected as much. I'll keep you posted. And… Theresa, I'm sorry about your girls. They were a hoot on Saturday. We'll get them back."

Her eyes filled with tears, and, chin trembling, she nodded but couldn't get words out.

Ezra, with a quick glance her way, said, "Later," and clicked off the call.

"I can't believe you all are doing this for me," she said when she could, feeling awkward, yet as though she was where she was meant to be in that moment. "I'm just a woman your mom knows because of her senile aunt. And you… You've only got a couple of weeks left on your vacation." She blurted the words more as a reminder to herself than because she thought he needed to hear them.

"All true, but you left out the part where you and your kids have snagged my attention in a way no woman with children ever has, and you took pity on a restless military sergeant being emotionally blackmailed by his family to spend time in a town he bolted from years ago. For good reason."

His gaze never left the road. She wasn't even sure he was fully cognizant of what he was saying. The tone of voice was a bit…distracted.

"Seriously, Ezra, thank you," she said and pulled out her own phone, making a couple of calls to arrange for a health-care manager to take over for her, starting immediately, at the Sunshine Senior Home until further notice. The first woman she contacted from the pool of traveling health-care workers, a woman who'd filled in for Theresa during the week Mark died, accepted on the spot and said she'd be in Blue Larkspur by nightfall. She also agreed to look after Charlie.

Hanging up, Theresa stared out the windshield, reminding herself that Claire and Neve needed her to stay focused.

They'd be counting on her to find them before dark.

"We have to find them before dark," she announced.

"We're going to do our best," Ezra said, and she heard what was in his silence, too. They might not succeed by then. Or ever.

The man wasn't going to lie to her.

But he reached out a hand over the console, and when

she took it, she believed they'd get through whatever lay ahead.

And that Claire and Neve would, too.

# Chapter 10

He couldn't give her false hope. Unstable people were also unpredictable—even to themselves. But Ezra believed that they wouldn't hurt the twins intentionally.

He had to believe it.

Never in his life had a battle meant so much to him. It had never been personal before. As he drove, keeping focus on his surroundings, the ditches, the trees, the road ahead and behind, looking for any signs of vehicles having pulled off the road recently, he kept his less understandable thoughts at bay, sending them to storage for a time when he could get them into order, label them and put them away.

And…there. He slowed.

"What's going on?" Theresa's question carried alarm.

He wasn't used to being questioned when he was working. He gave the orders.

Turning around, he drove back a few yards, got out of the Jeep, studied the fresh tire tracks in a pile of dirt and jumped behind the wheel again.

"A truck just turned right here," he said, heading down a one-lane side road. The vehicle's GPS system caught up quickly, showing him that the road was long, continuing on as far as he could see on the map. A likely road into open territory where one could dig a hole and hide forever.

She didn't say any more after that, just sat next to him, a second pair of eyes watching the landscape.

And he was glad she was there.

Once she knew more of what to look for, fresh dirt showing new tire tracks, for one, Theresa couldn't take her gaze off the sides of the road, the nearby ditches, as they drove. It wasn't like she actually expected the twins to be sitting there waiting to be picked up, but if they'd stopped, had a chance to leave any other telltale sign…

Claire had left her book outside the home on purpose.

She was a resourceful little girl. And Neve, once clued in, got things done. It wasn't that Claire was any more intelligent than her sister; she was just a lot more focused.

Kind of like Ezra.

The man's ability to concentrate on the moment at hand was a bit intimidating.

And wonderful, comforting and reassuring to have around. Ezra's attention to detail calmed her panic. Helped her focus and do her part.

As she actively worked to find her girls, just by looking for a minute clue like a clod of dirt that didn't fit, she grew in strength.

The ability to hang on.

And to think clearly. To use her knowledge of the Fitzgeralds to try to figure out their next move. Without attaching immediate panic to the answers that came to her.

The idea wasn't to imagine what the girls were going through, but to stop the Fitzgeralds before they reached their endgame.

And then Dominic called again.

"Yeah," Ezra said after a quick push on the steering wheel. She listened intently. She didn't take her gaze off the land passing by them.

"Pick up."

As Ezra reached for his phone, she shot out a hand. Stopping him. Grabbed his phone. Had he not been driving, there was no way she'd have succeeded. "No," she said to both men at once. "Whatever you have to say, I need to hear."

"The Fitzgeralds' truck has been spotted twice in Benson."

Oh, dear God. They were on the wrong road. Looking for signs of the twins in a place they'd never been...

Her thoughts were interrupted as Ezra did a far-too-rapid-for-safety one-eighty, managed it with expert skill and had them racing at twice the speed limit back in the direction they'd come as Dom relayed specific coordinates of the blue truck. One on the outskirts of town. "The other was twenty minutes ago," he said, "at an intersection two miles west of Main. Can't make out any occupants, but authorities are all over the area now."

Heart pounding, she almost cried out with glee. Their capture and her daughters' rescue were imminent!

"If you're in the area..."

"We aren't," Ezra nearly barked. "But we will be within the hour." In very succinct words, he told Dominic about their detour. "Good news is I was traveling slow enough to survey roadside. Backtrack will be quick."

As she listened to her vehicle mate relay what she already knew, it occurred to her that there was nothing in what Dominic Colton had said that would prompt him to tell Ezra to pick up. As in, prevent Theresa from hearing what he had to say.

There was no logical reason for the request.

"Keep me posted," Dominic said, as though ending the call.

"Wait!"

Ezra glanced her way, raised his brow, and she said, "What else is there? Why did you want Ezra to pick up?"

She imagined the brothers exchanging a glance in the silence that fell. And then Dominic said, "One of the cameras got a good shot of the interior of the truck," he said, his tone not good. And while for an instant she wanted to cover her ears, the instant passed as quickly as it came.

"And?"

"We were able to identify Eric and Jennifer Fitzgerald in the front seat, but the back seat was empty. I'm sorry, Theresa."

He was sorry. Meant something to be sorry for. Bad for her. For her girls.

"They could have dropped them somewhere in town," Ezra quickly asserted. His hand found hers again. Held on, though her fingers didn't clutch his back as they had before. She was too numb to move.

"That's the theory we're going with."

As opposed to?

Did someone think that the couple had…?

"They love the girls," she said emphatically. "They won't physically hurt them." Not knowingly. And you'd have to do it knowingly for it to have happened to both of them so quickly.

"They could also have been told to get down on the floor," Ezra said. "Could have been covered up by a dark tarp. Theresa has said these people are planners. They're unstable in their beliefs, but smart. Look at the way they pulled off the kidnapping. They'd obviously been watching the home. Had done their research on the security system…"

Which they could only have done if they'd been inside. On her phone instantly, she called the home, asked for the charge nurse on duty and had her get someone to start watching security cameras over the past week to see if Eric and Jennifer Fitzgerald had been inside. She texted a picture of the pair while she was still on the phone.

And when she was done, she glanced at Ezra. Saw the caring, and also the approval, on his face and knew that, whatever it took, she would get the job done.

Just as she knew he would.

They were a team.

For the moment only, she reminded herself.

But in that moment, there was no future.

There was only finding her girls.

What did you say to a woman whose children were missing and she'd just been told that they weren't in the vehicle they'd been reportedly seen in an hour or so before?

Way out of his league, Ezra didn't say anything for a bit. He drove like a bat out of hell, to get her to Benson with the hope that by the time they arrived, the Fitzgeralds would be in custody.

And he worked on a plan B as well. The plan where they got the older couple but the girls weren't with them.

Theresa had been scrolling on her phone since Dom had hung up. Knowing that keeping her brain occupied was the single most important thing she could do to fight off a feeling of powerlessness that led to loss of hope and panic, he didn't ask if she was okay.

How could she be?

He didn't tell her things would be all right. That the girls were fine. He had no way of knowing either.

"Oh my God!" Her exclamation sent shock sensations from his chest to his gut.

"What?" Had she received a ransom note? A text? An email?

"I've been researching bunker buildings," she said. "Just in case…you know… I mean, their goal is to get the girls to safety, and we know they have a bunker somewhere, or did…"

"What, Theresa?" he asked, in a sergeant-expecting-an-answer tone. Not mean, but firm enough to stop the stream of useless information. There was only so much emotional tension a guy could take.

"There's this guy. He builds bunkers for people. There are a few of them, actually, right here on the internet, but this one, for a pretty hefty sum, he'll build a bunker for you…" She glanced over at him, as if to see whether he was still with her or thought her misguided for her research.

He couldn't help but nod with encouragement before turning his attention right back to the road. Driving twenty over the speed limit wouldn't do well if he lost control of the vehicle.

"His address is Benson, Colorado," she said softly.

She'd found his backup plan.

He glanced at her again. He couldn't help it. She was smiling.

It was a teary smile, but there.

And he smiled back.

They made a good team.

# Chapter 11

Not long after the smile that had to be forgotten, Theresa's phone rang. Millie, her second-in-command at the home, let her know that the Fitzgeralds had been at the home on Saturday. They'd signed in as Frank and Janie Frederick, to see Alice.

Her entire body froze. With stark cold horror. Somehow managing to thank Millie, she dropped her phone in her lap, as though it burned her skin, and saw it sitting there, on the black material of her skirt…

She'd had a meeting with state health people this morning, hoping to win a grant to provide electronics for the residents who could use them. Had donned the black skirt and jacket so she'd be taken seriously…

"Tell me what's going on." Once again, Ezra's voice pulled her back into focus. Which sent her right back to despair.

"The Fitzgeralds were at the home on Saturday. They signed in to visit your aunt. That's how they got on the ward. They're diabolical planners, Ezra. I knew it. I knew it," she said, and continued right on, "They knew about the Colton barbecue, knew I was going to be there. Probably watched you come pick me up, followed us there and saw their chance. They've been watching me, us, all along. They knew when they were waiting when we got home Saturday that we were with you. That's why they were there. They were sizing you up. Sizing us up. I knew it. I should have…"

"What?" His tone had softened. "What could you have done that you weren't already doing?"

"Run."

"Someplace where there was no one to help you when they found you? Because if they're as good, and determined, as you say, they would have found you, you know."

"They've been preparing for the blast since Mark was ten. That's more than twenty years. He said it was pretty much all they did, all they talked about. But it was so many years ago, and people come to their senses…"

Or they didn't. They just got in deeper and deeper until planning and protecting their own from what they perceived as very real dangers was all they knew. And something they did at any cost.

"They're prepared for a blast, Theresa." Ezra's tone strengthened. A sergeant talking to his men, maybe? "They aren't prepared to be hunted by the best this state has to offer. They aren't prepared for me."

There was no bravado in what he said.

Just stone-hard truth.

She listened while Ezra called Dom, reporting Millie's news, and wanted to lay her head down against Ezra's chest, feel the rumble of his voice, and rest. When the thought struck, she sat straight up instead. And spent the next half hour perusing the internet on her phone, searching for anything to do with conspiracy theories about nuclear blasts, preparations for them, where to buy supplies. She read articles. Clicked on links to various outlets. Read a short piece about guns and ammunition—bunker living required stockpiling illegal types of both—and forced herself to see the Fitzgeralds, to try, as Ezra was doing, to predict what they might do next in an effort to get that one step ahead of them that they had to reach in order to save the girls.

If, peripherally, she was getting a glimpse into the life her sweet babies might be forced to live if they weren't successful, she pushed the impressions away. Just as she prayed that they'd be strong, cling to each other and continue to be smart as Claire had been in leaving her book, she knew they needed the same from her.

She had to stay lucid and capable, no matter what it took. She'd learned the hard way that there'd always be time to grieve. Her job was to prevent the need.

She'd get her girls back. And she'd do it without falling for a sergeant who'd be leaving. One who'd dedicated his life to danger and fighting enemies. She'd prevent reasons to grieve. Protecting her daughters from any more cause to fear.

They were six. Life was supposed to be about unicorns and rainbows. Horses and happiness.

She jumped as Ezra's phone pealing interrupted the concentrated silence in the Jeep. Every muscle and her fingers clenched, she waited to hear that the Fitzgeralds had been caught and her daughters were safe.

Stared at Ezra as he pushed the button on the steering wheel and said, "Yeah."

"Nothing." Dom's tone was equally stoic. "Not another sign of the truck, of the couple or the girls. More than fifty law enforcement personnel from various jurisdictions, and they manage to get by all of them."

"How does that happen?" she cried out, uncaring for the moment that she was supposed to be strong and focused. Unable to hold back her terror. "Where are they? How do they just disappear?"

But the answer came to her even as she asked it.

They went underground, that was how.

They were informed, prepared.

She'd known in her gut that they were making a plan. They'd had everything in place, down to every last detail, like using the magnet to fool the alarm system.

"We suspect that there's a network," Dominic said. "From what intel we've gathered, there is a whole group of these people, like a cult, spread all over the country. They meet on social networks, mostly on the dark web. We're on there and listening, but so far, there's been no chatter regarding grandparents with young girls. Or any special movement today…"

Dark web. Intel. Chatter. It was like she'd woken up that morning a normal woman and had somehow faceplanted in the middle of a TV show.

"We've checked property records from all over the state, and neither Eric nor Jennifer Fitzgerald comes up. Either they're renting, squatting, living on inherited property without legal deed change, or they've been living under an assumed identity for a hell of a lot of years. The address on both of their driver's licenses is to a rented mailbox in a postal center they used to own. Same for credit cards and cell phones. Phones are turned off, but we've got someone monitoring in case they come back on, even for a few seconds. We'll know as soon as it happens."

And she'd let these people drive off with her little girls? Even once? Nauseated, Theresa turned the Jeep's vent straight at her face.

Law enforcement had been alerted in all surrounding states. Dom let them know, as if that was cause to feel grateful. The pronouncement, the authorities' apparent belief that there was cause to make the call, scared her further. The Fitzgeralds were Coloradoans. Had always, as far as she knew, been in the state. The idea that they'd take her daughters farther than state lines…

Maybe it shouldn't surprise her. After Mark's diagnosis, she definitely knew that the worst did happen. But…

Dom said he'd stay in touch. Ezra told his brother they'd still head into Benson. Ezra wanted to do his own reconnaissance, and Dom agreed that he was the man for that job, like none other, and reminded Ezra to call him if he found anything. They hung up without saying goodbye.

She hadn't had a chance to say goodbye to the twins.

The last thing she'd said to them…she couldn't remember. Probably some reminder to keep a hand on Charlie's collar…and not to leave the memory ward for any reason.

Oh, God, did they think she'd be mad at them for disobeying?

Neve was better at discerning the difference between

disobeying and situations being beyond their control. Hopefully she was reassuring serious little Claire.

"This is a setback, not a failure." Ezra sounded like a teacher in front of a class.

Looking over at him still in his painting clothes, she saw the way his jaw clenched and wondered if he had as many doubts as she did.

"You talking to yourself or to me?" she asked, hanging on to reason by a thread.

"Just stating fact. You don't stop until you fail. We haven't failed. Not by a long shot."

"You stop trying to do something the first time you fail?" The question had nothing to do with anything that mattered, but came out anyway. She wanted to know his answer.

"In battle, when you've failed to achieve your mission, you fall back," he said. "Doesn't mean you give up on the war, only the battle. It's not time for us to fall back."

It wasn't time to fall back. It was time to continue moving forward. He'd just given her hope.

Again.

"You're a good man, Ezra Colton." Emotion filled the words. The tone shocked her, revealing something she would not, could not, own.

If he heard it, received it, he didn't say.

And she didn't ask.

Or apologize.

Best just to leave it alone.

There was no place for personal emotion in their brief acquaintance.

He was just helping her find her daughters.

And then he'd be gone.

Like the girls' princess lunch, she was experiencing a prince investigation.

Nothing more.

Ezra thought about calling Dom back, letting his brother know that he was planning to visit the bunker maker—Tom Smith. Thought about the fact that the authorities, his triplet included, would demand that he let them know first, if they could.

He dismissed the thoughts almost at once. Then had another one. Theresa had a say.

As they neared Benson, he broke the silence that had fallen between them. "I have a plan."

Though he kept his gaze straight ahead—not wanting to deal with another jolt like their earlier shared smile had given him, or the tone in her voice when she'd proclaimed him a good man—he saw, peripherally, when she turned to look at him. "I'm not surprised, but I'm glad. What do you need me to do?"

No questioning what the plan even was?

Her trust in him hit him hard. Humbled him.

The woman was putting her daughters' lives in his hands. Was he up to the task?

He wasn't a good man. He was the guy who'd run out of town at the first possible opportunity. Run out on his family and their myriad problems and challenges.

He most definitely wasn't a good man. He was just good at what he did.

Still…with Theresa, those two endearing urchins, he was out of his league.

In the army he had lives at stake every time he went to work, but everyone understood, going in, that you couldn't save them all. There were going to be casualties. Your job was to minimize them as much as possible.

This wasn't that.

"Ezra? I'm not just going to stand back and wait."

"I know." Knuckles clenched on the wheel, he took a breath and plunged in.

"As soon as we get to town, we stop at a box store and get a couple of changes of clothes for each of us. Pants, button-up long-sleeved shirts, boots, in colors that match camo, but not actual camo pattern. Survival wear that also blends in. I'm going to buy a burner phone and call Tom Smith, tell him we're a married couple interested in a bunker, but need to see more. I'll tell him we're in town specifically to meet with him. From there, the plan is fluid. Our goal is to get inside his place—if we get lucky, even see a bunker—and collect as much information as we can. Anything could be a clue that might lead us to Eric and Jennifer."

He meant to give her time to speak, to question, disagree, but started talking again, justifying, before she could get a word in. "Law enforcement can question him. But as soon as he tells them he's never heard of Eric or Jennifer Fitzgerald, as soon as he looks at a picture of the couple and denies ever having seen them, and then asks them to leave his property, they'll be done. There's no known tie between him and them, and even if they could find one, that could take time, which we don't have. And if they do find a connection, it would have to be more than just that they've been in contact at some point in order to be enough to compel a warrant to search his place…"

The plan was solid. The best.

He needed her buy-in.

"I'm not going to lie to you about the danger. I don't foresee any, but when you're dealing with someone who builds bunkers for conspiracy theorists, you never know."

He would have insisted on going in alone, in spite of the fact that he believed the cover of a married couple would work in their favor, except that she'd refused to be left out of the search for her girls, and this part of the plan posed little danger. No matter what kind of business you were in, you wouldn't get far if you went around hurting potential clients.

He waited. And in the silence, found the flaw in his plan. Theresa was a nurturing, compassionate woman who spent her life taking care of others. She wasn't a soldier prepared to don the gear and go into battle. He'd misjudged...

"I'll have to get a wedding ring. Something cheap that can pass for real. They'll have a jewelry counter at the box store."

He glanced her way.

She was looking him right in the eye. "To support the cover," she said. "Guys always seem to look for wedding rings."

He glanced down. She wasn't wearing one. "When did you take yours off?"

"A month ago."

Before she'd met him.

A sign that she was ready to move on with her life? That she'd be looking for more than a barbecue with a guy who was only visiting town for a few weeks?

He'd told his brothers she was a grieving widow who wouldn't be looking to him for anything other than a momentary acquaintanceship.

He'd told himself the same thing.

So how did he explain the looks?

The smile?

The tone of voice?

He couldn't have her seeing more in him than was there.

And no way in hell could he abandon her, either. Not while her girls were missing.

He might be a runner, but he didn't leave jobs he'd taken on until they were complete.

So…what?

Did he let her know what was what…make sure she wasn't falling for him…or imagining something that wasn't there…tell her that she could only rely on him to find her girls and nothing more…before or after they posed as a married couple?

"I need to get something out there." She interrupted his thoughts, relieving him of the immediate need to make a decision that wasn't feeling in any way pleasant.

"What?" he asked, both hands on the wheel as the traffic picked up slightly on the way into Benson.

"I just…don't want to give you the wrong impression here. I could be speaking out of turn, and I hope I am, but…you asked me out, and here you are, risking your life for my girls, and…it kind of feels like we've had a personal moment or two, and now here I am, telling you I took off my wedding ring, something everyone knows is a sign someone is moving on and…"

His knuckles turned white as she paused, and he silently swore every word he'd ever heard. And then made up one or two.

She was really going to do it? Force him to hurt her in the middle of the race to find her daughters? To add insult to injury to a woman who was already at her brink?

Could he pretend that there was a chance for them? Just until she got her girls back, when she'd be over-joyed and better able to handle the rejection?

The idea took root, was the most logical, consider-ing all aspects of the situation.

"I just… I'm so thankful for what you're doing, Ezra. And…having you by my side is about the only way I'm getting through this…"

*Yes. Definitely. Go the pretend route.*

She could find out later what a creep he was to lie to her. Women got over creeps all the time.

"But I need you to know that…once the girls are home…" She took a deep breath. And he just knew that she was saying a prayer that the girls made it home safely. "What I'm trying to say is that I can't get in-volved with a man whose career doesn't allow him to have a real home. And most importantly, not a man who faces danger every day of his life. I can't put my girls through it, either. We've already lost one man. We can't lose another…"

Talk about having the wind knocked out of you…

"No worries," Ezra told her. "I'm not a family guy, and most definitely will be leaving at the end of the month. I've never even dated a woman who'd ever had a kid." All true.

As was the huge wave of disappointment that hit him when she finally got out with what she'd been try-ing to say.

She didn't want him.

It was good. All good.

Right.

What he needed. What he'd need to tell her.
A huge relief.
And still…wow.
The light in his world had suddenly dimmed.

# *Chapter 12*

Ezra gave her ten minutes in the store to get what she needed, change clothes and meet him by the exit. When he'd suggested that she grab clothes for a couple of days, just in case, her heart had dropped, but it didn't slow her down. Every minute they were in the store meant more minutes before she could see her daughters again.

In addition to clothes and toiletries, she managed to grab food supplies as she ran her basket past displays, and she snagged a big package of cleansing wipes as well. The mother in her couldn't pass them up.

In dark green jeans, a long-sleeved, lighter green cotton shirt and a pair of tie-up, waterproof, tan ankle boots, she met him, bags in hand, at exactly ten minutes.

Tried not to take a second look at the way the jeans and long-sleeved light brown tee hugged his muscles, failed, and then noticed the thirty-six-pack of bottled water in the cart behind him.

The fact that she hadn't thought of getting the life-sustaining liquid herself told her how far off her mark she really was. Shaking, she followed him out to the Jeep, promising herself she'd do better.

And kept her mind on that goal as Ezra handed her a new burner phone and then sent a text from a second burner phone. "We have no idea how connected the Fitzgeralds are," he told her. "For now, use that phone."

Of course, there were conspiracy theorists with friends in high places. Governors who had bunkers in case of a nuclear blast. She'd just read about them that afternoon.

And she'd grabbed candy, as though she and Ezra were on an adventure. A road trip.

She had to do better. Be better.

"We're Jack and Molly Wallace," he told her as he stood the phone in a cup holder beside him and handed her a cheap metal band, motioning toward the one on his left ring finger.

Feeling surreal, she slid her matching band in place.

She could think about being Molly Wallace.

She had to not think about what could be happening to her daughters. Not think about Claire's worries or Neve's need to make things seem okay when they weren't. Not think about them afraid and crying.

As anxiety rose up, ready to choke her, she turned to reach for one of her bags in the back seat of the Jeep, intending to get the bag of candy she'd snagged, to grab a piece of chocolate to give her immediate distraction, and instead, her gaze landed on Ezra's bag.

More particularly on the new package of underwear visible through the thin plastic.

A three-pack—red, blue and black—of cotton boxer briefs.

Ezra's…

Anxiety dissipated.

And she no longer needed the chocolate.


Not liking going into battle with someone to protect beside him, Ezra drove toward Tom Smith's known residence with trepidation building within him. He only ever took armed and trained soldiers into battle with him.

A team of men who knew how to read each other and the situation, who knew how to preempt the unexpected and deal with it if it slapped them in the face.

Theresa was most definitely not armed or trained.

But if he hoped to get a good look inside Smith's premises, and around his property, he had to have an in, and Theresa was it.

With the Fitzgeralds seemingly off the grid, Ezra's chosen course of action could be the only way to get the girls back expediently.

Only if it worked perfectly, of course, and there was no guarantee of that.

As he thought over every aspect of the plan, he saw no reason to fear immediate physical harm. The man ran a viable business with a stellar rating with the Better Business Bureau. Smith was just an unknowing means to a possible quick and happy end to a kidnapping.

They were only a mile from Smith's place when he got an answering text, telling him that Smith could meet with him at his convenience that day. Not wanting to rush in like a fool, he texted back that he and his wife had stopped for a bite to eat, and asked if half an hour would be okay.

The confirmation came back within a minute.

And the thirty minutes he and Theresa waited were excruciating to him, as he ran the plan over and over in his mind, thinking about what to look for, where to look and what questions to ask.

"Dom's the undercover expert," he said aloud to Theresa at one point. She'd spent the majority of their time scrolling on her phone. After their very clear understanding that there couldn't be anything personal between them, he'd given up being friendly with her.

If only he could quit being aware of her as easily. Her scent. Her almost frantic touching of thumb to screen, more like jabs than the light touches that seemed more natural to her. Every breath she took…

"If I call him, to get pointers, he could very likely order me not to visit Smith, and send law enforcement there instead…"

"No!" Her gaze wide and alarmed, she looked straight at him for the first time since they'd exited the store. "Then we have the whole warrant thing to deal with. Please, Ezra, no matter how this turns out, I have to try."

"And I have to make you aware of all aspects of this situation, as best I can," he said. "I've never freelanced before. Or been on any job without explicit orders and protocols to follow. But here I am, listening to a gut that has led men into many victories, and I feel as though I have to do all I can to get those little ones back as quickly as possible, but they're your girls to save, not mine."

"And this is my choice," she said, her tone almost

calm, and most definitely filled with strength. "When Mark was sick, there were choices to make, different treatments with different risks and levels of success rates... I wanted to go one way, he wanted to go the other, but it was his life. He had to be the one to make them. And in the end, when the choices he made didn't pan out as he'd expected, he was at peace with having taken his life in the direction he'd thought best. That was one of the last things he told me. He'd lived on his terms. If we don't do this, and I find out that having done so could have helped my girls... I would never be able to live with myself."

He nodded, went back to his game planning while she went back to her phone, and they didn't speak again until he pulled through an opened chain-link gate. They drove across a dirt yard and up to what looked like a metal barn with a storefront sitting just feet away from an old, but well-kept, white-vinyl-sided house.

He turned to her. "Ready?"

"Ready." She didn't hesitate.

With a nod, he reached over to the glove box in front of her knees, opened it and pulled out his handgun. He slid it into the waistband of his jeans and covered it with the loosely fitting shirt. "I have a concealed carry permit in my wallet," he told her.

"I wasn't asking."

"I'm Jack and you're Molly," he reminded her.

"Wallace," she confirmed, exiting the Jeep and meeting him at the front, visibly calm when he knew she had to be shaking inside all the way to her core. God, he admired the woman.

He took her hand in his as they headed toward the front of the store. To get into character.

And because he wanted to connect with her.

When she linked her fingers with his, squeezing tight, he was glad.


Tom Smith was nothing like she'd expected. A short, thin man, with dark-rimmed glasses, a clean shave and short hair, he welcomed them to his store as though they were friends. Showed them to a table toward the back of the partitioned-off front room, offered them water or coffee or a bottle of soda and gave them a couple of notebooks loaded with page protectors filled with photos.

Walking around to the back side of the table, against the wall, Ezra pulled out a chair for her, and then scooted his right up next to hers, so they could look at the same photos at the same time. Smith, returning almost immediately with the bottled water they'd both requested, and a pad and paper, took a seat opposite them.

As the men started their conversation, Theresa felt surreal. Enjoying the imaginary story of Ezra and her as Jack and Molly Wallace more than anything else she'd had to face that day. Wishing she could lose herself in the make-believe and rest awhile. She couldn't remember ever taking as much solace from the warmth and nearby presence of another human being as she did Ezra Colton. He was a man of few words during situations when she needed words, and yet he said enough. Said what she'd needed. She'd calmed more through his silence than she'd ever have thought possible.

Smith started by telling them basics, recommendations based on type of location—city, rural, size of lot—and then trenching specifics. He likened his process to what was done for subway systems, rather than digging, to prevent cave-ins. Finally he moved on to dimensions. He built his bunkers ten feet underground and recommended ten square feet of space per occupant.

Much of which, just like the photos in front of her, triggered every one of Theresa's panic buttons.

Were Claire and Neve already hidden away ten feet under? Experiencing for real what Theresa was only looking at in pictures? Would they both already be claustrophobic for life, being trapped down there? Were they scared out of their minds?

As her imagination started to run away with her, she felt Ezra's hand on her knee under the table. And remembered that she had a job to do. Covering his hand with hers, she forced her focus to the room in which they sat, taking in whatever she could, in case Ezra needed it later.

"Do you recommend all steel construction?" Ezra asked, perusing pages so thoroughly she almost believed he was in the market for a bunker for himself. He talked about things she hadn't even read about, and it quickly became clear to her that Ezra Colton was no stranger to bunker construction.

And, of course, he wouldn't be. He was a career soldier, on special operation assignments. Dangerous ones. Where they'd need bunkers to keep them safe.

"I mostly do metal sheets with cement, reinforced with rebar in between them," Smith was saying, "but we can do steel if you prefer and are willing to pay for it." The man went on to talk about ventilation, generator sizes, furniture built into the wall to make more use of a small space.

"What about plumbing?" she asked. She was there to convince the man she wanted to live in a bunker. It was time to take ownership of the home, or she'd fail the task, and possibly her daughters. "I read about toilets that grind and then pump and dump up to one hundred feet horizontally, where the compost becomes natural fertilizer, keeping any odor from collecting inside the dwelling." She pulled from what little she'd remembered from her afternoon reading.

"We do pump and dump, yes. I don't generally add the grind feature. It adds a lot to the cost, and as long as you don't throw sanitary napkins or condoms in the tank, you won't need to grind."

He spoke pragmatically.

She could feel her face turning red as embarrassed heat crept up her skin with condoms and Ezra sharing her space at the same time. And celebrated the fact that she was doing her job well enough to feel something besides panic and growing despair.

"I'd still like the grind feature," she said. "I'll borrow the money if I have to, but we have quite a bit saved already from my father's life insurance policy. We're..." She glanced at Ezra, allowing herself to show the deep regard she felt for the man she barely knew, and continued, "We're trying to start a family, and I want to be prepared for a stray something to get flushed..."

Ezra held her gaze. The warmth in his eyes made her want things she couldn't ever have with him.

"Yes, we'll definitely want the grind feature," he said, blinking and straightening his shoulders as he turned back to the bunker builder.

And she wondered...did he have the information he needed? Could they get out of there?

Had he seen something in her that he'd wanted?

"Do you have any clients who would be willing to

give testimonials about your work?" her soldier man asked as Tom made a list of their dimensions, preferences and specifications.

"I do," the man said. "They're designated by type of bunker, and type of location, too, so you can contact those who have interests and needs similar to yours. I'll get you the list when we're through here."

Her heart started to pump. So hard she could feel her pulse in her chest, thumping through her. Hear it in her ears. Was it really going to be that smooth? They'd get the Fitzgeralds' bunker information, and maybe even an approximate location, handed to them on a printed piece of paper?

Clamping her hand down on Ezra's knee, she took the sustenance she needed without apology. For that moment, he was as a husband to her.

Tom asked questions. Jotted on his list. Retrieved a laptop and moved notes onto a form that would give them an approximate cost for their personalized bunker, to be set out on an old hunting lot in the middle of the Colorado wilderness. Something Molly had also inherited from her father.

Whereas Theresa Fitzgerald had never even known who her father was. Her mother, either, for that matter.

Feeling rather fond of the imaginary deceased figurehead, she gave Ezra a glance as, figures done, Tom slid them across the table. Assuring Tom that they'd look everything over and get back with him before they left town the next day, she watched as the man left them to collect his list of references.

Tom's phone buzzed, obviously a text, as he pulled out the cell and looked at the screen rather than answering it, and Theresa couldn't help but touch Ezra's knee one more time. "Thank you," she said, her heart pretty much in her throat, making her voice soft and guttural.

When Ezra stiffened, his immediate tension noticeable to her hand still on his lower thigh, she tried to snatch her hand back, but it didn't leave its location.

His hand held her fingers where they were as he leaned over to kiss her cheek and said, "I think we've been made. Stay behind me and follow my lead."

Clinging to the hand holding hers, she stood as he did, not questioning his judgment for even a second, as he walked her behind the man bending beside a desk in front of a tall filing cabinet and out of the odd little store.

"Keep to the wall," he said, his free hand under his shirt where she knew he'd shoved his gun. And then, "See that wall of trees? Run behind it, and follow it back to the far side of the Jeep. Climb in the back seat and stay down. Now. Go!"

She went. She didn't think. Didn't question what she wanted to do. She just ran. Reached the trees, hugged the first one she came to with her arms up against her chest, not spread wide, and looked to the next trunk, getting there as quickly as she could. Two minutes was all it took for her to reach the Jeep and scramble onto the floor of the back seat.

Two minutes, and then gunshots rang out.

# Chapter 13

Ezra heard the bullet hit the tree just to the right of his shoulder. And then tossed the rock he'd grabbed on an upward trajectory, to arch down and hit the ground near a tree a few feet over from him. Waited for the bullet to hit. And repeated it twice more, throwing the rocks up on an angle to land a few feet farther each time. When the fourth shot rang out beyond his last throw, in anticipation of where the path would go next, he spun and made his way stealthily through the woods, behind the barn and out to the trees on the other side where he'd sent Theresa. The side with more covering.

Years of training for battle had taught him how to move undetected, but he couldn't be sure how long Smith would be distracted by his movement in the woods before advancing on the vacant Jeep. He went on the hunch that the man wanted his prey badly enough to follow the path Ezra had laid. Keeping down, he slid into the Jeep and started it. With only enough of his head above the dash for him to see, he spun them around to head toward the property exit before Smith had a chance to figure out what was happening.

"Stay down." He bit out the words through gritted teeth.

Bullets flew at them, but Ezra had expected that. A couple hit the Jeep, breaking glass, embedding in the back of his seat. The doomsday preparer was an excellent shot. He'd counted on that, too. The bullets would have hit him if he'd been sitting in the driver's seat, instead of half lying across the console, his legs in a split formation, with one foot on the gas and one bunched up by the radio. He had one hand on the steering wheel, the other holding his gun, as he sped down the road that led to Smith's place.

"Stay down," he said a second time, less forcefully. "He might follow us."

"I don't think so." Her tone was…fine. Considering she could have been killed. And he wondered if she'd lost it back there—thinking that just because they'd managed to evade the bad guy once, they were automatically safe.

"Mark talked about how his folks were always teaching him how to defend house and home," she continued, as if conversing from the back floor of a Jeep was part of a regular day in her life. "They were always really careful about not breaking laws—no way you could save yourself from the blast if you were locked in a cell. They knew when and where they could fight with force, shoot their guns, whatever. And chasing someone down on a public road, shooting at them, wouldn't qualify. Legally, if Smith had hit us while we were on his property, he could have claimed self-defense."

He couldn't believe it. The woman had just nearly lost her life and she was conversing as though they were on a picnic or something. Almost chuckling with relief as half a mile passed with no further bullets flying at them, he slowed the vehicle, chanced a quick glance behind them, saw the roadway completely empty and stopped in the middle of the road just long enough to get himself in the driver's seat.

"Wait. I'm coming up," Theresa told him as sirens sounded.

He did as she asked, keeping watch around them for any activity in the woods on the sides of the road as well as the road itself, and saw the row of vehicles with lights flashing coming from the opposite direction toward Smith's property.

"I called the police," she said.

Of course she had. And Tom Smith would tell them that everything was fine. That Jack and Molly Wallace had been potential clients who'd left unexpectedly. Lay any trouble on them. If he was questioned about shots fired, he'd say he shot in self-defense.

"Did you use the burner phone I gave you?"

"Yes."

He had to call Dom. But first, when she looked over and smiled at him, giving him the urge to pull her against him and thank God she was okay, he put his foot on the gas and got them the hell out of there.

Thirty seconds after she'd climbed in the front seat, Theresa started to shake. Adrenaline dissipated, survival mode faded, and she was left with vivid sensations that wouldn't let her go. She'd heard shots. She surveyed every visible inch of Ezra's body for signs of red. Found none. Not even on his shirt.

"I didn't know if you'd been hit." He hadn't wanted authorities involved in their hunt. Protocols would slow their process. And if they were ordered to stand down and didn't…

Freezing in her long-sleeved shirt, she rubbed her arms and tried to get herself back under control. "I had to call for help."

"You did the right thing. I'll call Dom just as soon as there's a little more distance between us and the Smith residence," he said, sounding not at all upset or disappointed with her. "He'll be pissed, read me the riot act, but he'll arrange for us to have another vehicle. And he'll get his people looking at what they can legally access of Smith's business dealings and associations."

The slow route he'd wanted to avoid.

"I'm sorry you're in hot water with your brother."

She most definitely didn't want to get him in trouble with the law.

And she didn't want him to give up on them, either. She needed him.

Just until the girls were home and safe.

Then she'd be able to wish him a blessed life and say goodbye.

She'd never forget him. That was a given.

"If Dom were in my position, he'd do the exact same thing. And he'd expect me to do so as well. He'll be more pissed that I'm out here getting stuff done while his hands are tied," Ezra told her, giving her another glimpse into the man who was so quickly growing to mean so much to her.

Feelings that would dim as soon as life got back to normal.

"The aftershock will wear off in a few."

"What?" Looking over at him, she saw the concerned glance he was sending her.

"What you're experiencing right now. The aftershock. Every sense is on high alert. Emotions temporarily shut down. Your mind is in full charge. And when the battle is over, when all of that starts to subside, it takes a bit for all parts of you to come back in sync with each other."

He sounded so…normal. Like someone who'd just watched what had happened on a screen, not in real life.

Almost like a teacher in class.

The once-in-a-lifetime potentially debilitating experience she'd just lived through was only a day's work to him.

The reminder was another shock to a system that she was pretty sure couldn't take much more. And yet she wasn't backing out.

Wasn't quitting. And if he thought she was…

They'd turned onto another country road, surrounded by more woods and very few homesteads. He parked on the side, kept the Jeep running and pulled out his personal cell.

"Where are you?" The bullet-tattered Jeep filled with Dom's voice.

In succinct phrases, Ezra filled his brother in on Tom Smith, the plan to get inside the man's shop. "Everything was coming down perfectly, almost had a list with a very good chance of including the Fitzgeralds. It would tell us if not specific addresses, at least details about the physical location of the bunker and type of bunker. Then he gets a text. Looks over at us, looks back at the text, at us again, and bends down to his file cabinet…"

That was how he'd known…

"Getting a gun…"

She'd thought he'd been going to a file for a copy of his reference list. And seconds later, if she'd been there on her own, she'd have been looking down the barrel of a gun, instead of fleeing one.

Ezra continued his half-sentence statements, telling Dominic about his game play with Smith outside the shop, his escape.

"Then we got the hell out of there," Ezra said, while Theresa kept her own counsel.

"And the anonymous 911 call that couldn't be traced?"

Wow, they knew that already?

"Theresa. From the burner phone I gave her."

"How bad's the rental?"

"I'll need something else."

"Smith knows what we look like," Theresa finally blurted. Which meant the police might soon know, and they'd be ordered to stand down.

And maybe authorities would believe that Dom had been involved with his brother's off-the-grid vigilante enforcement? Would he be told to stand down as well?

Panic filled her anew.

Her daughters, who could have already disappeared off the grid forever, needed more than protocol at the moment…

"He'd have to reveal more than he wants to, maybe even give access to the information you were after, if he admits he saw you. If he's going to report it officially," Dom said over the line. "More than likely he'll say he thought he saw movement and shot, thinking it was an animal."

She hadn't thought of that. But clearly Ezra had. He was nodding his head. And reached out a hand, tucking a lock of fallen hair back into her bun. Automatically reaching up to tighten the scrunchie holding her hair in place, she accidentally brushed her ascending hand against his descending one.

Ice against warmth.

Dom said he'd get back to Ezra shortly with details of where he could pick up a new vehicle and leave the damaged one to be retrieved by the rental company. "You're lucky you paid extra for their insurance, bro," the FBI agent said.

He was lucky he wasn't dead, Theresa thought to herself, recalling the cat-and-mouse game Ezra had told Dom he'd played with Smith while she'd been facedown on the floor of the Jeep, listening to gunshots.

Neither of the brothers seemed to get that the danger they were taking for granted, their escape from it, wasn't at all normal life.

Because to them it was.

To her, it would never be.

As it turned out, Dom used Smith's shooting at Ezra and Theresa as a means to tie the incident to the kidnapping of Claire and Neve Fitzgerald, and by the time Ezra and Theresa were in a new, slate gray Jeep, picked up at a rental place in Benson, the FBI was attempting to get a warrant to search Smith's place.

"So our plan worked after all!" Theresa said when she heard the news. "Not like we'd hoped, but, as you said, once we got inside, the plan was fluid…"

They'd just pulled off the rental lot, and he had more to tell her. "There's been no sign of the Fitzgeralds." They'd agreed to drive through for something quick to eat, and then he had to come up with his next move. "No credit card use, no sightings of the truck, and their phones are still turned off." He knew his words had to be striking terror within her, but if they were going to get through however long it took to get her kids back, she would have to be able to deal with the hard stuff.

No way, as darkness fell soon, that it wouldn't be coming.

He couldn't let her slow him down.

Because to do so would let her down.

"That's with reports from multiple law enforcement agencies across the state and in bordering states, and a check of all Benson surveillance cameras." The truck was seen twice in Benson and then disappeared.

He pulled into the lot of an Italian place that offered a drive-through window. Pasta was filling and easy on the stomach. And then he asked, "Do you like Italian?"

He didn't look her way. Couldn't afford to be compassionate at the moment. Either she had what it might take, or she didn't. With the chance for a quick rescue gone, he was going off the grid.

"Look at my hips. What do you think?" The somewhat waspish comment drew his gaze to hips that, while maybe a little filled out due to childbirth, looked way too good to him.

"No, don't do that," he told her, shaking his head.

"Do what?"

"Distract me. Look, here's how it is. I'm given a goal, I figure out battle plans, and I only work with the best of the best. At the moment, that's me. Alone."

"We've already been through this."

The car in front of him pulled forward, making it his turn to order.

"I want baked ziti," she said. He asked for two. Saw her reach for her credit card as he inched the Jeep toward the pickup window, and pulled out his own wallet.

She stuck her card in front of his chest. He handed his own card to the teenager leaning out the window.

"Why are you being this way?" she asked, her tone marked down several notches. "I was good today. I helped."

He nodded. He'd like to have her along. When he found the twins, there was no telling what emotional state they'd be in, and they'd need her.

She had a right to be with him since he wasn't working in any official capacity, but rather, at her request. If it were his kids who'd been hauled off, no way he'd sit out the search.

It wasn't like there was going to be some kind of ransom call. No reason for her to be home. Worse, there was nothing for her to do there but worry.

Not his concern.

She wasn't even a friend.

"I need to know that you aren't going to fall apart on me. I have no idea what I'll be doing, or what I might find along the way. If I have to tend to you, it could make the difference between completing the job successfully or not."

"The credit card, that was a test, right?" she said, her brows drawn together as she pinned him with a knowing look.

How did she do that? How was it possible that a woman he barely knew could read him when no one else, other than Dom and Oliver, had ever been able to do so?

What was taking the damned ziti so long? He glanced toward the window.

"I'm the boss," he said. When it came to split-second decisions and life and death, there had to be one.

"And I proved that I won't fight that. You won. You paid. I conceded gracefully. And earlier, when you told me to leave, to run, where to run and how to enter the Jeep, I followed every command without question."

Yeah. She'd done good. He had good points, too, but he was being a jerk. Because the woman turned him on, and he didn't want her to do so. Had given no permission for that to happen.

Had no good outcome for the malady.

And that pissed him off.

The fact that he hadn't found her daughters before nightfall was eating his insides out.

None of which was her fault. Nor should she be bearing the brunt of his frustration.

She'd suffered enough for a lifetime.

And was carrying a burden far, far worse than his would ever be. Nighttime fell on his failure, but it fell on her children.

He couldn't even imagine…

"You showed me what I needed to see in terms of your ability to do what's asked in the heat of battle this afternoon." He glanced her way again, really looked at her, into those overflowing brown eyes, and let himself soak for a moment.

He shouldn't have doubted her ability to hold up even for a second. "I'm sorry."

"You're risking your life for my daughters, Ezra," she

said softly, the glow in her eyes growing, not diminishing. "You have nothing to apologize for."

He needed to kiss those lips. To hold her tight and make the bad things go away.

"Here you go, sir." A hand reached a bag out to him.

He took it.

And drove off into the setting sun with a sinking feeling in his gut.

For the first time in his life, he was in over his head.

# Chapter 14

He hadn't quit on her. From the time they'd talked to Dominic, Ezra had been chewing on something, and Theresa had been prepared to hear that he was stepping back to let law enforcement do their jobs.

She'd been prepared to beg him to stay, even though he'd already done far too much for her.

Instead, she'd had to beg to be allowed to stay.

He drove out by a river they'd passed, pulled into a lay-by and parked. Wanting, first and foremost, not to hamper his process, she didn't attempt to converse with him while they ate. And forced herself to chew and swallow a good portion of the pasta crammed into a very full Styrofoam container.

She might not be skilled in battle, and sometimes her imagination ran away with her when it came to worry-

ing about her kids. But she would not hinder the finding of her children.

Nor would she abandon them solely to the abilities
of others.

"You're too quiet." Ezra's words washed over her
like warm water.

"I didn't want to interrupt your thoughts."

"Might have been better if you'd pulled me away
from them." The statement was odd, most particularly
from him, but she let it go.

And said aloud what she'd just started thinking
about. "When I was two, I was abandoned at a church.
Just left there, inside the vestibule, with no note, no
identification. I'm told I wandered around for several
hours, at best guess, and eventually crawled up onto a
lone pew that was out there and fell asleep. I was found
there early one morning."

She took a bite. Chewed. Appreciated his silence.

"Authorities spent a lot of time trying to find my
parents. They couldn't put me up for adoption without
knowing that I hadn't been kidnapped. Maybe one parent not wanting the other to have me or something. In
any case, I grew up in a children's home associated with
the church. I was well educated. Well loved. But until I
married Mark, I'd never had a family of my own. Two
things about this are pertinent," she continued. "First,
the authorities, through all of their effort and access
to information and databases, were never able to find
who'd left me at that church. I cannot just leave my
daughters' fates to authorities. I trust them to do everything they can. I appreciate all that they're doing. But
whether you're with me or not, I will be on the hunt for
Claire and Neve until I find them."

There was nothing he or anyone was going to do to stop her.

"And second?"

She glanced at him, noticed that he'd completely cleaned his container. "What?"

"You started with 'first,' and I wanted to know what second was."

"Second, I will not abandon my children as I was abandoned. I'm not prepared for battle, I get that…"

"I'll prepare you as best I can every step of the way." The old Ezra was back. The one who'd spent an entire afternoon at her side while his family hovered around them. Who'd made her daughters' horse-riding dreams come true.

"We're a team again, then?"

He nodded. Didn't really smile, but he was looking her in the eye again. Telling her things that she couldn't really translate into words, but things that mattered.

Things that gave her strength.

And hope.

"The good news is that Eric and Jennifer Fitzgerald's end goal is to protect their son's children." Ezra started in before they'd even pulled away from the river. "Which means that this kidnapping is different from many where hope for the child's physical safety wanes as the hours pass."

"I'm counting on that fact." Theresa was putting their containers and plastic silverware back in the bag they'd come in.

"Until we can figure out where they're homesteading, where their bunker is, we need them to feel confident in their ability to pull this off." He was thinking aloud. But also doing what he'd just said he'd do—preparing her.

If the Fitzgeralds were cornered, feeling desperate, the twins could get hurt.

"So, we need to make sure that today's situation with Tom Smith doesn't happen again," she said. "We don't want them to know we're closing in on them."

She was good.

But he'd known that.

"We'll need to be more discreet, yes," he agreed. "I'm not a profiler, per se, but before we go into battle, we profile our enemy as a whole. We have to be able to predict what they might do given various situations. We need to know what kind of weapons they have, for instance, how many days' worth of supplies, or what kind of barricades, physical or otherwise, they'll be using to stop us. I need to know these kinds of things about the Fitzgeralds. So what I suggest is that we get a room someplace in town and sit down and talk. I need you to tell me everything you can remember Mark ever telling you about his parents. And any and all details you can recall about the time you've known them. Things the girls have said, but also your own impressions."

They had to get a room. No way they were heading two hours back to Blue Larkspur when they knew the girls had been driven as far as Benson. And it wasn't like they could scour wooded miles in the pitch-black for any telltale signs of recent occupation.

Realizing her little girls were going to be spending at least one night with the unstable couple had to be soul-destroying, but Theresa was sitting up straight. Engaging rationally with him.

She was there, as she'd sworn she'd be, and he admired the hell out of her.

"There was that place kind of in the middle of town," she reminded him. "It had rooms with windows that look out over Main Street. And parking outside each door." So much for thinking the room idea was going to be a problem for her.

If only he could be so sure it wouldn't pose serious issues for him.

He'd shared bunks and slept sleeping bag to sleeping bag in bunkers, too, with both male and female soldiers.

He'd never, ever spent a night in a motel room with a woman he was hot for without sex being an already-agreed-upon mutual desire.

And there were considerations so much more important at stake…

"I just thought of something," she blurted as he pulled back into town. The streetlights were coming on to brighten the falling dusk. "Tom Smith had a pamphlet sitting on that desk when we walked in. I remember wondering if it was part of a packet he gives to all prospective clients."

He'd been sizing up the man, looking for weapons and planning escape routes. Not glancing at brochures on the furniture.

"And?"

"It was for guns and ammunition, Ezra. That store right there." Sitting forward, she pointed an obviously shaking finger at a small corner place attached to a long string of storefronts all under one roof.

He drove slowly past, taking in the nearly all glass front and what looked like cases in a U shape around the long, narrow room. Several businesses down, outside an ice cream shop, he parked. "You up for a walk?" he asked, studying the street and the area around the ammunition shop on the corner intently.

"Of course." She'd opened her door and was out of the vehicle faster than he'd have liked. Remnants of having been shot at—of knowing she was a target as well—still tightened his nerve endings.

He didn't see any sign of unusual activity. The street was calm. Shoppers, but not so many that the sidewalks were crowded. A few cars. A family sitting on a bench eating ice cream.

If Claire and Neve had been there, they'd have ordered chocolate...

"Let's go inside," he said, heading up to the door of the soda fountain and sweets parlor. Pulling his phone out, he spoke with the manager who'd been working all day, spoke with anyone who'd been there for more than four hours, showed the picture he had of the twins without saying who they were or why he was asking about them.

No one had seen them. And it wasn't like six-year-old twins who, while not identical, looked alike would be forgettable.

"How about these two?" Theresa asked, showing a picture of the Fitzgeralds standing by their truck, smiling. "We were supposed to meet them here, but we're later than expected, and I'm afraid we missed them."

She was good. Damned good.

Better than he was.

Interrogation wasn't his business.

"Yeah, them I recognize." A young guy with dark hair tied back in a ponytail nodded as he wiped his hands on a long white apron over jeans. "Mostly because they bought like two cases of ice cream sandwiches and paid cash for 'em, too. They wanted all we had, and I emptied out the back of the walk-in to get them. They got dry ice, too, you know, like they were going on a road trip. But they didn't have any kids in here with them, if they were all supposed to be together or something."

"The kids were probably still out in the truck," Ezra said, to cover for Theresa's suddenly white face and tighter expression.

"Oh, well, maybe it's not the same people," the kid said. "They looked an awful lot like that, but these guys were driving a van."

"A van?" Theresa voiced the question.

"Yeah. I offered to help load it, but the guy was pretty definite about being able to do it himself. I figured he was one of those OCD types, you know. Everything has to be just right. The van was older, from the eighties, maybe, brown, and sweet, really. Not a scratch or dent that I could see. Tires were fairly new, too, great tread on them."

The kid asked if he could get them anything…on the house…but Ezra shook his head. Took Theresa's hand. Making an excuse about hoping to catch up with their family, he got them out the door, and as soon as they were far enough down the block for the observant ice cream scooper not to see, he was on the phone with Dom. Authorities were looking for the wrong vehicle.

"They got the warrant and are on their way to Smith's," Ezra told Theresa as, still holding her hand—for show, he told himself—they headed down to the ammunition shop.

She missed a step, clasping harder at his hand as she

righted herself, and looked up at him. "Oh my God! We might still get them tonight!"

He didn't want to get her hopes up, but he couldn't deny that he, too, saw the plausibility of such a possibility. And needed it to come to be.

Every second he was with Theresa, every breath of her he inhaled, he was getting in further over his head.

One step in front of the other. It was all she could do. Life had spiraled so far out of control, out of any comfort zone, out of all realms of anything she'd ever imagined herself doing, that Theresa couldn't find any sense of a self she knew. So, she took the self she had and determined that that person was going to do whatever it took to find her children.

"Act natural," Ezra said, his tone striking a new shot of fear through her. "We're a couple on a stroll…"

About to get shot at? She clutched his hand harder. Whatever happened, holding his hand made it easier to bear.

"The guy behind the counter in the gun shop is watching us. And texting."

He'd told Dominic that Tom Smith's doing the same was what had alerted him to their danger at the bunker store. Was the ammunition shopkeeper going to reach for a gun as well?

Ezra wasn't urging her to run. Or hide. He wasn't rushing her to face-plant on the floor of their new Jeep. She walked as casually as she could beside him. Looking toward the window of the antique shop next door to their destination. Moving close enough to Ezra that their hips were touching.

"You okay to go in?" Ezra asked as they approached the gun shop.

"Of course."

She saw the shopkeeper, a skinny guy with a mop of curly red hair falling down around his face, coming around the counter as they got close. Her heart pounded as her gaze flew to his hands, her entire system rushing into flight mode.

The man's hands were empty. He reached toward the door handle just before they did.

He was going to hold the door open for them?

She'd just started to adjust to the information when she heard a click. And saw a shade come down over the door. Followed by quickly pulled shades on the windows on either side of it.

"He just locked the door on us," she said, standing there nonplussed.

"Yep." Ezra moved them quickly toward the antique shop storefront. "Not smart to stand in front of shaded windows," he said. "Most particularly when the room behind them is filled with arms."

It was as he said that last word that the blood drained from her face, and what felt like her entire body as well.

His statement brought a picture to her mind's eye, the glance she'd been taking in of the shop in the seconds before she'd expected to enter it—just before she'd heard the click of the turned lock.

She made it back to the Jeep, hand in Ezra's, and dropped down to the front passenger seat, hands shaking as she fastened the seat belt. Sweating, she shivered.

"We've done what we can do for the night," Ezra was saying as he climbed in beside her and started the vehicle. "We need to find a room."

She heard him. Accepted his words. They weren't enough to bring her out of the horror she'd been catapulted into.

"What is it? Are you hurt?" Ezra's tone, sharp then, drew closer as he leaned across the console, his gaze running intently over her. Looking for blood, she figured. He didn't know it had all drained away.

"Theresa." The tone was compelling.

She blinked. "Mariette." She barely got the word out. Coughed. Then said, "I was wrong."

"About what?" With a finger on her chin, he turned her head until she was looking into his very intent gaze. "Wrong about what?"

His hand dropped away. She had to hold her own head straight. Felt driven to lay it on his shoulder, to turn her head in until she got lost within his strength.

But couldn't do that, either. She couldn't escape, no matter where she went.

Her girls… The danger was so much worse than she'd even imagined.

"Mariette. That antique gun in the case in the middle of the gun shop. I saw it just before he closed the blind. Mariette. Not marionette. Claire was right."

He didn't look away and his gaze didn't weaken, either. "I'm not following you."

Looking at him hurt. Everything hurt. Tears filled her eyes. She knew it. Couldn't stop them.

"The one solo visitation. Eric and Jennifer gave the girls presents. They each got a wooden box. Pretty wooden box, Neve said. Claire said they were heavy and wouldn't open. Neve thought that part was stupid, but insisted the box was pretty…"

Who cared about the way the damned box looked?

And yet her mind clung to Neve's impression. Couldn't let go of her baby girl's positive take on her world. Issued a prayer from the depths of her soul that Neve would hold on to that perspective.

"Still not following." Ezra's voice brought her attention back to the black moment sucking her in.

"Jennifer told the girls they couldn't open the boxes just yet. Not until they were someplace where they could get set up to use what was inside. Mariettes, Claire said. That was what was inside, Mariettes. *Marionettes*, I corrected her, thinking that the Fitzgeralds really were trying to be good grandparents, buying the girls real marionettes to play with, and keeping them for them until they had a stage set up to stand behind and put on a show. The girls said their grandparents were going to teach them how to use them. I pictured a puppet play. Was relieved…"

She saw the change come over Ezra, as though in slow motion. He stiffened. His eyes grew harder. His jaw tense.

"They gave those little kids Mariettes?"

She nodded, knocking tears over her lids and down her cheeks. "Oh my God, Ezra, they bought my babies their own guns!"

# Chapter 15

Mariettes were small guns, but precise and designed to kill. Ezra burned from the inside out as he drove to the motel Theresa had mentioned. The inn was well lit, beautifully manicured with gardens and fresh paint, and had a lit waterfall pond feature with benches out in the spacious, freshly mowed lawn. The type of place he was pretty sure she needed to be.

She was a natural nurturer, and beauty and peace had been horribly vacant from her day.

He asked for two rooms, adjoining if at all possible, and was told there was only one left, period. And that due to a cancellation.

He turned to Theresa, ready to offer to try one of the other two motels on the outskirts of town, when she said, "We'll take it," and slapped her credit card down on the counter.

Ezra had intended to pay. With no mortgage and very little upon which to spend money, he'd amassed far more wealth than he needed over the eighteen years since he'd left home for the army, while Theresa was a single mother who'd struggled with massive medical bills.

And he recognized that Theresa needed to be in control of something in a life spiraling out of control.

He recognized it because he'd been there since he was sixteen years old.

Five minutes after they'd registered, they were using a key card to enter a much more welcoming, homey place than he generally frequented. Bare-bones was good enough for him. He was glad that Theresa would have nicer than that.

It did feel a bit low-life to be entering the spacious accommodations carrying box-store plastic bags as their only luggage—a firm reminder that they weren't there on vacation.

Or even because they'd planned a trip.

They'd be in the room only until they had their next maneuver planned out and had gotten at least a little rest.

Or until Dom called and gave them a more immediate assignment.

Like picking up Claire and Neve.

"Obviously you've got the bed," he told Theresa, scouting out the room for safety and defense purposes. Only allowing himself to think about being on the job. Period. Might be a self-imposed, unofficial assignment, but he was there for only one purpose. Win the most important battle he'd ever fought. "I'll take the sofa thing."

"That doesn't make sense, Ezra," she said, moving

over to the window alcove and dropping her bags on the iron-barred mattress filled with pillows and frills. "I'm fine with the daybed. You're a lot bigger than I am. And you're the one who is more apt to be called upon for physical exertion."

He'd just determined that he needed to let her win, to call the shots, wherever he could. This wasn't that. "I take the window," he told her unequivocally. "You take the wall." He nodded his head toward the bed with a wall at the head and another one right beside it.

She gave him one glance and moved her bags. He dropped his in one of the four chairs pushed up to a round table set in the twenty feet of space between the bed and the window. Opposite a two-cushion couch and two armchairs also sharing that space. They'd passed the door into the separate, private bath as they'd entered the room.

Feeling slightly as though he'd landed in a minefield like none other, Ezra grabbed the pad of paper and pen he'd purchased, along with his cell phone and a bottle of water, and sat down at the table. He made columns. Filled them in with what he knew. Heard movement in the room. The bathroom door closing. Silence. Water running. Door opening.

And stared at the page that he hadn't touched since the door had first closed.

It had been a while since he'd spent the night with a woman. Heard her moving. Couldn't look. Not for a minute or two, at least.

"What can I do to help?" Her phone landed softly on the table. The chair next to him moved. And...she'd taken the band out of her hair.

Long dark strands cascaded...everywhere. For a

second there, they were all he could see. Thick dark strands, with those hints of fire in their depths.

And then he noticed the eyes in the middle of the array. They bore…agony.

His mind clicked into immediate gear. He asked her to start with everything she could remember Mark ever saying about his home, growing up. "I'm hoping that Dom's going to find that referral list in his search of Smith's place, and that we'll have good direction in terms of finding the Fitzgerald bunker, but in case he doesn't, we need to know where to head in the morning." He turned his phone around, showing her a topographic map of the state. Asked her to call up Smith's website and get his list of suggested bunker locations, to designate the most likely bunker sites. "Knowing as much as we can about the Fitzgeralds' choices—do they prefer woods or open fields, for instance—will help us more accurately pinpoint where they might be."

"You think they've already taken my girls down into their bunker."

Lying only added insult to injury. "I think we want to assume the worst so that we're prepared to fight under the worst-case scenario and win." He looked her in the eye as he spoke, and then continued immediately. "What do you know about where Mark grew up? Were they out in the country? In a neighborhood? Anything about the surroundings might help."

She didn't know much at all. "Mark had to fight hard not to be brainwashed, manipulated or influenced by them. When he left, it's like he locked off that part of his mind. I do know that he had a dog that got in a fight with a bear once. The dog won. The bear ran off."

Her smile, though distant, was genuine. Like fresh water to look at. A massive lake of it.

In Colorado, bears could come into neighborhoods, but it wouldn't be as likely. And it made sense that they were looking for someplace isolated, though from what they'd been told by Smith that day, people had bunkers in the middle of big-city properties, too.

"And he learned to shoot a gun in his own backyard."

Very likely more remote than city or neighborhood living.

"Did he ever say how he got to school?"

"He was homeschooled."

Isolation.

Everything was leaning toward the Fitzgeralds living off the grid.

Which was going to make finding them a lot more difficult.

And also made him one of the best men for the job. He'd spent more time in foreign desert and mountainous land off the grid than in his home country in recent years.

What he didn't add was that Colorado had a load of state land—mountainous, nearly-impossible-to-access land—where someone could live an entire lifetime and never be seen.

No point in giving her more than one mountain to climb at a time.

"Tell me about Mark's skills. What was he good at? What were his hobbies? What did he enjoy doing?"

He had to ask the questions. And wanted to know the answers, too. Not just because he needed them. Who was this man who'd won Theresa's love and life partner commitment? Who'd fathered two very special little girls.

"He was a good swimmer. Insisted that the girls start taking lessons before they were even a year old. But he didn't particularly like swimming. He liked food trucks and festivals. He liked going to the zoo, and he loved amusement parks. I always kind of thought that he was a kid having the childhood he'd missed, but he never said so."

She caught Ezra's eye and didn't look away. He couldn't desert her, even as he knew he should. Eventually, she blinked. Looked down. Pulled at a string on a cloth thing set in the middle of the table with a bowl of fruit on it. And then said, "He was great around the house. Knew how to fix anything and everything."

Mark's parents had trained him to be self-sufficient. Something Ezra hadn't learned until after he'd accepted the fact that his father hadn't been the man he'd thought him to be.

"Oh, and he must have been pretty good at mountain climbing," she said. "We never went, but one time when we vacationed at a little resort in the Rockies, Neve asked if we could go to the very top and sit in the clouds, and he'd told her that he'd climbed that mountain to the very top once, and there were no clouds there. It just looked like they were the same from down below."

And…damn.

The man the Fitzgeralds had raised was proficient enough to climb a mountain. One that, considering his daughter thought it was high enough to be in the clouds, could likely take superior skills to scale.

Unless… Did Ezra dare hope that the guy had just been spinning a yarn for the sake of his little girl?

It was possible.

But he couldn't risk going with that more palatable theory.

He couldn't risk reaching out and touching the fingers that were unraveling a corner of the table's center decor one thread at a time, either.

But, God, how he wanted to.

Some seconds, Theresa felt like she was holding on by a thread. And then she'd have some question to answer, some task to do, and she came back into her strength again. At some point, was that ability to persevere going to run out?

She couldn't let it. Whatever it took, whatever she had to do, she would acquire the capability by any means to find her girls and bring them safely home.

"I know this is hard, Theresa." Ezra's tone had softened again. She didn't need or want his pity. Sympathy weakened her.

But his personal attention... Life kindled inside her just a bit. Keeping her...present.

Giving her impetus to sit forward and tend to his next question. "Anything else you need to know?"

"I need anything you can think of."

"Jennifer and Eric risked discovery to stop and buy ice cream sandwiches. Probably because they thought the girls would be thrilled with them. Means they are trying to tend to the girls' happiness." It meant that they didn't even know their granddaughters well enough to know their food preferences. It also meant they were planning to keep the twins someplace where they wouldn't have access to purchasing ice cream sandwiches for a long time.

Ezra's hand covered hers on the table, stopping her fingers from moving. And she realized she'd been pulling at a string on a doily to the point of damaging the lacy work. "You can talk about it," he said, giving no definition to his vagueness. "I know I'm not the most sensitive guy in the world, but I get that this has to be killing you and you're stuck with me at the moment, and…if you need to talk…I can sit and listen. Not too many ways to screw that up." He grinned with the last line, probably trying to lighten the moment—and kind of screwing it up, too.

She wanted to smile back. Was tied too tightly to do so. She couldn't show any loose threads. The slightest tug and she'd unravel.

"I'm fine," she told him. "This isn't about me." And she didn't need him wasting any of his precious brain cells on worrying about her. She needed him coming up with a plan by morning that would get them closer to her children.

"So, you've been shot at before today?" he asked.

Of course not. And, yeah, she'd been shaken there for a bit. She was over it. "Technically, I wasn't shot at. Only trees were shot at." Thanks to his training and skills. "And the Jeep, of course," she added, remembering the terrifying moments when she heard breaking glass so close by and a horrifying thud as bullets pierced the back of the seat just above her head.

Her heart had cried out for Ezra as she'd braced for a wreck. And worse.

But she was over that, too, she told herself, pushing memories, emotions away from conscious thought by focusing on other things.

"It's okay, you know. The aftershock. I've gotten many of my men through it…"

His men were part of his team. She was…a blip in time. They could afford to lean on him. She couldn't.

"Believe me, I'm far more ripped up inside about my daughters than I am about a few flying bullets." Truth.

Ezra sat back, was studying her. "Those bullets could take your life." The words were calm. Matter-of-fact. Just like she was being.

And she answered without a second's hesitation. "I'll die if I have to to save my children…"

"Death is the end, Theresa. If you'd been shot today, how would you then go on to save your kids?"

Good point. She started to shake, as she had after they'd escaped from Smith. He leaned forward again, took her hand and held it on top of the table, sandwiched between his much larger ones. Warming her.

"Your girls have already lost one parent," he said quietly, and yet the words hit her core. "They need you to be waiting, healthy and ready, when they return." He was right. And had understood something she had not. The girls didn't just need to be found. They needed her to be present and ready for them.

Ezra Colton might not be in her life for long, but his impact was huge. The man was one of those special beings who'd always hold a place of importance in her heart. He was leaving. She knew that. Just as she knew she needed him to go. But she would never forget him.

"One way you prepare to be capable of providing whatever emotional sustenance and understanding they're going to need once we find them is accessing the help offered you," he continued, unaware that he'd just been on the stage of her heart, being awarded top honors. "Finding your daughters, bringing them safely back to you… This isn't something you can do alone."

"So why do I feel like I have to?"

"Because it's easier than opening your emotions up to the help that's being offered." His statement was like a confession. She had the thought, sat there studying him, and he said, "I adored my father when I was a kid. And as I grew, I idolized him. I wanted to be just like him. To help so many people…and to rid the world of the criminals that hurt people." He paused, pulled their hands down from the table to his knee, bringing them closer. Playing with her fingers, he continued, "When his duplicity first came to light, I didn't believe it. I fought anyone who tried to speak evil of him—and at that point, pretty much everyone was talking about him. On the news and everywhere else. I would have died defending him. Even after he called me into his office alone, and told me what he'd done and why, I still didn't believe him. I thought he was protecting someone…"

Her heart aching, Theresa swallowed back tears. She could feel the grief of the young boy he'd been. Wanted so badly to make the pain go away.

"Once I realized that he'd really done what everyone was saying he was doing…" He sat up, letting her hand drop. Leaned back in his chair. "I needed no one," he finished. "Let's just say it wasn't a pretty last two years of high school. Not until I joined the army, became a part of a unit of people again and found my purpose. I found my way to being the man I'd thought my father was."

If there'd been any minute hope that Ezra Colton would ever decide to hang around Blue Larkspur, or change to a less dangerous career, that hope had just been dashed.

If possible, her respect for him had grown. And her trust in his ability to find her daughters had expanded so far there was no room for doubt.

"My whole point here is that I know what I'm talking about, Theresa, and I know how to minimize the fallout. This is what I do for a living—get soldiers prepared for battle and go into battle with them, yes—but a big part of my job is also teaching them how to cope with the aftershocks of shooting and being shot at or walking through a field that could explode under your foot at any given moment. If you don't deal with the residual emotions, you might survive or even win the battle, but you won't be good when the war is over."

He'd drawn the curtains across the window, mostly hiding the darkness that had fallen. A somewhat blinding light shone through a crack where the two sides of the drapes came together. The parking-lot security lights.

She appreciated that they were there. Knew she couldn't stare straight at the light or she'd be blinded.

Much like Ezra. She was thankful for his presence, but she couldn't get too close and be burned.

"I'm not saying you have to speak to me," he said then. "Obviously, the kind of coaching I know how to do is vastly different from a parent dealing with child abduction. I just… You haven't made a single phone call to anyone since we've been together. Other than to get your duties covered at work. If you need some privacy to talk to someone, I'm fine to provide it."

She'd texted a few people, a neighbor, the day-camp coordinator, and the mother of the twins' closest friend.

Their horror and sympathy had only fed her own at a time when she couldn't afford to be weak.

"In a way, I've been going it on my own since I was two," she told him then. "And with Mark's illness ongoing as it had been, I learned how to carry the weight on my shoulders." She was going to leave it there. Meant to. Looked over at him, held his gaze…and couldn't keep it in. There was something he could do for her. Right then. Right there. Something that would instill some good feeling in the midst of all the debilitating pain.

Something that would give her a few minutes of escape from the horror that had become her existence.

In the morning, for the rest of her life, she'd probably regret opening her mouth. The morning seemed light-years away.

And uncertain. For over a minute, he'd sat there maintaining their visual connection.

"You know what would help?" She was doing it. That in itself was a relief.

"What?" And then, with a softening in his expression, "Tell me."

Leaning forward slowly, she opened her mouth… and his phone rang.

# *Chapter 16*

Ezra and Theresa turned at once to look at his phone vibrating against the table, the screen fully visible.

*Dominic.*

Reining in the chest-weighting disappointment that hit him, he turned from his chance to receive Theresa's confidences and find out how to help her and picked up the cell.

"Yeah."

"Am I on speaker?" Code for *don't put me there*, which couldn't be good.

"No."

Something had happened and he sat unprepared. Seconds too late. Lacking in the knowledge he needed to help an incredible woman over the impossible hurdle in front of her.

"We got the client list. It's as thorough as you'd hoped, but the Fitzgeralds aren't on it."

Steeling his face to show nothing—another talent he'd honed to perfection—he didn't respond, either, waiting for his brother to lay it all out for him before giving Theresa any board from which to dive off.

"He didn't build their bunker. Doesn't even know where it is. Four years ago, they bought a plumbing system from him to pump water into the bunker from an underground well. And two years before that, a pump-and-dump toilet with one hundred feet of piping to shoot waste one hundred feet from the bunker on a diagonal to the surface, where it apparently composts and fertilizes. We've got the paperwork for both, and the measurements of the diagonal, which tell us that the bunker is ten feet down from the surface. They paid cash for both, picked both up at Smith's shop. He assumed by the questions they asked that they were doing the labor themselves."

Feeling Theresa's gaze on him, and because there were some good points in the conversation, he nodded. "Sounds like they trenched it in," he said, speaking of the bunker based on what Dom was describing about the plumbing designs he'd also seen.

"Trenching's good." Theresa's words drew his gaze to her. He left it there. Holding her up in whatever way he could. "Prevents cave-ins," she told him.

At the same time, Dom was saying, "He claimed self-defense on the shots fired. Said that you two acted odd by just getting up and leaving without a word, and he saw you go for your gun…"

"He did not. My hand was on it, but it was stuffed in my jeans, under my shirt."

"No cameras to prove that. And all he'd need to do

is convince police that he had reason to believe he saw a gun."

"That's bull…" He finished a string of words Dom had heard from him before.

"You were on his private property," Dom continued. "Colorado law gives him the right to defend himself…"

Yeah, yeah, yeah. He got it.

"So what now?"

"We've got a specialist looking for underground wells starting around Benson and branching out three-sixty from there. And we've got the referral list. Dooms-day preparers tend to be in close-knit groups. Hopefully one of them knows something…"

"You think they'd turn on one of their own?"

When the line went quiet, he knew Dom had hung up.

His brother had told him what he could. And hadn't hung around for Ezra to say something that Dom would have to warn him against.

Theresa sat watching him, her features the most beautiful thing in the world as they reflected the woman glowing inside her. She was waiting.

Not demanding.

"We don't have an address. Or bunker type." He laid it out clearly. "What we do have is some building specifications. We know that the plan is for long-term underground living…"

"And that it's trenched," she said, as though need-ing some encouragement to help her hold it together.

"Six years ago they bought a pump-and-dump flush-ing toilet system. And then two years later, a plumbing system that taps into an underground well for water."

"They bought the toilet system the year the twins

were born. You think they somehow knew? And have been planning this since then? Even before Mark got sick? I mean, they don't have just a bunker. They've got an underground home," she said, her lips pursed as she nodded. "I saw some pictures. They have actual flooring, not just dirt. And furnishings. Neve might convince Claire they're on an adventure..."

He had to give it to her. The woman knew how to make lemonade out of lemons.

And he needed to get to work. "I've got enough specifics here, and with a topographic map, we'll at least be able to pinpoint some possibilities... Generally, the pump and dumps go straight up or horizontal. I'm guessing the diagonal angle of theirs means that there's rock face in the way. Which would most likely specify mountain terrain. And we want to stay within a couple of hours of Benson. Can't be too far out with the Fitzgeralds making frequent trips to Blue Larkspur."

"They could have stayed in motels. It's not like they chose to build to be close to Mark. They had no idea where he was."

"A simple assessors records search for his name could have shown them property owners in the state. And with probable dark-web access..."

"But you said credit cards hadn't shown any motel stays..."

He had said that. They could have paid cash. Or used assumed names. But since they hadn't been hiding their presence in Blue Larkspur, why would they do either? Most motels didn't even allow check-in without a credit card to pay for any damage done to the room.

"Okay, we'll narrow our start to within sixty miles of

Benson. Obviously, they shop here. The ammunitions guy knew to watch for us. And keep us out."

He texted Dom. He'd failed to relay that information and wanted his brother on it.

Out of the text app and back to his search engine, he found a topographic map that allowed him to narrow down regions with specific geographic qualifications. No lake or stream nearby—the ground would be too vulnerable to flooding and caving. No underground utility lines, probably not a huge consideration out in the middle of nowhere. And probably not in a wooded area—trenching with trees would be a nightmare of roots. Mountain region…

"Do you know exactly what mountain Mark climbed?"

She nodded. Named a peak. And he narrowed his search to there. He could be wrong. Had to start somewhere. Typed in various coordinates, looking for areas that would fit trenching and diagonal dumping coordinates.

Theresa, sitting so close that her knee was touching his, worked her screen with a thumb that didn't quit. "You a speed reader?" he asked at one point, giving his eyes a rest from the small screen he had to work with.

"Yeah. I sing, too," she added, and he didn't know if she was being sarcastic or really had a good voice. He wanted to ask.

Specifically did not allow himself to do so.

He'd expect, with all of the specific guidelines narrowing his search, that there'd be one or two areas of interest to him. He had seven. In three different directions from where he sat. Could take three days to a week to get to them all.

He looked for roads into the regions. No way Eric

Fitzgerald could haul a toilet system up a trail, even with determination and trolleys.

And it wasn't likely Claire and Neve were going to be up for serious climbing, either. Not without training.

"Did Mark ever say whether or not his parents were preparing right where they lived? Or was their bunker elsewhere?"

"He didn't specifically say…" She drew out the word. "But he was claustrophobic. Not in any debilitating sense. But he didn't like to have the curtains closed in the house. And when we went to Disney World, he opted not to go on any of the rides that took us underground or in tunnels…" She looked at him, her gaze wide. "It makes sense, doesn't it, that he spent time in their bunker?"

"It sounds like they could have been living there, at least part-time, even then. Maybe they slept down there? I know some doomsdayers do that." He knew a veteran with PTSD who did. Granted, the bunker was more of a tented camping spot, but it was down an incline into a cave in Arizona. The bunker gave Dave peace. Highly unlikely that Mark Fitzgerald had had the same reaction.

And Ezra had thought he'd had it rough with a famous, revered father who turned out to be a lying, bribe-taking criminal, sending innocent people to live in dark cages.

But not Ezra. Ben Colton had only ever treated his children with love and respect.

An hour later, Ezra had a map with possible bunker locations, with road access, charted on it. They intended to head out at daybreak. If they got lucky, and were able to quickly eliminate places, they could get five narrowed down to one in a day.

And have the girls home before darkness fell a second time. One night of adventure might be fun. Two nights trapped underground, with no contact with their mother, could prove to be emotionally scarring.

"It's probably a good idea to order room service for breakfast," Theresa said, as he saved his map and went to plug in his phone. "The kitchen opens at five, and we can have it packed to go. Eat on the way." She'd already retrieved the padded brown in-room dining menu from the desk not far from his bed. Was perusing it while he made plans to sleep in his clothes on top of the bed serving as his bunk—something he'd done many times in his life.

"Oh," she said, looking over at him standing there looking at the daybed by the window.

"What?"

"Prickly pear."

"What about it?"

"They have prickly pear jelly on the menu. Mark hated prickly pear anything," she said. "We were in Arizona once before we were married, and some friends of his from college had told us we had to try these prickly pear margaritas, which I did, and they were fabulous, but Mark wouldn't even try it. Said he couldn't stand the stuff. I just figured he'd had it before and really had a distaste for it, but now…with you asking me about him, our backdoor way of learning about Eric and Jennifer… what if a memory from his childhood had something to do with his reaction?"

"Prickly pear grows in the Rockies, mostly lower elevations," Ezra said, moving over to join her by the desk. He stopped a good foot away, had almost grabbed her shoulders with hope as another thought occurred to

him. "Say the Fitzgerald bunker has prickly pear growing nearby and Mark stepped back into it. Or walked
into it in the dark. Maybe he never had a bad incident
with it, but it was something he saw by the bunker entrance, so the thought of it just reminded him…"

"Maybe his parents made him drink juice from it
if the plant was growing in abundance on their land,"
Theresa joined in.

Her comment spurred another. "Now add a six-year-
old compost fertilization on the surface within fifty
yards of the bunker surface," he continued. "It stands
to reason that vegetation would grow more profusely
with fertilization…"

"So tomorrow, when we're driving, we look for areas
with healthy prickly pear growth…" Her voice faded,
but the light in her eyes did not. "Maybe it won't be the
prickly pear. Maybe it's one of these other things we've
homed in on. We're going to find them, Ezra."

It was a long shot.

A really long one.

Mammothly long.

But any kind of shot at all was better than none.


They had a plan, and they needed rest.

She needed some distance from the man who'd become a lifeline to her. A few hours of sleep to give her
some perspective.

In the bathroom, Theresa went through her shopping
bags, found the sweats she'd grabbed from an endcap,
the gray, doomsday-appropriate T-shirt she'd snatched
without even looking at the price because it had a uni-
corn on the front of it. Toothbrush, toothpaste… She'd

done well, considering the state she'd been in when she'd been given ten minutes to shop.

It took her less than ten minutes to get ready for bed. Ezra headed into the bathroom right after she came out, giving her a chance to get into bed, snuggle the soft, fresh-smelling covers up to her chin, turn toward the wall—with her back to the daybed—and will herself to sleep.

She heard the water running. Heard him pee and flush, too, though she tried really hard not to listen. Heard water running again. And his bag rustling some more. She heard the turn of the doorknob. And the swish of his feet on the carpet as he passed by the end of her bed.

With a click, the light went out.

And…her nightmare started.

As though the light switch in the room also controlled a mechanism in her brain. As soon as darkness consumed the room, and the moment became officially designated as sleep time, Theresa's mind went from rational to worry mode, igniting a series of scenarios that scared her to death.

The girls trapped in the ground, in the dark, lost and clutching to each other as they cried for her.

Visions of bad things that could be happening lingered around every mental turn she tried to make.

Eric losing his temper with them as they failed to conform to his idea of who they should be.

Were they hiding someplace? Under something?

Had they eaten?

Claire was such a picky eater… Had Jennifer been patient with her as she tried to find something the little girl could eat without triggering her gag reflex?

Mark had never understood that one—always thinking that Claire just had to be taught to eat her food. She
had to understand that even if she didn't like something,
she just had to chew and swallow and make it gone.

Until the night he'd forced her to sit in her seat across
from him, put a spoonful of peas into her mouth, and
chew and swallow them. She'd done so. She'd adored
her daddy.

And as she'd swallowed, the peas had failed to make
it past her throat. She'd gagged and spewed peas all
over the table.

Neve's laughter had saved that day. After a moment
of shock, Mark had laughed, too, and then Claire had.

Theresa had been cleaning up the mess...

Her stomach ached, muscles clutching against each
other, and she pulled the bed's extra pillow down to
apply soft pressure, hoping to ease the pain.

Had the girls been crying for hours? Were they de-
hydrated?

Had her babies learned how to hold guns? Had they
been forced to aim and fire?

She moved again, trying to find comfort where there
was none.

*Oh my God.* What would happen if one of them got
sick? Or fell and broke an arm or cut themselves? It
wasn't like their grandparents were just going to waltz
them in to see a medical professional. They had no
paperwork, no records, no insurance information.

And there was an Amber Alert out on the girls. Eric
and Jennifer would know that. They'd avoid any chance
of being recognized.

The Amber Alert had to be canceled. Immediately.
Someone had to get one of the band of doomsdayers

who all hung together to get word to Eric and Jennifer, letting them know that they'd be free to get medical treatment for the girls with no repercussions.

Tom Smith. They could make him do it. He owed them for shooting at them. And he'd want his compatriots to have the immunity she was offering. Should she get up and call him right then? If Neve or Claire got sick in the night, the morning could be too late.

She could use her burner phone. Text him…

Or call for a rideshare and go see him herself. That way she could sign whatever she'd have to sign saying that no charges would be pressed. He could hold her hostage in the event that someone tried to intervene and take Eric and Jennifer into custody.

Could the police charge them anyway, even if she said no, since there'd been a kidnapping?

Oh, God.

Her babies had no medical protection. They could already be hurt.

What if there'd been an accident during gun training?

Chance of that was huge. Six-year-olds with loaded guns?

And Neve…bless her…she didn't always listen the first time around. Her little mind spun with such great stories of her own that sometimes things just didn't sink in.

A vision of Neve calling out to her sister, telling her to look, and a little finger hitting a trigger…

Claire!

Neve would scream. There'd be blood…

*Stop.*

She could say the word. Fear, despair, dread…they didn't dissipate.

For the first time since her baby girls were born, she hadn't been there to kiss them good-night. To tell them to have sweet dreams.

Hope was gone as tears trickled out from tightly squeezed lids. She couldn't cry. Her nose would run and then she'd either have to sniffle, which would be loud, or get a tissue, blow her nose, which would be louder.

With the hand clutching the comforter to her chin, she wiped at the tears.

Through all of Mark's illness, times when she'd had to work the night shift at the home, the time she was sick with the flu, she'd always kissed her babies' cheeks good-night—albeit with a face mask on when she was sick—and told them sweet dreams.

All the years of never missing, and her record was broken.

Tears spurted from the corners of her eyes, fell across her nose and to the pillowcase. Her nose ran. Burying her head, she tried to stifle her sniffle with the covers.

The girls were gone.

What if she never saw them again?

What if…?

Her mattress moved, sinking from weight on the edge of it. "Hey."

She knew the voice. Trusted it.

But there was nothing that it could say to help…

"Talk to me."

There was nothing to say. Nothing anyone could do that would…

"Help me," he said.

What? She stilled. Waiting. Of course she'd help. If

# Chapter 17

Shockingly, Ezra slept. Lying with Theresa snuggled up to his chest, breathing softly, evenly, he'd thought he'd give her a bit and then gently extricate himself to return to his own bunk.

The next thing he knew, daylight was peeking around the edges of the drapes he'd drawn the night before.

They'd never said a word. From the second he'd slid down on her sheets, there'd been not one attempt at conversation. She'd relaxed against him and within minutes had been out.

All the anguish she'd been putting herself through, and in his arms, she'd found peace.

You had to like a woman who knew what she needed and had the guts to ask for it.

Because he couldn't focus on the rest of it. Her peace.

His arms. There was no future in it. So no permission to go there.

She awoke as he started to slide away from her. Pulled herself off his chest. Let him go. He didn't look back.

Or speak.

He just made a beeline for the shower. A cold one. To wake himself up. And to calm himself down, too.

And by the time he'd reentered the room, she'd been up and waiting for her turn in the bath. He already had breakfast there and waiting when she exited twenty minutes later, dressed in a pair of brown cotton pants, another long-sleeved lighter brown shirt and her boots. Breakfast in hand, they hit the road.

They discussed the omelets. The route they were on. Filling up with gas. And the clear skies. Neither mentioned the night they'd spent in each other's arms.

The first two locations on his map were a bust. One area was off from a single-lane dirt road that had been blocked for some time by two fallen trees that had clearly been the result of a lightning strike at least a year before. Vegetation had already grown and covered the spot. There was a scattering of prickly pear, though, and Ezra scouted the mostly flat, open area on foot anyway, with Theresa in the truck researching message boards and websites for information about doomsdayers. He'd found no sign of any kind of human presence, period.

They'd wasted a couple of hours.

Another single-lane dirt road, miles off from a county highway, led them to the second area. Badly rutted—to the point that Theresa was holding on as they bounced along—the road had clearly not been traveled on recently. Still, he persevered, and they spent an hour walking the flat land that met all bunker criteria, with no sign of footsteps, tamped-down vegetation from someone or something having gone through the space, and no sign of any kind of cover or cave opening.

"There's prickly pear, though," Theresa said as they made their way back to the Jeep. They'd scared up rabbits, too, and had walked to the chorus of multiple birdcalls.

The sun was climbing steadily, and Ezra felt the tension start to build again. Within himself, but in his companion as well. Theresa's expressions were growing stiffer, her sentences less wordy.

Dom hadn't called yet that day.

They'd rushed out just after dawn and had gotten nowhere.

While time ticked and Claire and Neve experienced life unknown to them.

He needed a plan B. Didn't have one.

Every soldier knew you didn't enter the battlefield without a plan B.

"We're doing something," Theresa said as she climbed back in beside him. "If nothing else, we're narrowing down areas they might be by knowing where they aren't."

He and this woman were in sync. There was just no denying it.

He glanced her way. Smiled.

And she smiled back.

Theresa didn't even see the little store at first. Set back from the road—down a single-lane road, that continued past it up the mountain—its brown shingled siding and roof looked more like a dilapidated shack than a place of business. She frowned when Ezra slowed, then glanced over at him.

"We're going in there?" It was the first time they'd spoken in a while. She'd been busy reading a doomsday message board she'd landed upon. He'd been doing… whatever it was he did when he went into himself.

"Fresh tracks," he said, nodding off to his left. The mountain road was one lane in places, two in others, mostly paved, though badly so, and climbed slowly by going around the mountain, not straight up, with very little shoulder. They'd seen other vehicles, but sparingly. Mostly campers and trucks.

And had rounded bends with drop-offs that were straight down one hundred feet of rock or more. She'd done better reading on her phone, trying to get into the Fitzgeralds' mindset, than watching the road. If nothing else, when the girls got back, they were going to have heard things, and she needed to be prepared to refute them. With fact, not just motherly assurances.

A rudimentary, handmade painted wood sign hung over a wooden screened door. Miller's Deli and Market, it read. The screen was dirty, but she could see a couple through it—older-looking—sitting in chairs behind a counter. They both looked up as Ezra and Theresa entered.

The place might have been a deli at one point. Any hint of fresh meat and cheeses had long since departed. Dust covered…everything. Much more aware of what she might be walking into than she'd been a day before, Theresa looked around for any sign of guns and ammunition.

Found the latter stacked neatly on shelves along the back wall.

"You camping?" the old man asked. Up close, she'd guess him to be eighty, at least. "Camping supplies is along the far wall, middle set of shelves. And water's stacked in cases of four gallons to a case in the closet back there to the far right. You can't miss it. You'll have to help yourself with that. Can't lift the damned things like I used to."

"Chip, the guy who delivers them each month, has to do it," the woman offered.

Smiling at her, Theresa felt Ezra close to her side. But not nudging her like a warning or anything.

"We'd like a box of crackers and some peanut butter if you have it," he said to the couple. And was told to take a look around.

"There should be some out there somewhere," the man offered. "Water's in the closet in the far back right corner," he said and pointed again to the opposite corner of the store. "Comes in four gallons a case, but you'll have to lift it yourself if you want some."

"I think we will take a case." Ezra nodded, starting to walk around one of the two small center aisles of goods.

"I'm Nancy. This is Howard," the woman offered to Theresa while Ezra "shopped."

"I'm ninety-four years old."

Though she tried to school her features, her shock must have shown, as the woman laughed. "Howard's ninety-six," she added. "He robbed the cradle when he married me." She laughed again, and Howard chuckled, too.

Theresa couldn't smile with them. "I have a degree in senior health management," she said, "and I have to say…I'm impressed. Do you two live around here?"

She sure as heck couldn't picture them in the Sunshine Senior Home.

"Around that corner," Howard replied, pointing to a closed door behind the counter, off to the left.

"Been here five years," Nancy told her, rocking back with her hands crossed over a belly that was only slightly protruding beneath the rose-and-white housedress she wore. Pride rang through the elderly woman's words.

"I met a couple who said they live up this way," Theresa said then, not forgetting for even a second that her only purpose for being there was to find her daughters. She pulled up a picture on her phone. "You ever see them?"

The couple leaned forward together, Howard pushing his glasses up, and Nancy raising her head to look through bifocals that were as thick as any Theresa had ever seen.

"Yep," Howard said, as Nancy spoke over him with, "They're nice people. Just wanting a safe place to live."

Ezra moved farther along the opposite side of the shelf separating them. Theresa could still feel his energy coming her way. There'd been no plan for her to be in charge—ever—but the opportunity had presented itself, and...

A deep breath helped her steady her shaking limbs.

"You see them recently?" she asked then.

Nancy looked at Howard, who looked at Theresa and shook his head. "Not for a while, I don't think. But we don't open every day. Mostly all's that ever comes up here is campers, and they buy their stuff in town. Cheaper that way. We're just here for locals who don't like to go to town, and they know to knock hard on the door if it's locked."

"Locals?" Ezra came up beside her. "There's a settlement up here?"

"Just folks looking to live safe," Howard said. "Next hundred miles or so, they're scattered about." And Theresa's stomach churned with roosts of butterflies. "We had a safe place up here ourselves, been here forty years, but it got hard to haul the water in."

"I'm ninety-four," Nancy piped in. "I told Howard, what we staying safe for anymore? I wanted some flowers and blue skies overhead. So we bought this place and sit and watch the birds and look at sunshine every day." She smiled again.

"And wait for the Good Lord to take us," Howard added. "There's water in that closet back there in the far corner. Comes in cases, four gallons to a case..."

Ezra pulled a couple of twenties out of his pocket and laid them on the counter, handing Theresa an older-looking unopened box of saltines and a dusty jar of peanut butter as he went to collect their water and head out. She followed him with a chorus of "Have a nice day" from the husband and wife.

Waited while Ezra pulled open the only closet in the place.

The skinny space behind the door was completely empty. No water in sight.

"Their memory issues were age-appropriate," Theresa said the second they were outside the store, hurrying across gravel in the hot sun. "That doesn't mean that they didn't really recognize Eric and Jennifer."

Heading to his side of the Jeep, Ezra climbed inside and had the engine going and the vehicle in gear by the time she'd fastened her seat belt beside him.

"Whether they recognized them or not, they just told us that the next hundred miles contains bunkers," he said, feeling energized in a way he hadn't been since he'd come home for his brother's wedding.

He was closing in on his target. "We've only got one area on the map over the next hundred miles—about halfway up this road to a turnoff that I'm going to assume is more of a dirt drive than an actual street." He didn't want to get her hopes up.

But he wasn't going to lie to her, either.

The Fitzgeralds weren't going to give up those girls easily.

And they were well armed.

He called his brother. Gave Dom the coordinates of the area he'd be searching. The war wasn't won. Hadn't even started.

The battle was still ahead.

But at least he had one to fight.

With only one troop out of his usual hundreds. Himself.

He had fifty miles to prepare her.

"They might see us before we know they're there," he said. "I can almost guarantee they will." Even if they weren't on the run, doomsdayers would likely have traps set to alert them if anyone got close to their domicile. It was all part of protecting oneself.

"And when they do, they're going to come out fighting. At this point, not only do they stand to lose the girls, but they'll be arrested, separated and sent to live in a cage with criminals if they're caught."

Theresa broke in. "It would make more sense for them to leave the girls, as a distraction—because they know that Claire and Neve are who we want—and run. They'll have an escape route, Ezra. From all the reading I've been doing today, I'm sure they already have a secure plan in place in case we do find them."

He hoped to God the plan wasn't to take the girls with them, risking them getting killed, to keep them from suffering through the slow burn of a nuclear blast with their mother.

And knew he couldn't rely on hope alone. It was up to him to make sure that Eric and Jennifer Fitzgerald didn't detect them in time to take the twins and disappear off the grid forever.

He was the front line in the fight of his life.

With a very special untrained soldier at his back. He had to keep her there. Behind him. So he would take any hits that came their way. And be the only one to see if something horrible happened.

That was his plan.

It was weak.

Unfinished.

And it was all he had.

# Chapter 18

The mountain road climbed and then rounded and seemed to slope back down. She'd seen the map they were traveling. A half circle around Benson. Since Ezra had already mapped out the areas without underground utility lines, lakes or streams nearby, or a lot of trees, there wasn't much reason to keep her eyes peeled out the window during the interim miles.

The challenge then became keeping her mind occupied so that fear didn't take possession of it.

Because while she much preferred the scenario where Eric and Jennifer sent the girls running at them, as a distraction, while the couple bolted through some underground escape hatch that would lead to a vehicle aboveground somewhere—maybe even a garage only ten feet away with a ladder up to it—she knew that another, probably more likely, possibility existed.

They'd take the twins with them. Why not, if they believed their escape plan was viable? And then, if something went wrong, they could all die together...

And...*cut*. She blinked, stared at the phone screen in front of her—her own phone, because the burner was only for use if she had to assume Molly's persona again.

Molly and Jack. Yes. Molly and Jack. A lighter feeling entered her system for a second. Easing the panic that her mind had brought on once again.

Molly and Jack. Her and Ezra.

He'd held her. No questioning or warnings. Just a wordless sliding under the covers and pulling her into his arms.

And the weirdest part was...she'd laid her head on his chest, closed her eyes, listened to his heartbeat and fallen asleep.

She couldn't remember the last time she'd drifted off so quickly. Or slept so peacefully.

Was it wrong to want to do it again?

If thinking about it kept her emotions from spiraling into panic, then that was definitely okay. Conversation might have helped, too. About the night they'd spent, or anything else. But Ezra was...Ezra. He was on a mission, and there was no way she was going to interrupt his process.

No way she'd do anything to save herself if it meant putting her daughters further at risk.

Thinking back over the way he'd gotten them out of Tom Smith's place, the way he'd read the second that congeniality turned into danger, even the shooting at trees as a cover to get himself back to her...

It was like Charlie had known exactly what he was

doing when he'd burst into Alice's room the afternoon Ezra had been visiting his great-aunt.

Ezra was only with them for the moment, but she'd spend the rest of her life being thankful for him. Maybe when the girls were home, and Ezra left for his next assignment, they could keep in touch…just a text or email now and then, letting her know he was okay.

He might want to know she and the twins were okay, too. Since he was risking his life right now to save theirs.

What if Eric and Jennifer really did see them coming and grab the kids? What if Ezra foiled their escape plan and they felt trapped and chose to die together rather than risk leaving them to suffer what they believed to be an unbearable fate?

Jerking her head in Ezra's direction, she said, "It's more important to me that you rescue those girls than watch over me," she said as they drew closer to the area where he suspected the girls were being held. He had his phone lying on the console. She could see the live map on his GPS. "I'll distract Eric and Jennifer while you get the girls."

So much for staying out of his process.

He glanced her way. Briefly. Frowned. Then said, "Let's see what the situation presents, first."

Of course. That was a given. But… "I'm just saying, if it comes down to protecting me or saving them, there's no question. It's them."

The words garnered her another serious look.

But no verbal response.

Ezra had never felt so ill prepared.

As he pulled off the dilapidated paved road onto an

even more unkempt dirt one, he had a bad feeling. If it weren't for the fact that every second could make a difference between saving those kids or losing them to off-the-grid nothingness, he'd pull back. Gather a team of trained professionals, study a map and discuss parameters.

Law enforcement was already doing just that. And so far had much less than he did. There were only so many of them, and they couldn't spend an entire day driving in the wilderness on the off chance that the landscape might produce a lead.

The first part of the road was wooded, so he passed through it with only cursory glances for signs of recent habitation.

Saw newly trod tracks from large-sized wheels quite clearly. Determined to follow them as far as they led.

Took his gun out of his waistband, safety still on, and laid it on the console.

"I know you don't know how to shoot, but if you have to pull the trigger, do so." He explained how, with one quick move, she would need to turn the safety off.

He saw her peek down at the gun. Was looking at her as she then turned to look up at him.

The road grabbed his attention almost immediately.

Which was a good thing.

No way he could afford to drown in those expressive warm pools of her eyes. Not then.

Not ever.

"The bunker entrance might just be a flat piece on the ground like a trapdoor. Oftentimes with brush over it so you wouldn't ever know it's there," she said, drawing another quick glance from him. Her voice was a little shaky, but her thoughts seemed to be steady.

As was her gaze.

He didn't blame her for her fear. He'd been living with his own version of it all of his adult life.

She feared for the lives of her daughters. He did, too, in that moment.

Overall, his biggest fear was failure.

He wasn't going to be able to live with it. Didn't set himself up for it.

And yet there he was…driving into God knew what, with no idea what he would actually need to do to rescue those little girls.

"Some of the fancier ones have actual shed-sized structures with a front door that opens to steps down into the living space below."

Climbing a ladder ten feet underground to be home didn't appeal to him. Nor did sleeping under all those feet of earth. With an inner shudder, he tried not to think about what two innocent little kids would think.

Unless their grandparents had made a fairy tale out of it. Like the hobbits, or Alice, who passed through the looking glass.

And…there. Foot on the brake, Ezra brought the Jeep to a slow enough stop not to kick up a lot of dirt. The tracks turned onto a rudimentary road that was little more than two tire tracks of tamped-down earth. As though the road had formed from being driven on over and over, not by formal construction.

"I've been following recent tire tracks," he told Theresa. "They turn here."

"But it's wooded."

"Yeah, but look around. Trees at the edge of the road, but none on either side. And while they're alive, they aren't particularly thriving."

"You think they were purposely planted here? Like… as a cover?"

"I think it's possible. Or they're natural, but not predominant in the area."

He didn't like what he was going to say next in the event that she argued with him, and he knew she would. But he saw no other option.

"I have to do the rest on foot," he told her. Which meant she'd be left on the open road alone. "Do you have phone service?"

She shook her head. He didn't, either. Hadn't since they'd turned onto the dirt road.

"I'm leaving the gun with you," he said. "I've got my knife." Pulling up his right jeans leg, he showed her the weapon.

"I'm not staying out here." Knowing the objection was coming didn't make it any easier to take.

"Theresa." He said her name firmly, not kindly. "I have no idea what I'm walking into, what kind of maneuver I might have to do…"

"Which is why you need your gun. And if it comes to you going into action, I can always lie flat on the ground and wait. And pray. It'd be a lot harder to hide sitting out here in the open in a Jeep."

She had a point.

"Besides, I might be able to help."

Looking at her, seeing the stubbornness, and knowing their time was wasting, that they could have already been discovered, he did what he did. Came up with a plan.

"You come with me as far as the edge of the trees. And then you wait. Your job is lookout. Do not come out of the woods for any reason. You get seen, you likely get dead. If you see the girls and they're in danger, you scream once and change your location within the trees immediately. If you're in danger, you scream twice. If I find the girls, and have to use myself as a distraction and can't escort them out, I'm sending them your way and you take them to the Jeep and then straight back to the main road to alert Dom. Got it?"

"What if I'm in danger and can't scream?"

That would mean she was either comatose, or someone was preventing her from opening her mouth or using her throat. "Then the mission failed," he said, not wanting to consider that option. "This isn't Blue Larkspur, Theresa. You're going to have to be aware every second…listen to every sound. Anything that doesn't fit, a crack of a twig, or birds suddenly squawking all at once…you pay attention." He handed her the gun, but she shook her head.

"Someone would be more likely to get it from me before I got a shot off," she said. "But I'll take the knife, if you don't mind. I've done a lot of carving of fowl in my lifetime. And right now, Eric and Jennifer are both about as foul as it gets."

If they hadn't been fighting the clock and walking into way too much danger with no backup, Ezra might have kissed her right then.

And regretted it later, too.

Because the mission wasn't going to fail.

There would be a tomorrow.

A next week.

And the day after that, when he got his assignment and left Blue Larkspur for the life he needed to live.

Ezra walked and couldn't be heard. Very quickly he taught her how. "We're in a hurry, but to get in there without being discovered, we have to move slowly," he said. "Keeping all of your weight on your left foot, knee bent, put your right foot down, pinkie toe first, then slowly roll to the ball of your foot. And repeat. You can't walk standing upright or you'll have less control of your balance, and it's always weight on the standing foot while setting the walking foot down, pinkie toe, ball of foot."

She practiced once. "What do I do with my heel?"

"Lower it as you roll to the ball of your foot." She tried, and he tapped her knee and said, "Knees bent, Theresa. You lose your balance, you fall. That leaves you fallen prey."

His words struck her cold, and the skin of her thigh still burned from the touch of his strong, thick fingers through her pants.

The man was going to drive her wild.

But his weird magic over her was keeping her focused long enough to find her girls, and that meant more than life.

By the time they'd reached the edge of the woods, completely without incident or any sound other than an occasional bird or quiet breeze in the trees, she was confident in her ability to move as he'd taught her. Had an idea of what he'd meant about paying attention to the sounds around her as well, to notice sudden change.

Which, he'd told her, would denote foreign occupation. Could be the enemy, because she'd been discovered. Or it could be a bear or other wildlife.

She had her knife. Was ready to use it.

She *was* a bear. A mama bear protecting her cubs.

The wildlife didn't worry her nearly as much as the thought of an armed former father-in-law did.

Ezra stood so close their bodies were touching as he used the last cluster of tree trunks for cover and surveyed the land before him. At first glance, she saw peaceful meadow.

And then, off to the right, so far away she could barely make it out, she saw the van. An impeccably kept brown van. Nudging Ezra, with her elbow to his side, she pulled her forearm up to her chest and pointed, with one finger only. Big motion, just like big steps, could be more easily detected.

He'd already seen the van. She got that when he nodded, leaned down, his head nestled into her neck, and gave her succinct, softly whispered instructions. "Do as I said. And don't watch me. Watch your six."

Putting her lips to his neck, she replied, "There are two of them and two of us. We've got this." After which she kissed him.

Right there on the neck.

A promise that she'd follow orders. A thank-you.

And a sip at his well of strength, too.

No matter what happened, the man was in her soul for keeps.

# Chapter 19

Did she just kiss his neck? Ezra had no idea what to make of the possibility, and while the idea of it lingered, he couldn't hang on to it right then. Moving stealthily, he headed to the front corner of the woods, leaving Theresa behind him, and didn't look back. Not even once.

A glance could cost him a missed detail, and one detail could be the difference between life and death.

If he didn't hear her scream, she didn't need him.

At the edge of the trees, he dropped to his stomach, arms stretched out in front of him, gun in his hand, with his head up only enough to be able to see his path. He'd chosen the shortest angle between him and the van, which was the only visible sign of human habitation. But as he lifted his head from the ground, looking upward, the view was different.

He noticed the glint right off. A camera lens in a

tree to the left of him, pointing toward the prairie land into which he was heading. Rolling over to his back, he studied the lens, and then returned to lying stomach side down. He'd detected three cameras on the front line of the trees, and could assume there were others, most likely on the ground, but all of them were facing approximately three feet aboveground. The cameras' owners were interested in large intruders.

Maybe bear or bobcats, but most likely those of the human variety.

So he became a snake, slithering in the foot-high grasses slowly enough not to be obvious, gaze peeled to the point of dry eye. Every blink could come with a price.

Oddly, as he moved, he came back home to himself. Was comfortable, at home, with the activity. And trusted his ability to complete the mission.

Nostrils filling with the slightly sharp scent of grasses and plant life mixed with the sour smell of mildew, he moved along slowly and steadily, the van in sight at all times. Earth scraped against his stomach as his shirt pulled from the waistband of his jeans. He knew. Didn't care.

Blades of various straw-like growths tipped at his cheeks. His nose. Accepting the itch without scratching, he watched for any sign of movement. Burning with one need in those moments—to see Claire and Neve. Once he had them on his radar, he could formulate the exact rescue plan.

They could be tied up. Or guarded by an armed grandparent.

More likely, they would be safely down in the bunker, which was going to make Ezra's job trickier. It wasn't like he could just pull open the hatch and trot downstairs.

Not if he wanted to make it without bullet holes in his legs and possibly torso.

He was going to have to get Eric and Jennifer Fitzgerald to vacate the bunker. To join him on the surface. The guards had to be dealt with before he could free the prisoners.

He'd looked the old man in the eye just four days before. Had seen the steely resentment at Ezra's presence around Eric's dead son's family. At his dead son's residence.

The grandfather wasn't going to give up.

He'd have to be taken.

Blue skies and sunshine shone a bright light over the land, and beat down on his neck, too. Gray and rainy would be better. Keep him in shadows rather than in a spotlight. And camouflage movement in the growth.

Cool him down, too.

And make sliding on his gut less onerous, as rain would make mud.

Weather was always part of the battle challenge. He'd slugged through snow and ice, for an entire night, with exposed skin. And had survived twelve hours in one-hundred-fifteen-degree desert heat without water.

Still several yards from the van, he popped his head up far enough to get a good look at his surroundings, another take on the same view he'd been studying throughout his half-hour trek. And...there it was. On the opposite side of the van from his approach, a piece of steel, set in a thick frame six inches off the ground, protruding with a locking handle on it.

Holy crap. He had eyes on the bunker.

His gaze shot sideways, first right, then left, looking for prickly pear, or any well-growing vegetation
that would signify compost fertilization. Nothing stood
out as any different from the rest of the landscape, but
he didn't have a full three-hundred-sixty-degree view
of the seventy-five or so feet that the angle of his dia-
gram had projected.

Inching his way to the van, intending to use the vehicle for cover, allowing him a more thorough look around
without alerting cameras to his presence, he contemplated various ways to get the Fitzgeralds out of the
bunker, if this was theirs.

Considering their irrational fear of blasts, he knew
an explosion wouldn't do it. A gunshot might not, either, as both were sign of attack, and the bunker was
their protection from that. It would have to be a threat
to the bunker itself.

A threat to the entrance. No way he was equipped
to drill down ten feet to reach the steel-enclosed mini
home itself.

Of course, someone, maybe even the girls, could be
in the van. He checked, as he drew closer, to see if anyone was visible through the windshield from his position on the ground, and saw nothing, but maybe they
were all in the back? Eating a late lunch?

Not at all likely.

If the girls were in that van, it was more likely that
they were tied up. Pray to God not drugged. Didn't make
sense that the Fitzgeralds would hurt the twins. Eric and
Jennifer's goal was to save their granddaughters' lives.

But irrational people did irrational things…

*Crack!* He saw the earth a foot to the right of him
puff up in a cloud of dust a second before he heard the

shot. Freezing in place, flat on the ground, he waited for a very brief breath, and then, moving sideways, he slowly inched his way closer to the van. Needing the metal for bullet protection while he assessed his enemy's strengths against his own weaknesses.

The one shot didn't mean for sure that he'd been made. Could have just been reaction to the possibility of someone on the premises—maybe a movement in the grass that triggered suspicion. A flash of color.

Could be someone thought his movement had been created by a rabbit, and the human was only seeking dinner.

Could be that Theresa had heard the shot and was panicking, thinking her girls had been hurt. Or that he wasn't coming back and she'd have to save her children on her own.

If she came any closer, she'd likely be shot.

No way for him to tell her that.

Best-case scenario, she was already on her way back to the Jeep to drive to where there was cell service and get Dom's butt in there to help Ezra get the girls to safety.

A knife against a bullet, long-distance... The knife would lose every time. Didn't matter how many turkeys she'd carved.

Another shot fired. Also landing barely a foot to the right of him. And it hit him... There weren't just cameras. There were motion detectors. Set within however many feet of the bunker he'd just reached.

His best hope was that the van would block the sensors. So thinking, he sped his pace, figuring that if he'd been seen, he was already a sitting duck, and if he hadn't been, his best chance at remaining undetected was the lone brown vehicle to which he'd been headed.

A third shot fired, following his progress. If he continued on the same path, he was going to lead his attacker straight to the van. Which would most likely bring Eric out of the bunker, but he'd leave Jennifer down in safety with the girls.

Should Ezra take out the grandfather?

Was it his only hope of getting those kids safely home with their mother?

Backtracking a bit, he rolled and slithered, rolled and slithered, on no sensible course, but inching his way closer to the back side of the van, the driver's side, as it happened to be. If sensors were showing movement, it wasn't going to look human. That was the best he could do in the moment.

That and plan. His heart pounded, his body hurt, but he couldn't waste thoughts on either situation. Feelings didn't matter. Staying mentally alert and ahead of his enemy was the only way to stay alive.

All three shots had come from the same spot. As though the gun were stationary, not being carried by someone on the move.

And they'd been rifle blasts, not from a pistol or shotgun. He might not be able to distinguish one from the other in a battle of many shots—but one at a time, he'd get it right.

The bullets had each been a single shot. Not with pellets, like a shotgun would emit.

Scratched and sweaty, he made it to the van, taking cover behind the front wheel, surveying the area around the bunker door from beneath the vehicle.

And saw the rifle. Attached to a telescoping apparatus coming up from underground. The shooter was down in the bunker. Aiming and firing from there.

Fancy setup. Military style.

Had Eric Fitzgerald served?

Was he up against a brother in arms possibly suffering from PTSD?

The thought came—and went. Two defenseless little girls made the point moot.

Knowing the source of the gun, more particularly knowing that its location wasn't going to change, made his job less harrowing for the moment. As long as he kept the van between him and the barrel, he'd stay alive.

He had to stay alive. Theresa and her daughters were counting on him. There were no troops behind him, fighting beside him, no one else to back him up in that particular maneuver if he failed. And the Fitzgeralds would have time to move the girls, to sequester themselves and the twins, and they might never be found again.

With a quick lift of his body, he glanced inside the driver's-side window of the van, noting the mess on the floor—blankets, fast-food trash. And the lack of seats in the back.

Shots were fired again. Straight at his head. From a handgun, not the rifle. And based on the trajectory, the shooter was traveling—and could be using children as cover. At that point, with the older couple feeling cornered, who knew what they'd do? Would they rather the girls die with them than have to live through a nuclear blast?

Ezra couldn't shoot back unless he could make certain the girls weren't in the vicinity.

His gaze fell to the van's ignition. He knew how to

hot-wire a vehicle, but couldn't do so just by… The keys were in the ignition.

Shots fired again, hitting the van's passenger window, and Ezra jumped in. Head down by the console, he turned the key, threw the vehicle in gear and pressed the gas pedal.

Another loud crack sounded, followed by a large thud to the van that shot him up in the air and back down. A tire had blown out. Sitting up enough to monitor his destination, Ezra kept going. Thumping over the ground, skidding and having to floor the gas when the blown tire got stuck in ruts, he continued toward the tracks leading back to the bunker, headed toward the road. There'd been no other vehicle in the area. His pursuer would be on foot.

And he prayed to God that if Theresa was still on the premises, she'd made a run for the Jeep.

If they were going to stay alive, they had to get the hell out of there.


Shaking, heart thumping so hard she wasn't sure how long it would last before giving out, Theresa sat behind the wheel of the Jeep, watching for any sign of human activity. Ezra, the girls, coming at her from any direction— she was ready to get them to safety.

She'd heard the first shot ring out, had never been able to figure out the source. Not even after the fifth had sounded. She'd seen a blur of movement by the far side of the van. Hoped it was Ezra, but didn't know that it was.

And she'd run for the Jeep.

Was Ezra lying shot and bleeding?

Would the Fitzgeralds be coming for her next?

Were the girls hurt?

Should she go for help or, if she left with the Jeep, would she be taking Ezra and Claire and Neve's only chance at getting to safety?

They could need emergency attention. Should she drive toward the main road until she got service, call Dom and then head back?

If the Jeep was their only hope of safe refuge, and she took it, then what?

Ezra was good at what he did, the best, but he'd never dealt with children before. Any children. Normal, happy children.

He most certainly would be in over his head with a traumatized set of twin girls who'd already been through so much.

If any of them were injured, they wouldn't be able to travel far. Or quickly. Not on foot, at any rate.

Biting her lip, blinking back tears, she sat with the Jeep in gear, worried about having enough gas, afraid to turn off the engine, as it was the only source of escape, and keeping her gaze focused on the landscape around her. Both sides. Front and back, too.

Two days in a row of hearing shots fired had taught her quickly.

She searched for clothing, movement, any sign of Ezra or the girls. And for Eric Fitzgerald, too. If he'd killed Ezra, and was coming for her, he wasn't going to succeed. She'd gun the Jeep she'd already turned to face the way out, and get help back there, or die trying.

The Jeep rocked, and she screamed as she realized the passenger door was opening. Mouth open to scream again, she had her foot on the gas, ready to floor it, sending whoever was there to the ground, when she recognized Ezra's head as he catapulted in beside her.

"Go!"

One look at his dirty, disheveled body, and she asked no questions.

She just went.

Trembling with fear, nauseous, she sped up the dirt road, leaving a large cloud of dust behind them, afraid to death for her daughters.

Afraid to ask questions.

Afraid of the answers.

Was Ezra hurt? Bleeding? She didn't look. Didn't dare take her gaze from the road. Half a mile passed, she rounded a corner, and he said, "Okay, you can stop. I'll take over."

"But…"

"We're not being followed" was all he said, exiting as she pulled to a stop. He rushed around to the driver's door. She didn't want to get out or waste precious time. Climbing over the console, she dropped her butt in the passenger seat he'd just vacated, allowing him to shove in behind the wheel and get the Jeep back in motion.

She tried to keep silent, to let him concentrate and do what he did, but after a couple of minutes, her throat clogged with tears, she asked, "Did you see them?"

"No." He focused only on the road, except to keep close watch in the rearview and side mirrors.

If he hadn't seen her girls, it stood to reason that he didn't know how they were. She digested the news, accepted it as best she could, and watched her side mirror as well as her phone, waiting for service.

"Are you okay?" she asked.

She just needed basic facts.

"Fine."

He didn't look fine. Not only did the tight line of

his jaw and the steely glaze over his eyes tell her he wasn't fine, but his clothes were filthy, and his shirt was ripped. She was pretty sure, when he moved and she caught a glimpse of his stomach through a rip, that she'd seen red.

His stomach was bleeding?

Horrified, she asked, "Were you hit?" She should never have let him drive.

"No." He glanced at her then, once, quickly, and for that second, his gaze softened. "I'm fine, Theresa—scraped up, maybe. Right now, we have to get word to Dom so they can get aerial surveillance out before the Fitzgeralds have a chance to lose us again. The van isn't drivable, but we have no idea what other plans they might have in place, maybe two-way radios that allow them to communicate with someone in a bunker close by. Some kind of signal they send. The technology back there was expensive."

That was why he kept looking behind them. And was racing to get off the road before someone else came at them, too?

They might not just be fighting one older couple. There could be a whole community behind the grandparents, believers in the cause, who'd help them in their fight to keep their granddaughters safe.

Sitting stiffly, feeling like she was dying an excruciating death one emotion at a time, she watched in all directions and imagined her face lying against warm T-shirt-covered chest muscle as she counted heartbeats.

# Chapter 20

The second Theresa told him she had cell service, Ezra pushed a call into his brother, leaving the audio on the vehicle's speaker. He gave Dom the exact coordinates of the bunker, listed camera locations, the telescopic gun site, how many shots had been fired, and a moving shooter who was invisible to him. And noted that he wasn't sure it even belonged to the Fitzgeralds. He described the brown van, down to tire type, listing all of the bags he'd seen from various fast-food outlets so someone could check their security cameras.

"It's no longer drivable," he relayed. "Tire rim meeting rock took care of that. Broken axle guarantees it. Reconnaissance says you're going to have to go in aerial first," he finished.

"I'll get drones out immediately." Dom's tone held urgency, which calmed Ezra's a bit. A good soldier knew when to back off and trust the man with superior ability to get the job done.

"There's a scenic pull-off a quarter of a mile down the main road," he said then. "We'll wait there."

Ezra hung up before Dom could argue. Or advise.

If his brother had something pertinent to say, he'd call back.

"We're staying in the area?" Theresa's tone sounded much better than it had the last time she'd spoken.

"Of course. Strangers go in and get your daughters out, you need to be one of the first things they see." He might not be child-savvy, but he wasn't a moron.

She looked at him, and he had no excuse not to look back. He read the panic, the pain, coursing through her. Swallowed hard.

He couldn't tell her there was no reason to fear.

"What are the chances of getting them out unharmed?" Her gaze, more than her voice, demanded honesty.

He had a much easier time telling a platoon of soldiers that they might die than telling Theresa that her two little girls could end up with the same fate. Easier, but still, excruciatingly hard.

"Reason says to look at the motivation of the captor." He changed the word from *enemy* at the last moment. He was talking about her dead husband's parents. People who'd been devastated by the death of their only child. "They are motivated by love for those little girls. Their goal is to ensure that they're safe when the debilitating blast that they believe is coming actually hits. We aren't dealing with narcissistic psychopaths," he finished. "The Fitzgeralds love deeply. They have consciences."

And their minds were misguided. While the last bit

of his thought remained unsaid, he knew Theresa was fully aware it was there.

And that the older couple's instability gave possibility to any scenario.

He also knew that he'd met the woman of a lifetime in the person sitting upright next to him. She wasn't immune to her emotions. But she took them and still managed to present herself to the problem.

He admired the hell out of her.

The way she'd not only held up over the past two days but had managed to think and act in a rational, beneficial way, as good as many trained soldiers. He was...beyond impressed.

He'd recommend her for a Purple Heart if she was a soldier. Although she hadn't been physically wounded, the emotional wounds she was bearing while continuing to serve effectively weighed far more.

And he knew that though he'd be leaving her, he wouldn't do it until he'd brought her daughters home.

One way or another, he was going to be there.

Theresa managed to stay logical for about five minutes after they'd pulled into the lay-by, which was really a fancy word for gravel at the side of the road. The scenic view was across the street—looking out from the mountain down into the valley stretching all the way to Denver, not that they could see that far if they went over and took a peek. Glints from Benson were visible, cars moving, probably, like little stars on the ground, from where they sat, Jeep turned and pointed toward the road in the direction heading to the Fitzgerald homestead. Land with a door to the home underground.

From what Ezra had described, there was no way

anyone was going to get those girls out. At least, not until Eric and Jennifer ran out of ammunition to shoot in the legs anyone who attempted to descend the ten feet down to them.

Unless the rescuer had head-to-toe body armor, and such a thing didn't exist.

Although, some military gear came close...

The Fitzgeralds likely had enough ammo to last through more law enforcement manpower than existed in the state of Colorado. They'd been stockpiling for decades.

And Claire and Neve would witness it...

You didn't ever forget something like that. Her sweet little ones, if they survived, would be emotionally scarred for life.

She couldn't fix that, no matter how much mother's intuition or love she poured into them.

And what was her other option? To leave them down in that bunker for the rest of their lives? They had to be rescued...

Sitting there contemplating options, she felt as trapped as they were. Flying out of her skin as she sat quietly within it.

Feeling the darkness closing in as it had the night before when she'd crawled into bed. Her stomach swarmed. With dread and fear-induced butterflies. Her mind careened to a place where emotion ruled and created thoughts.

Her precious little girls were being irreparably damaged, and there was nothing she could do about it and no way she'd ever be able to make them better. Were they already hurt physically? Restrained? Bruised? Or...

Ezra shifted in his seat, drawing her attention. Watching out the window, he seemed to be on the lookout every second. As though the Fitzgeralds might drive past them at any moment.

Because…that was Ezra. Always aware. Always prepared.

Always focused.

Butterflies flitted away with that thought.

Focus dissipated them.

Thinking about Ezra wiped them out.

And the moment she tried to concentrate on the occasional car driving past, on whether or not the drones were in place yet, what images the powerful cameras might be portraying…she catapulted into darkness.

Was reminded of the night before…the despair.

If they didn't find the girls, she'd be right back there that night. Only eight or so hours in the future, she could be climbing back between the sheets of the bed she'd left back in Benson that morning.

She couldn't do it.

But she'd already done it.

So…if she had to…maybe she could…

"If we don't find the girls tonight, will you hold me again until I fall asleep?" The words blurted out of her, born of panic, pushed out by desperation.

"Of course."

The certainty, the rapidity, of his response reached deep within her. As did the promise within it. She glanced at the unusual, one-of-a-kind man at her side and knew that, no matter what, she'd survive another day.

So that she could be the mother she was meant to be.

Dom's caller ID showed up before Ezra was expecting it to. Dread filled his gut as he grabbed his phone.

The Jeep and thus its audio system were turned off, conserving gas. No reason for him to make it obvious that he wanted the call to be a private one. There hadn't been enough time for surveillance and then a successful extraction.

Even Dom wasn't that good.

But if the cameras showed death...

"Yeah."

"It's not them."

Feeling Theresa's gaze hot on him, Ezra said, "What's not?"

"The people in that bunker... It's a young guy and his pregnant wife."

He didn't say the string of words that ran through his mind, but he sat with them for a couple of seconds. Avoiding the woman seated to his right completely.

"You've trespassed and have been shot at twice now, bro."

Yeah. And he'd let Theresa down twice, too, which hurt far worse.

"Guy's claiming self-defense and is well within his rights to do so. He saw your gun. He wants reimbursement for the van you damaged. He agrees not to press theft charges against you, considering the circumstances, as long as he gets a new van."

"Fine." He could afford to buy a guy a van. Even without a financial wizard as a sibling, like Oliver looking after his investments for years.

"I get what you're doing, Ezra," Dom said then, sounding a bit like he needed a beer—and maybe a night alone with his fiancée. "I get why. But you're making me look bad here."

"Yeah."

"Don't call again until you've confirmed their location."

Dom had stopped short of ordering him to cease and desist. Ezra owed him one. "Yeah, okay."

"Caleb called," his triplet said then, the comment random enough that Ezra knew it was important.

"He's got verified intel that shows evidence of Ronald Spence smuggling, just like I suspected. In or very close to Blue Larkspur. Hitting us at home."

"Thumbing his nose at all of us." The idea made Ezra burn. As did the fact that he'd failed his older brother. He'd told Caleb he'd help look for evidence on the guy Caleb and Morgan had erroneously helped get out of prison, thinking he'd been one of their father's victims who'd been sent to prison for a crime he didn't commit.

Ezra couldn't remember a time when his family had needed him. Now Caleb had, and he hadn't been there for him.

The knowledge didn't sit well, not that Dom knew what Ezra had told Caleb. His brother was just filling him in on family business.

None of what Dom was telling him sat well.

"Hey." Dom's tone was firm. Like a slap upside the head.

"Yeah."

"Don't give up." Dead silence followed the words. Dom had ended the call.

Leaving Ezra alone with one of the strongest women he'd ever known. A woman who was hanging on by a thread that he was about to cut.

It was like she was in a free fall that just didn't stop.

"...a young couple..."

She heard Ezra's voice filling the Jeep sitting on the gravel lay-by. Only caught a few of the words that came after the ones that kept replaying themselves over and over in her mind.

*It wasn't them.*

Such innocuous words could mean anything. *Them* could mean anyone. It might mean that Eric and Jennifer weren't the ones shooting at Ezra, because they were down in the bunker playing the girls' favorite princess board game with them and a friend had been visiting and taken care of the intruder for them.

Or…or…it wasn't the Fitzgeralds there at all. What if the girls had been left in the care of a babysitter who'd been told to protect them at any cost, so she'd pushed the button that set off an electronically manipulated rifle to shoot at sensor movement?

*It wasn't them.*

*A young couple…*

"You were shot at…could have been killed…for nothing." The words fell from her lips, born from the depths of despair into which she'd fallen.

And she hadn't finished descending the downward trajectory inside of her. The longer she sat there, the deeper she went into a darkness that had no beginning and no damned end.

Starting the Jeep, Ezra pulled out onto the mostly deserted road. Drove without saying where he was taking them. She didn't ask.

Just sat frozen, watching trees go by, seeing mountainsides and distant vistas, and hearing *It wasn't them.*

A whole day had passed, and all of the law enforcement agencies looking for her daughters had made no progress. The Fitzgeralds had planned long and well.

For a crime that had obviously been spurred on by their son's death. They were successfully completely off the grid. And might not ever be found.

With no power to change the circumstances, she had to face facts...

"It wasn't for nothing."

Ezra's words were a long time coming. So long, in fact, that the shock of hearing his voice again got her attention, and she heard every one of them.

"How can you say that?" What good could possibly have come of that afternoon's debacle? Of the wasted time? Darkness was going to be falling before they could make it to the next destination on the map.

She'd done the math. Unless some miracle happened and her daughters came walking up the road toward them, or showed up on law enforcement's radar, her wish for their sweet dreams was going to be delivered to them via angels again that night.

"We're on the right path, Theresa." The cadence of his voice flat, he didn't even glance her way. Whatever he was giving her, it was no pep rally. He wasn't trying to convince her. To build her spirits. He was giving her facts as he believed them.

So she didn't argue with him. She just sat there, arms crossed over her aching body, and wondered if he was hurting, too. The man had spent close to an hour dragging himself along on his stomach on her behalf.

Glancing over, she saw the tear in his shirt again. And felt something besides death inside.

She felt gratitude. Toward him.

And toward a world that held people who got up every day to risk their lives for others.

"The authorities can't go and search private property," he reminded her. "And today we proved that our theories are accurate. We found a bunker. Just not the right one. Yet."

*Yet.*

"We know they're out there. And we know enough to reasonably assume that their bunker is in the state and out there, too. It's just a matter of time until we find it."

Time was something he didn't have. A couple of weeks, maybe, was all he had left before he'd be off on assignment again.

Panic soared within her. Taking over mind and body.

"We have two more areas on our list," he continued, speaking without inflection. And yet somehow getting through to her. "We knocked off three today. Tomorrow, instead of heading west, we head north from the motel and hit both of them."

There were two more areas on their initial list.

There could be another list, too, expanding farther around the state. They had the recipe for bunker search parameters. They just had to stay in the kitchen until… until…

"I'm sorry."

Those words drew her gaze in a flash. "Sorry? For what?"

"I honestly have no idea. This is war. You make the most logical plan with the best chance of success, you go out, you fight like hell, and you keep doing it until the battle's won. I've just never had someone with personal investment in my platoon before. I've never fought for someone I knew personally, and it feels…"

He broke off midsentence.

And just like that, Theresa's panic-filled pity party

was gone for the moment. She was outside of herself, caring for someone else.

Ezra wasn't just a body on the job. He was a man, a person, with a good heart, a great heart, and…a friend with his own struggles.

"You might be out of your element, but you're doing far more for me than I would have thought anyone ever could, Ezra Colton, and I don't just mean finding bunkers and getting shot at."

He continued to stare straight ahead, but she saw his jaw tensing. Showing, to her, that he cared.

And she cared, too. Even if she hadn't…she'd never been one to make the world all about her. Doing things for others felt better. And Ezra, whether he knew it or not, had just given her a job to do. She had to be okay, to show him that she was holding up; she had to hold on to her hope, so that he could focus on getting his job done.

"What's your favorite food?" she asked him. Yeah, it was random, but feeding others was what she knew. Everyone had to eat—Maslow's lowest level on the hierarchy, food in the belly and roof over the head.

He glanced at her. Finally. Probably checking to see if she'd lost her mind. "Filet mignon."

"So before we head back to the hotel, how about we find the best steak house in this part of the state and have a decent meal?"

She might choke on it. She might not. She might not be able to keep it down. But she'd do everything she could to tend to him as he was tending to her.

"How about we find the best steak in Benson?" he asked then, the lines on his forehead and around his eyes finally fading a bit. "I need to change my shirt." She looked at the torn cotton hanging over his flat belly.

Worried again about the damage he might have done to himself.

He glanced at her again then, almost as though he could read her mind.

She smiled her gratitude, her regard for him. A smile she knew was tinged with the desperation and agony that hung in the air, but still a real expression.

And he smiled back.

The same way.

# Chapter 21

Ezra almost welcomed the sting of the soap to his scraped skin as he stood beneath the shower, thinking about the day, replaying the information that had come at him, the way he'd processed it, the choices he'd made. He found he'd done all he could possibly have been expected to do given the circumstances.

Satisfied that he'd lived up to the ideal he'd once thought his father to be, to the best of his ability, he rinsed, determined that his stomach wasn't nearly as bad as he'd thought, the skin more surface-burned than actually pierced, and pulled on his last set of clean clothes.

Jeans and another long-sleeved T-shirt, this one in green. Balling up the dirties, he headed out to rejoin Theresa in the room they were sharing. She'd redone her bun. Was sitting at the table, scrolling on her phone.

"I need to make a stop at the washer and dryer before we go," he said, telling himself not to notice how incredibly beautiful she looked, sitting there so quietly, so still, while he knew emotions raged inside her. In some ways she was more like him than even his own brothers. The way she could be calm, collected, and raging inside at the same time. The way she could hurt, and yet wall herself off from the pain enough to get the job done.

"I was just thinking about that, too," she said. "Between the two of us, we've got a load. You mind throwing them in together?"

He shouldn't mind. Didn't mind, really.

Except that...he did.

From the time he was eighteen, his clothes had usually been washed on their own. By him...

"Of course," he said. "Fine..." He held out his spare arm. "Load me up."

"I'll do them," she replied, grabbing the clothes out of his grasp before he knew where she'd been headed. "Your others are here, right?" she asked, bending over to the shopping bag he'd used for a laundry basket. She had his skivvies there...

Grabbing her purse and a similarly filled shopping bag to his, she headed for the door. "Be right back," she said and walked out.

Ezra stood there, watching her go, hard as a rock.

Because a woman—Theresa—was doing his laundry.

As though it was all in a normal day. And then it hit him... Of course it was all in a normal day. She would have done laundry for three every time she did the chore. And had done it for four, too, back when her husband had been alive. As sick as he'd been at the end, there'd been no way Mark could have, or would have, gotten up to wash his own dirty clothes.

Ezra's growing erection shrank right up at the thought of her late spouse by the time Theresa returned. She let him know that the clerk at the front desk had just told her the best steak in town was right next door, and out they went, to have their first dinner together while his underwear soaked back at the motel with hers.

How sick was he to be jealous of his own skivvies?


Dinner was as nice as a dinner could get when you were a woman adrift with her children in danger in an unknown location. As if by silent declaration, neither she nor Ezra spoke about bunkers, their search or the day they'd just had. They didn't talk about Mark, his illness or how difficult the past year had been for her. And they didn't discuss his family, or his father, either.

They talked about the movies they'd seen, some the same, some not, held the same opinions on some, disagreed on others. He'd listened to classic rock growing up. She'd preferred the female pop singers of the time. Their favorite vacation spots both included the beach. He ordered a beer. She had a glass of wine.

She'd had a high school sweetheart. He hadn't. She had a college degree. He didn't.

She'd been married. He'd never been in a long-term serious relationship.

What they didn't do was expound on much of anything—except maybe the movies they'd seen. And by the time the waitress brought them their check, Theresa was shocked to see that she'd almost emptied her plate.

He paid for dinner, and then walked with her to move the clean clothes to the dryer. She wasn't sure whose idea it was to take a walk around town, just up and down the main drag, but it did her good, seeing normal people milling about, having normal lives. And it made her incredibly lonely and antsy, too, because everywhere she looked, she thought about the twins, what they'd like, where they'd want to go, what they'd be saying if they were with her.

The length of the walk was predicated by the dryer cycle, and Theresa wasn't at all ready to head back to reality as they stood side by side at the laundry table and, each grabbing their own things, folded and bagged separately.

They could have been strangers at a Laundromat, where bras and panties were handled in every city, every day, by tons of people without incident or undue thought.

Except that she'd had thoughts.

Of him taking an interest in her underthings. She'd noticed his, after all.

And when those thoughts raised such sorely needed good feelings inside her, she allowed more of them. Wondering if he'd like to see her wearing her underthings.

If he'd like to take them off her.

If he'd thought about undoing her bra and touching her breasts...

If he'd seen her panties there on the table with his underwear and thought about their respective body parts together...her crotch on top of his.

Then his phone rang.

His brother Dominic again.

An officer from Padillac, a small town just west of Benson—not far from the gas station where she and Ezra had stopped that first day—had found the Fitzgeralds' old blue truck nose-first in a river. There was no sign of any bodies.

But there'd been some blood inside.

Some. Not a lot.

*Some.*

Ezra stressed the word. Over and over.

There'd been no melted ice cream sandwiches in it, though.

And based on the water's rise and fall and the debris, the truck had been there less than a day. Which meant the nosedive happened after the brown van had been at the ice cream store.

Had the girls been hurt in the accident? Had they even been in the brown van? Did the Fitzgeralds have two vehicles?

Had a friend loaned them the van?

Maybe even the young couple who'd shot at Ezra earlier that day?

FBI forensics were going over the truck, lifting prints, and the blood would be tested. They wanted Theresa's permission to access her daughters' medical records for possible matches.

"To rule them out," Ezra said. More than once.

She listened. Gave permissions. But floated in and out of focus. And when it was time for bed, and Ezra crawled in beside her, wrapping her in his arms, Theresa allowed herself to rest her head on his chest and lose consciousness for a little while.

\* \* \*

He ached. Hard as a rock. Needed release.

Movement on his chest. Fingers. Heading slowly downward.

Excruciatingly heightened sexual desire pounded Ezra, bringing him from sleep.

Not unusual. He was a healthy guy. And…

He wasn't alone. The weight against him…wasn't just in his sleep.

Full consciousness hit with a slam. Holy hell.

Theresa.

She was moving her fingers softly down to his penis. She palmed him there.

How was he going to get his body under control with her doing that?

Rubbing her face against his chest, she moaned, more like a hum, sounding pleased, and he lay there, trying to school himself into not reacting, but unable to stop her. Not that he wanted to.

She was obviously dreaming, thinking he was Mark, and if he woke her…

She had enough emotional crap to deal with. The day ahead was going to be rough, no matter what, and if she had to go into it with an embarrassingly awkward sexual component between them…

Her hand stilled, and he told himself it would only be a few minutes. Then he'd get himself back to size and quietly extricate himself from the bed.

No. No. Her fingers were on the move again. To his side…his other side…circling around his belly button area while his groin ached painfully.

He was going to have to stop her. Sorry for the embarrassment. But it would be much worse if he exploded right there.

Her hand slipped lower. Just an inch from the tip of him, and she lifted her head. Slid up to place her mouth on his, kissing him full-on.

His lips knew what to do. How to respond. They did it.

For her.

Surely that would be it. She'd lie back down and drift off, with no conscious memory of doing anything more than having a dream. She'd been so distraught. Bottling up more emotion than any one person could reasonably expect to keep contained.

Forcing her subconscious to seek an outlet in the only way…

Her lips came at his again. Open and soft, her tongue looking to tangle. And…oh, God…he tangled with her. Just for a second.

Because the incredible woman who he'd been wanting for days and couldn't have was sticking her tongue in his mouth.

Meaning him to be her husband, he figured.

With her lips still on his, she moved, throwing one leg over his, straddling his thigh, and rubbed her core on him.

Using every ounce of the rigid self-control he'd honed over the years, he lay still, prolonging the sweet torture as long as he could before being forced to wake her.

Maybe she'd stop. The dream would end as if it had never been. She'd wake in the morning with no knowledge of…

With her lips on his throat, sending delicious shards

of desire through him, her hips moved upward on him, and her knee gently rubbed against his way-too-sensitive privates.

He almost embarrassed himself. Barely held it back. Took a second to let things simmer lest he move and explode, fully aware in that second that what he was doing was wrong.

He couldn't pretend to be another man even if he was doing it to help her. It wasn't right and…

"Ezra?"

No trouble freezing everything then. He didn't move. Had no clue what to do.

"I just… I know you aren't much for words, but… I just need to know that you're okay with this. That I'm not taking advantage…"

Her body lay against his. Still, but for the heart that was beating hard against his chest.

"It's just for tonight," she whispered. "Just to get through the night…and only if you really want to do it with me, too."

He still didn't speak. The right words didn't come. But he rolled with her, arms supporting his weight on each side of her, cradling her. Gazing into her eyes, seeing himself reflected there amid her want, he lowered his lips to hers.

*It's just for tonight.* Even as she kissed Ezra, Theresa heard her own words again. Silently. A reminder.

She'd known, when she'd woken up with her leg thrown across Ezra and had felt his hard-on, that he hadn't been reacting to her specifically. His even, slightly raspy breathing had told her he'd still been asleep.

She'd carefully removed her leg, but continued to lie against him as she dozed off again. To dream about him.

Waking to see her fingers splayed on his chest.

And to find his entire body tensed. His breathing too rhythmically controlled.

Clearly awake.

The rest… There hadn't been thought. She'd just acted.

Him lying there awake beneath her, still hard… The surge of feeling had been so good, so energizing, she hadn't been able to resist.

There'd been no plan to seduce him. Or even to do more than explore the expanse of muscles and hard stomach she'd been finding irresistibly hot over the past week.

Thought returned briefly as she lay under him, looking up at his strong, gorgeous face. An acknowledgment that she was about to have sex with a man who was not her husband, for the first time since she and Mark had met.

Her heart knew…and was okay, too.

Her body needed Ezra Colton in a way she'd never craved a man in her life. The desire coursing through her was alive, an entity that was in control, demanding strong response.

Tenderness was there as well, but almost as an afterthought.

Urgency came first.

Feeling as much of him, taking as much of him, as she possibly could, the only goal. He was familiar and brand-new.

Exciting beyond recognition and safe.

His lips didn't just kiss hers. They consumed her,

mingling tongues and breath into a taste that hadn't existed before that night.

One that was exclusive to them.

She loved it. Couldn't get enough.

When he sat up to pull his shirt over his head, she started to pull hers off, too. He reached out a hand and helped, tugging the material over her head and tossing it away.

Cool air hit her breasts, while his hot gaze warmed them. She liked sitting there for him, watching him enjoy the sight of her.

And that made her too hungry again. With her hands on his chest, she pushed him over, lying fully on top of him, moving her breasts and her hands over his chest, learning the feel of his springy hair, rubbing their nipples together.

With one arm around her back, he rolled them again, lifting himself up to slip out of his sweatpants, taking his underwear with them, and Theresa stared.

He was male perfection. Truly beautiful. Muscled and strong and so gorgeous.

And his penis was…clearly ready.

She went for the elastic waistband of her sweat bottoms, but his hands were there first, one on each hip. With his thumbs hooked in the waistband, he pulled down slowly.

Very slowly.

Revealing her mama hips, and what lay in between them, with a glow in his eyes that she'd never forget.

It had been a long time since Theresa had felt beautiful. Desirable.

Too long.

And that moment was hers.
All hers.

Ezra never looked away from Theresa as he left the
bed only long enough, and only far enough, to grab his
wallet and the condom he always carried, tossing it to
the pillow as he lowered himself beside a woman like
none other. Over the next while, he committed every
inch of Theresa to memory. He touched every part of
her, with the intention to give her as much pleasant feeling as he could, to offset the bad consuming her world.
To create a good memory for her in the middle of hell.

It wasn't about him. He'd had sex before. He'd have
it again.

It was always good.

And then she pushed him to his back on the mattress,
straddled his stomach and started touching him. Every
inch. Watching herself do it.

At one point she grabbed the condom. Ripped it open
with her teeth, while her free hand teased his nipple,
and then gave him a mouthwatering look at what he
was going to feast on.

Turning, she sucked on his neck, kissed him long
and wet and hard, and moved to his arms. Sliding her
hands up and down them. Kissing them.

Her gaze was focused, and yet…ethereal, too. As
though she was on another plane, being guided, knowing full well what she was doing to him and getting
hot doing it.

He'd never had anything like that before.

She wasn't rough, but she wasn't gentle, either. And
when she suddenly scooted lower, impaling herself with

one movement, he hissed and almost came right then and there.

He held on, and thanked fate that he had when she started moving on him, eyes wide open, watching him, and bending to watch them coupling before looking him in the eye again.

If there'd been any doubt at all that the woman knew who she was having sex with, even though he knew she was aware, it would have vanished. Her voice was loud and clear, telling him she knew that she was with Ezra.

And that was what made him come.

# *Chapter 22*

Theresa slept naked, still slick with sex, cuddled up to Ezra's chest. She was exhausted, satiated, mind blown, but more, she'd poured so much energy into him. Her emotional well was drained dry for the moment, allowing her the respite necessary to refill.

A few hours later, she woke before dawn, knew exactly where she was, what she'd done, and was glad she'd done it.

Slowly and gently removing herself from Ezra's body and the bed, she used her newly learned silent walk to get to the bathroom and closed the door before turning on the light.

The sight of her wild dark hair tangled and falling around her shoulders and breasts made her smile for a second.

The one second she gave to herself.

And then it was into the shower, taking care of her ablutions quickly and concisely, barely pausing over the sore parts of her that hadn't been used in too long. The tender nipples that she soaped just as she did every morning.

There was no lingering, no prolonging what was already over.

She would be ready for whatever the day needed from her the second Ezra said it was time to go.

There were also no regrets, she found, as she looked herself in the mirror while applying a light coat of makeup with sunscreen to her face.

She'd made a choice and didn't feel sorry about it.

Was it going to be harder to tell him goodbye when the time came for him to go?

Probably.

But it wasn't like it would have been a piece of cake to see him depart, even if she hadn't slept with him.

Was she going to ache to the bone for a bit after he left?

Obviously.

But she'd rather have been alive in a moment than let her libido lie dormant forever. The thought made a sad kind of sense to her, and with one last look in the mirror, she became only the mother who desperately wanted more than anything for her daughters to be returned safely to her care, and went to face the rest of her life.

Ezra had learned at sixteen how to compartmentalize. More importantly, he'd perfected the talent of putting anything that made him feel emotionally vulnerable into one particular area. That part of him received and never opened enough to allow anything to escape.

That Thursday morning's dawn came with a major malfunction there, though. It was rejecting Theresa Fitzgerald. Wouldn't let him pack her away, emotionally speaking.

And, of course, it happened on a day when he didn't have the time or resources to deal with it. He couldn't head to the gym, take a long run or climb a mountain. He couldn't go to target practice or make a surprise visit to the nearest boot camp in his area to join the recruits in their training.

Those resources, and others like them, had helped seal away his emotions every single time.

Without them, he did the only thing left to him—carried on with baggage in tow. And he'd make damned certain that his growing feelings didn't slow him down or get in the way of successfully completing his mission.

While Theresa was in the shower, he went for breakfast, ordered it to go, ate his on the way back to the room and waited long enough for her to get out of the bathroom before he reentered the room. No listening to her shower or entertaining thoughts about being in there with her.

What was done was done.

She'd made clear the night before that what was between them was just for that evening.

By touching her back, he'd agreed to that stipulation.

Wanted it, even.

And so it was.

He went in only far enough to set her foam take-out container on the edge of the dresser. "Eat up while it's hot," he said, and without more than a glance in her direction, seeing that she was all put together, green pants and shirt again, hair in that perennially messy bun, he shut himself behind the bathroom door.

A cold shower and quick shave later, he gathered his things, left them in the bags on the counter as he'd done the day before—on the other side of the sink from her bags of things—and headed out to find her standing, purse on her shoulder, in the middle of the room.

Looking lost?

"Ready?" His tone was a little softer than normal. He'd work on it.

"Thanks for breakfast," she said as she left him to follow her. Her response was short and to the point. No words, just meeting him at the door and opening it before he could.

And so it went for most of the morning. They tended to the business at hand. Neither of them spoke of what they'd done in the darkness.

If she thought about it at all, it didn't show. No covert looks, chance glances or accidental touches.

As soon as he was on the road, he didn't notice as much. Keeping his mind on the job was second nature to him, and he settled into his skin gladly.

Traveling the other side of the U on their map that morning, they had all-new scenery to canvass as they passed. He noted more prickly pear than he'd seen the day before, but there were fewer of some of the other plants natural to the Colorado mountains.

Still, he took note, with a check mark in the positive instead of the negative column. Could be a sign they were finally on the right track.

"I widened my search while you were in the shower this morning," he told Theresa as the miles sped past and they drew closer to their first destination. Silence

was fine, but he had to know that she was really okay—
and up for whatever might lie ahead.

Partially because she was putting her own life at risk,
as well as his and the kids', if she couldn't hold her own.

Or if she wasn't willing to follow orders.

He had no God complex, but the truth was, on any
job, there could only be one boss. On that particular
job, that particular day, the boss was him.

She wasn't jumping into the conversation. So he
eventually told her, "I included old homesteads in the
parameters. Maybe they happened upon an abandoned
one in the mountains someplace, set up shop, and no one
came along to question their right to be there."

The idea had occurred to him when they'd first gone
to bed the night before. He'd had to keep his mind firmly
on the case to keep it off her snuggled up against him.

"That would explain why they show up in no property
searches," she said, her voice even. Her brow furrowed,
more in consideration than displeasure, he figured from
the brief glance he took, and he felt better.

She was with him. Holding up.

"For all we know, they could have raised Mark there,"
she added. And his gut clenched a little.

Was the reference merely because they were seeking
her deceased husband's parents? Or did she have Mark
on her mind? Were there deep regrets for what she'd done
with Ezra, given Ezra, the night before?

He didn't blame her.

He was mostly all right with having been a probable
substitute. He totally understood. Searched for a way
to tell her that it was okay.

He didn't find one.

And didn't see that it mattered where Eric and Jennifer had raised their son. What mattered was finding where they were planning to raise their granddaughters.

But he and Theresa would be rescuing them.

Returning them, safe and sound, to their mother's arms, to their freshly painted little home with a dog named Charlie.

And then he would be getting the hell out of Blue Larkspur before he made any major blunders.

Like asking a grieving widow if he could sleep with her one more time for good luck before he set out.

They'd been in the Jeep a couple of hours, and Theresa was having a hard time keeping hope alive by the time Dominic's call came in.

She'd tried not to worry about that nose-dived blue truck, but she'd known from the second she heard about the accident that there was no good scenario for it.

When Ezra pushed to answer his brother's call and said, "Yeah," she almost covered her ears. She didn't want to know.

But she had to know. She couldn't help her children if she didn't know...

"Blood in the truck is no match," the FBI agent said right off.

"It's not Claire's or Neve's?" she called out to him. No room for misunderstanding on that one.

"Correct."

"Oh, thank God." Tears spurted and she looked away, sorry to appear like a weak link to the two strong men helping her so diligently.

Peripherally, she saw Ezra's head turn a few quick

times, but she didn't so much as glance over. Didn't dare allow herself the chance to connect with him at the moment.

She'd had what she could have.

Because even if Ezra was aware of the powerful feelings she had for him, even if he shared them, she'd never love him enough to be okay with his career. To the contrary, the more she fell in love, the more problematic his career would become.

And by all accounts, Ezra Colton was a soldier. To not be okay with that was to not be okay with him.

And even if she'd risk her own heart, there was no way she could put her daughters' hearts out there again. Not with such a strong chance that they could lose Ezra, after having already lost their father.

And, yes, she'd fallen for Ezra Colton. She was fairly certain she'd had no choice in the matter. It wasn't one she'd have willingly made. But she wasn't going to lie to herself about it, either.

She'd learned the hard way, with Mark's illness, that lying to oneself only hurt more in the end when you had to accept reality.

Dom's words flew in and out between her thoughts. The FBI had gotten no hits in the fingerprint database that matched the prints taken from the truck. And no DNA match off the blood, either, for the girls or their grandparents.

The area search produced no evidence of a struggle or recent footprints—but it didn't rule them out, either.

Personnel had combed the banks of the river for several miles both ways from the crash site. No sign of a body, or even clothes, had turned up.

"We did get one hit, though," Dom said. Theresa

swung her gaze straight to the car's audio system, as though she could see the man on the screen that currently displayed his name. "Doesn't help us much today, but officers have been canvassing the area between that first little gas station you visited outside Blue Larkspur and Benson, going door-to-door, which was a feat since places are so few and far between…"

"Today, Dom." Ezra's tone carried definite tension.

"Found a home security system. Got an older brown van, mint condition, heading from Benson, and later the blue truck heading toward Benson, coinciding perfectly with the time we catch it on the two cameras there from two days ago, and just a bit later, we get the brown van heading back toward Benson again."

"They switched vehicles someplace along the way."

"And if it really was them in the brown van, they headed back to Benson as we'd thought."

Maybe it wasn't much to people like Dominic and Ezra Colton, who fought bad guys every day and knew that two-day-old news wasn't going to help them find the girls that day. But to Theresa, who'd just had confirmation that it was *likely* that the Fitzgeralds really had been buying two cases of ice cream sandwiches, the news was a gift from heaven. You didn't buy perishables by the case unless you were planning to spoil the intended recipients for a long time.

To her, that ice cream symbolized hope that her daughters were being well cared for—to the extent that unstable conspiracy believers could administer good care.

"Good to have a piece fall into place," Ezra said, almost as though he'd read Theresa's thoughts.

"Doesn't bring 'em home." Dom clearly wasn't into

sugarcoating. Ezra hadn't been, either, the two prior days they'd been on the road. If he was suddenly changing his tactics, thinking he needed to protect her...

"Nope, it's up to us to do that," Ezra replied and clicked off before Dominic said another word.

"I won't be coddled," she said, almost glad to have something to be angry with him about. "I prefer Dominic's honesty to false hope."

His jaw tightened. He stared straight ahead, both hands on the steering wheel. White-knuckled. Were they about to have their first fight?

Probably their only one?

Shoulders visibly relaxing, he gave her a quick glance. "Point taken. I apologize."

*Good.* She sat, staring out, watching ahead, and on both sides of the road, too, as had become habit. Glad that she'd set him straight.

So why, now that she'd made sure that Ezra wouldn't give her any special treatment, did that fact sadden her?

He wasn't trying to give her false hope. Ezra knew full well how damaging a fake sense of reality could be.

But *damn.*

When his brother started spouting off facts, without any regard as to how hard his words would hit Theresa...

He had to find the girls. Get them safely home.

And get his ass out of Blue Larkspur. New assignment or not.

He could spend a few days at the beach, drinking beer. Or take a side trip to Malaysia to shoot pool with Oliver.

Maybe even let him win.

"Ezra, stop!"

He hit the brakes gently. And then again. They'd been traveling for nearly forty miles on the same dirt road without slowing. Locations number four and five were both accessed by it, with fifty miles in between them. If she...

Theresa was out of the car before he'd even come to a complete stop. Thinking she was ill, he barely got the Jeep in Park before he rushed to join her.

She was bent over, but she wasn't heaving. Or peeing, either, which could have been another emergency necessitating a quick stop, he realized too late.

She was pointing toward the rock face that covered much of the ground around them. "Are those tire tracks?" she asked.

Following the point of her finger, he saw the black, almost grease-like markings on the mostly whitish rock, prepared to tell her kindly that she was seeing earth misplaced from a storm and cooked into the rock.

And then he noticed the glint...off to the right, several yards away, embedded in the mountainside that mostly lined the road. A camera.

"Get down," he said. He lowered himself to the ground, scooping her toward him, to make sure she landed on him, not the rock.

He rolled over immediately, keeping her under him, as he surveyed the area. It was all overkill, he was sure.

They were on the edge of private property. Fence line had been clearly marked by posts and flags on both sides of the rock face, which had made installing fence on that one spot impossible. And needless.

The flat ground she'd seen could be a gully or could lead back behind the rock face to something more. Entire towns could be erected back there, and from the road, it would look like nothing.

He knew there wasn't a settlement of some sort, though. His topographic map had told him so.

But he couldn't be sure there wasn't another hermit who'd shoot them off his property.

"Stay on your belly and get back to the Jeep." He bit out the words as he slid her his knife. "Stay low and get around to the driver's side and climb in the back. Get down on the floor." He moved off her. "Go."

Ezra waited until he heard the far side door close, and then he moved forward, inch by inch, to get a better look at the marks she'd seen.

Adrenaline kicked in when he got close enough to see that she'd been right.

The markings were tire tracks.

Recent ones.

He was still ten miles from the map's designation of the ideal location for the Fitzgeralds' bunker, but his quest wasn't science. Or exact.

And he could once again be on private property owned by an inhabitant, or inhabitants, who only wanted to be left alone.

He had no right to be there.

And absolutely did not want to put Dom in a tough situation at his job.

The visible track, a bit of mud mixed with tire tar, was on an angle. That told him the vehicle was headed away from them around the rock face, blocking his view from what might be beyond. And the tread was larger than a car's. Not as large as a work truck's. A van?

The tread was solid. The kid at the store in town had noted the van's tires being in good shape.

Was he so desperate to help the woman he'd had sex with, so desperate to find two little girls who'd shown him how cool being around children could be, that he was going to turn a mark on a rock into a reason to break the law again?

His life was about order.

And absolutely upholding what was right and just.

He would not be his father.

Peering carefully at every inch of the rock face upon which he lay, smelling dirt and fresh air, listening for anything, Ezra questioned himself as he never had before.

His number one rule of engagement? Don't hesitate.

Sliding forward, he tried to get a glimpse of where the vehicle might have gone, without compromising any potential landowner's privacy. Twelve inches at a time. Then another foot.

What was he doing?

What kind of real evidence did he have?

Had he been so desperate to help Theresa Fitzgerald, to fight her fight with her, that he'd been leading them on wild-goose chases all along?

And why?

Why did he think he could do any more to find those little kids than all of the law enforcement agencies in the state? Like he was better than the entire FBI, which was taxed with kidnapping cases all the time?

He knew nothing about kidnappers.

Or kids, either, for that matter.

He knew about fighting terrorists and cartels in Afghanistan.

Why in the hell was he lying on a rock face in the middle of nowhere?

Because Theresa had intrigued him?

Because he'd wanted to ask her out on a date, even though he knew that it could lead nowhere?

With the new van he'd be paying for, he had to admit he was certainly on the most expensive outing he'd ever taken with a woman.

Strange, though, that the same kind of camera as at the first homestead, set at about the same angle, had been protruding out of a cliff face.

Maybe it was because those who lived off the grid were a kind of community of themselves, buying their supplies from those who were like them.

Continuing to mountain climb the flat surface on his belly, bending one leg to push him along, and then the other, he just needed a glimpse of where the vehicle had been headed. If it had been headed anywhere.

The driver could have just pulled off to take a leak. A nap. A photo.

Could have been turning around.

But just the one tire track. At that angle…

One more push and more mountain wall…with a breakaway, flatter surface that led farther into the mountain range. And there at the bend was a healthy bed of prickly pear cactus.

It was too much. Too coincidental.

Unless he'd been spot-on from the beginning of the day, and the Fitzgeralds *were* here after all. Heart pounding, he moved forward. He had good tracking skills. Knew to look at the basic things others missed. Like healthy growth at the site of a compost dump that turned into fertilization. Lusher vegetation than the rest of the landscape around him.

It was a stretch. He got that. And trusting his instincts had saved a lot of lives. Including his own a few times.

He had to make sure, though.

He crawled farther forward. Saw nothing but more flat rock running through hills like a path. Curving so that he could only see a few feet at a time.

Reminding him of a remote village he'd once stumbled upon in a foreign desert, a valley completely protected by three-hundred-sixty-degree mountain ranges.

And there was another tire print. He couldn't sit up, couldn't take a chance on other cameras being strategically hidden in the rocks towering above him. But he managed to pull his gun from his waistband and his phone from his pocket. They'd still had service on the road—the result of some satellite system.

He had to call Dom. To get drone surveillance out there. The tire prints would have to be evidence enough…

And he had no service.

He also had to turn around and go back, to make the call, and do things right this time. But as he made one slide to the side, he heard the loud crack of a gunshot.

Rocks crumbled not far from where his head had been, falling down on his hand, but he barely registered them. His ears were ringing, his brain was ringing, his heart was pounding…with the sound of a little girl's scream that had sounded right after a bullet flew.

# Chapter 23

With the sudden cry repeating like a discharging rifle in his brain, Ezra wasted no time. The shriek had carried bloodcurdling fear. No way would he turn his back on it.

Hugging the mountainside, his forearms pulled into his chest, holding his gun in front of his face, he used his elbows and his feet to propel himself quickly along the flat rock. The bullet had hit high, maybe a couple of feet above him. If he was lucky, it had come from a stationary gun with limited aim, and the ground would be out of range. He didn't need to tread slowly. He'd already been discovered.

The only thing that mattered was getting to that child before she was hidden away.

Or worse.

He'd heard only one scream.

Had no idea if Claire and Neve were even there. Could have been another little girl entirely.

Didn't much matter to him at that point.

The chilling terror in that scream required action. Two minutes later, he rounded a small bend and was transported to another world. A grassy clearing, several acres' worth. A private little valley in the mountains. An old farmhouse.

And…two little dark-haired people holding on to each other, and a tree, while a woman pulled at both of them.

Claire and Neve. Had to be.

And Jennifer?

Pulling his gaze from the children, he searched for Eric.

Stiffened at the loud crack of a shotgun being fired. Heard a bullet hit above and behind him, coming from the direction of what he was guessing was the trapdoor of a bunker. Eric was likely in the bunker using a telescoping rifle.

Another scream rang out, echoing across the valley. So closely surrounded by mountains as the area was, sounds would reverberate. Which was probably why Ezra had heard the sound at all.

His mind cataloged. Calculated. Possible positions of people. Sounds. The young girls he'd grown to care about in such a short time. Continuing extra carefully, aware that any small noise would travel, he rounded the side of the mountain and moved into the grassy clearing.

Those girls weren't going to be able to hold out much longer, and if the woman got them down in that bunker, trying to rescue them could push the unstable older couple to drastic measures.

They could also have an escape tunnel, with an unknown outlet, and a vehicle waiting to take them further off the grid.

He didn't see the brown van. Or any other vehicle.

One of the twins—Claire, based on the braided hair—lost her grip on the tree. Another scream pealed, and the woman gained ground, pulling the pair backward. Neve held on to the tree, Claire grasping her twin. And Ezra shot his gun on an angle, into the air.

A warning. A distraction. Hard to tell where it came from.

As he'd hoped, Jennifer—it had to be—loosened her grip on the twins just long enough for them to break free and run. Eric came around the trapdoor of the bunker, a rifle in one hand and a pistol in the other.

Jennifer also had a gun out, pointed, as she circled in place and then dashed behind a tree.

Ezra, aware of both of them, gave most of his attention to two pairs of the fastest running legs he'd ever seen. The children were heading for the house.

Pride filled him. As though he'd taught them himself. Keeping himself down was one of the hardest things he'd ever done, but he stayed in the prairie grass, working his way toward the old farmhouse, twisting his gun around and shooting upward and behind him.

His extended magazine held thirty bullets. He'd used up two. He was so far outgunned he'd be a dead man if he didn't think of some other way to get those children out of there.

And just like that, it came to him. *He* was their way out.

He had twenty-eight bullets to keep the Fitzgeralds more worried about intruders than about the kids. He had to make the grandparents feel as though they were surrounded. Keep them turning circles, while he got the twins' attention and sent them out to their mother.

And plan B—surrender himself to give the girls time to get out to their mother. Take whatever the Fitzgeralds handed out to him.

He'd risked his life many times for people he didn't even know.

He'd give it up in a heartbeat for Claire, Neve and Theresa Fitzgerald.

Clear plan.

Ezra moved, shot, moved more, shot again. His bullets flew from different trajectories to various parts of the compound, staying clear of the homestead. He was praying that the twins would run to the front of the house, keeping them out of view of their grandparents.

Ezra continued to shoot bullets that ricocheted off to the side of the structure. Carefully choosing his times, with pauses in between. He caught glimpses of the older couple, both with their backs to the house, watching their perimeter, keeping cover with trees that he realized had been strategically placed.

They'd planned for years. Had clearly practiced. Long before they'd even known the twins existed.

Above all else, they protected their safe space. Were focused and on task.

Reminded him of armies he'd fought.

And had fought in.

A semiautomatic unloaded into a mountainside.

Shots fired into the other side of the clearing.

They were gunning for him.

And if they thought the girls were safe for the moment, in the farmhouse, his plan would work.

If they even thought about the children at all. They'd let their son go rather than let go of the belief that they had to protect themselves from a nuclear blast at all cost...

He saw a flash of color near a small porch on the side of the house. Yellow. The twins had been wearing yellow shirts. Positioning himself behind a boulder in the yard, he grabbed a smaller rock and threw it toward the porch. Arched back, took a shot at the other side of the homestead perimeter and then threw another stone.

Ripped a piece of his shirt, tied it around one more rock and threw that. Letting the girls know that someone besides their grandparents was there. Hoping to God they'd peek to see who it was.

He was down to eleven bullets. And...

Neve peeked her head out.

He wasn't going to get another chance. Staying low, Ezra lifted his head, and one hand, above the grass. Saw Claire pop her head out, too. He motioned to the rock face that wound around the mountain and out to the road not far beyond.

Held up three fingers.

Counted them down and threw his hand in the direction he'd pointed. As both girls took off, Ezra stood up, running toward the house, and started shooting. One bullet headed toward Jennifer, a second later, one toward Eric, and then back toward Jennifer.

He shot until he ran out of bullets.

And then heard shots ring out toward him.

When the first bullets had been fired, Theresa had crawled from the back seat of the Jeep to the driver's side. Ezra had told her the day before to drive until she had cell service and call for help if she heard gunshots.

But if she left, and he came running back, needing a getaway, and she was gone...

Or if he sent the girls out to her...

She'd made a choice.

She'd stayed put.

And when the gunshots started to ring out in quick succession, and rapid fire joined in, she trembled, her heart thudding, and feared she'd made a gross, severely negligent error. She started the Jeep, but didn't move it.

Turned it off and jumped out.

She couldn't just sit there while someone killed the man she loved.

There was no long-term thought process on that one. Just a knowledge that prompted action. Seconds later, she was already at the first tire track when she heard footsteps.

Coming rapidly.

Frantically diving for an alcove in the mountain-side, she stood, panting, hardly able to breathe, knife in hand, and waited.

The noise came closer. More than one pair of feet.

Homesteaders protecting their territory? Thinking they were under attack?

Or...

Blood drained from her face, and she dropped the blade. Weak, thinking she was hallucinating, she watched first one dear little face come around the bend, and then the other.

"Neve! Claire!" She heard her joyful cry. Opened her arms.

But it wasn't until two trembling, crying little bodies plastered themselves against her, and four arms wrapped with strangulating strength around her neck, that she knew she wasn't dreaming.

"Are you two okay?" she asked, pulling back far enough to study both of them in rapid succession.

"I got gum in my hair," Neve said.

"It wasn't her fault, Mom," Claire added, her gaze wide and solemn, though her eyes were still wet with tears. "Grammy made her go to bed with it so she'd chew and not cry."

Theresa's stomach knotted, her heart ached, but... "But you aren't hurt?"

They both shook their heads, and she hugged them to her, never wanting to let go.

Ezra had done what he'd said he would do.

He'd sent her girls out to her.

Theresa barely managed to stay on her feet as she gathered those little bodies close, holding them as tightly as they held her. Her face wet, she buried it against dirty brown hair for one brief second. Then, shielding the children's bodies with her own, she quickly ushered the girls to the far side of the Jeep. Opening the back door, she helped them inside.

"Down on the floor and don't get up," she said. And then added, "I love you so much," before shutting the door after them.

"Wait!" Neve cried out, popping right back up and pulling on the door handle. Her sweet face wet with tears, she said, "You have to get Mr. Giant! They're going to hurt him!"

"Neve, get down here," Claire yelled. Theresa saw Neve's little body jerk downward, as though her twin had given her a huge pull.

God, she loved those kids.

Standing there at the Jeep, she glanced toward the flat rock face, not knowing what she'd see if she followed it. Looked at the driver's seat of the Jeep.

But in the split second, a sound—sirens—came from the distance. Approaching rapidly.

Looking up, she could hardly believe it when she saw several law enforcement vehicles, different colors from different agencies, converging upon them. Taking over the road, the cars parked all around and across from the Jeep.

Weak with relief, before she could fully process the fact that help had somehow arrived, she saw Dominic jumping out of a vehicle and running up to her.

"I've got the girls," she said. "Ezra's still in there. Lots of shots fired. Rapid-fire ones, too…"

He didn't say a word, didn't wait to hear any more, either.

He was gone before she could blink.

Theresa climbed into the back seat. Asked the girls to stay down, just in case, for a little bit. Not sure what, or who, Dom and his army of officers would be bringing out of the mountain. Not sure the state any of them would be in.

No matter what happened from there, she and her daughters were going to talk about Ezra for the rest of their lives, say continual thanks for him. None of them would ever forget who he was and what he'd done for them.

As if they could read her thoughts, the twins hugged her legs. Both girls were silent for once. They'd need to talk about what had happened, what they'd just seen, too, but not yet. With a hand on each of her very-much-alive daughters' backs, rubbing slowly, Theresa blinked back tears.

Uttering prayers for Ezra that hadn't been answered when Mark had been sick.

And waited.

She didn't have long to wait. Within minutes of disappearing around the rock face, officers were back with Jennifer and Eric Fitzgerald, the latter with a tourniquet tied around his hand, in custody. Looking for Ezra behind them, not seeing him, she felt her heart stop.

"Stay here and stay down," she told the girls. And then tapped Neve lightly on the shoulder and said, "I mean it. I'll be angrier at you than I've ever been if you so much as pop your head up, got it?"

The messy little head nodded, and as Theresa exited the vehicle, she saw the two six-year-olds holding hands.

"Paramedics are almost here." A female officer came up to her. "We can have them take a look at the girls…"

Theresa shook her head, not wanting the girls to face any more trauma. "Not now," she said. She'd have them checked, just to be safe, by the doctor they knew and liked back home.

At the moment, she needed to see Ezra come walking around that bend.

A few long seconds later, Dominic came forward, glancing back, and then stepping aside to let officers through carrying a long board by the corners. A makeshift stretcher.

With Ezra, blood covering his shirt, lying unconscious on top of it.

# Chapter 24

Antiseptic smell. Rhythmic swishing. Beep. Beep. Beep.

He'd rather sleep than deal with the noise. Ezra meant to drift off again, but couldn't quite let go. He had to know…

Had to know.

His eyes popped open. Claire and Neve.

With a swift glance around the room, he knew immediately that he was in the hospital. And that he was alone.

He remembered going into the valley compound. Telling the girls to run.

Running toward the old farmhouse as a distraction…

And then…nothing.

He fell asleep again and woke up sometime later. A look at the window told him it was daytime. The clock on the wall said seven.

Seven in the morning?

He'd been out overnight?

He tried to sit up, felt the immediate jabs of pain in his gut and lay back down.

Obviously he'd been hit.

How bad?

And most importantly...the girls.

Reaching for the call button hanging over the side of the bed, he saw his cell phone on the table beside him. Grabbed it.

Pushed speed dial.

"'Bout time you woke up," Dom answered on the first ring. "I sit there all night, leave for ten minutes to get a cup of coffee with Sami, and you call me," his brother continued, and as he spoke, Ezra could hear Dom's voice both over the phone and coming down the hall.

He'd said he was with Sami, but he came in the room alone, his expression serious, in spite of his tone, as he studied Ezra.

"What the hell, bro?" Dom said, shoving his phone in his pocket. "Coulda done without the scare..."

He shrugged. It hurt, but whatever. "Neve and Claire..."

"Are fine." Setting a foam coffee cup down on Ezra's table, Dom pulled up the only chair in the small, private room, where he'd obviously spent the night. "They've been checked out by their doctor and, other than understandable trauma from the unexpected separation from their mother, are doing well. They were glad to be home. Won't let Theresa out of their sight. Insisted on sleeping with her last night, I was told when she called to check on you, but overall...you saved the day."

Good. He was ready for that nap, then.

Turned his head, and when he woke again, Dom was still sitting there, scrolling on his phone. Clock said seven thirty. Still light outside. But nighttime?

"How bad am I?"

Glancing up, his brother said, "You'll live."

And when Ezra stared silently, Dom said, "You lost your spleen. Doc says four to eight weeks and you can get back to duty. I've already looked up army regulations and they allow for splenectomy when it's caused by trauma."

Relief flooded him, and he pushed the button on the bed to get himself more upright. He was still army.

Still capable.

And the better he followed orders, the sooner he'd be back with his troops.

"What about Eric and Jennifer Fitzgerald?"

"Ultimately it's up to the judge." Dom shrugged. "But Rachel is talking about recommending long-term mandatory psych admission for both of them, separately, with the possibility, sometime in the distant future, of supervised visitation, at the institution where they're locked up, with Claire and Neve if it's deemed to be a healthy choice for the twins."

He swallowed. Would have maybe taken the news in a more congenial manner if he hadn't been lying there without a spleen because of the older couple. From blood loss alone, he could have died. Because of them.

"Neither of them shot you," Dom said then.

And it occurred to Ezra to wonder, "How did it go down?" Had Theresa gotten him and the girls out of there? Had he stumbled out? Did she leave and go for help when she'd heard the first shot?

His lack of memory was pissing him off.

*Theresa.* The thought of her made him swallow. Hard.

"Funny thing," Dom said. "We had no idea you were there. We were following up on a lead... We took the van you messed up, ran forensics and found evidence that the Fitzgerald twins had been inside. And that it was registered to a guy who's been dead for thirty years. He had an old homestead on file, coordinates, not an address. Turns out the guy's son, Steve, is Eric's half brother, through their mother. But it was from Steve's father, who never married Eric's mother, that Eric was first turned on to doomsdaying when he was a young teen. And it was Steve's son, Jamison, Eric's half nephew, whose bunker you found yesterday. Jamison told us exactly where to find the old homestead when we hauled him in for withholding information in a kidnapping investigation. Steve is the one who shot you. The bullet was from his gun."

Wow. "Talk about all in the family..."

Dom nodded, gave Ezra a noncomedic half grin. "Guess we don't have a lot of room to talk, huh?"

Maybe. He hadn't been around enough to be all that close with his family in recent years. But when he came home, they certainly acted like he was one of them.

And...maybe he liked it.

Though a couple of hours later, he wasn't so sure about that. There were only so many visitors a guy could take, only so much mothering. Most particularly when there was only one woman he really needed to see right then.

And she wasn't there.

Theresa had to see Ezra. To assure herself that Dom had been telling her the truth that his triplet was going to be fine. But she couldn't leave her girls.

Claire and Neve were eating well. They'd slept well. They were playing, but the second she left the room, they stopped what they were doing and followed her.

Their first therapist appointment was already set for later in the week, but she knew there would be no quick or easy fix.

They'd been terrorized.

She got it.

Was up for it, for however long it took, to help them feel safe and secure again. When her children truly needed her, she was a mother first, a woman second. Her choice. In her world, the right choice.

And every second that passed that she wasn't at Ezra's side, she died a little inside, too.

When Isa showed up at a little past ten in the morning, two days after the shooting, pulling up to Theresa's little house, freshly painted but still in need of work, Theresa automatically assumed the worst. Met Isa on the front porch, with the door open and in full sight of the girls, but hopefully out of earshot.

"What happened?" she asked. "Is Ezra okay?"

Isadora Colton smiled, her beautifully elegant face showing genuine compassion, and maybe a bit of... pleasure as she sized up Theresa, who was standing there in an old cotton spaghetti-strap sundress that had aged about as gracefully as her house. "He's fine, dear," Isadora said. "A bit grumpy for my taste, but that's Ezra when he's feeling caged in. I think he'd like to see you, which is why I'm here. I know your sweet babies have been through a lot—Dom told me about them refusing to go to bed in their own room again last night. Certainly a hospital surgical ward is no place for them to be right now. I was thinking... They took such pleasure in being out at the Gemini, playing in the kids' hut and spending time with the horses, and if you wouldn't mind, I'd love to take them out for a visit while you go see my son."

Heart leaping into her throat, Theresa just had one thought… "Ezra said he wanted to see me?"

"No." Isadora shook her head. "You really think he'd come out and admit something like that?"

The question was rhetorical, but Theresa smiled then—a genuine, toe-to-scalp feeling of happiness—and said, "No, of course he wouldn't. And thank you. As long as the girls are comfortable with going…"

"Yes! Yes! Yes!" Claire and Neve jumped up in unison. Running to the door.

So much for out of earshot.

Half an hour later, Theresa stood outside Ezra's cracked-open hospital room door, shaking hard. She knocked, and blinked back tears when she heard his voice call, "Come in."

She couldn't stop tears from falling, though, when she saw her big, strong hero dressed in a tied-on hospital gown, propped up by pillows, with tubes taped to his skin.

"Looks worse than it is," he said, holding up his left arm and gesturing toward the IV bag. "This is done, just hanging around for another hour or so until they're convinced I don't need the pain meds they've been pumping through it. Switched to saline a couple of hours ago."

"Oh, Ezra…" She smiled, dropped to the edge of the one chair in the room, wanted so badly to touch him, hug him, kiss him, hold his hand. Instead, she held her own hands in her lap. "I just…"

Couldn't say most of what needed to have come tumbling out of her. Love meant thinking of those you loved as much as yourself. "I will never, ever be able to thank you…" She broke off. For saving her girls, first and foremost.

But for saving her, too. The days with him…making love with him. He'd shown her that while a part of her had died with Mark—the part that had seen them together forever—she'd become a different woman.

And that woman was still very much alive.

"Just doing my job, ma'am," he said with a shrug.

And while she knew she had to let him go, knew that he was a soldier who had to go out into the world and fight, she'd become a fighter, too.

"Technically, it was the FBI's job," she said. "And about a gazillion other law enforcement officials…" She let her voice trail off. Looked him in the eye, and when he looked back like he did, she couldn't turn away.

And knew she had to. But— "I just…would very much like it if maybe it would be possible for us to stay in touch," she said. "Even just a text now and then. Just to let me know you're safe."

"Sure." He smiled, though his expression seemed a bit cloudy. Medication, maybe. Or the pain.

"If you need anything," she said, "please call, this week, next, whenever…"

He nodded. The polite kind that said he would, but he never would. And then asked, "How are the girls? All I get out of Dom is 'fine.'"

She smiled then, spent the next five minutes telling him about the past forty-eight or so hours since he'd sent her back to the Jeep and left her there to rescue her children.

She'd heard bits and pieces of what had gone on at

the homestead in that little mountain valley and hoped
some of the details she'd heard through her six-year-
olds' perspectives were largely exaggerated, but feared
they were not. Ezra neither denied nor confirmed the
details. But he grinned from ear to ear when she told
him about his mother taking the twins to the Gemini.

"Great idea," he said. "Should have thought of it
myself."

As if he hadn't already done enough for them.

Silence fell. She feared she was outstaying her welcome and stood. She had to touch him, knowing that she
might never see him again. Leaning down, she kissed
his forehead. And then, because it would have seemed
wrong not to, brushed her lips across his, too. "Thank
you, Ezra. You gave me back my life and will always
hold an honored place in my heart."

With that, she turned and walked out the door.

Before she broke and begged him to let her stay.

Ezra watched her go. Stared at the door after she
left, too, because there was nothing else in the room
that he wanted. Why Theresa Fitzgerald had impacted
his head and heart so strongly, he had no idea. He'd
have bet every dime of his investments that he'd never
fall for one particular woman. But then, he'd have bet
against Dom ever doing so, too, and he'd have lost his
shirt on that one.

Not that Theresa was Ezra's Sami. There was no
happy ending for the two of them, and one seemed
pretty much a given with Dom and Sami. They weren't
just in love, both of them, with each other; their lives
also fit together, in spite of the fact that Dom had been

trying to take down Sami's father, and Sami's dad had died in the process. Sami loved Dom.

Theresa wasn't in love with him. She'd given him a place in her heart because of what he'd done for her girls. He'd take what she could give, remember her with fondness and get on with his life. Because while it had become clear over the past hours that Theresa and her daughters had a much more powerful pull on him than any need to travel the world, and while it had become clear that he felt much more strongly about being around to fight their battles with them rather than fighting for strangers, there was no way in hell he was putting her on the spot or misreading her gratitude. No way he'd make her feel bad by asking her for more than she had to give.

Her true love was a man who had died.

He'd known that going in.

And still...he'd gone.

He wasn't sorry about that.

Not even minus a spleen.

At that point in his thought process, he'd usually get up and go to the gym. Or paint a house. Strapped to the bed by the damned tube he no longer needed, Ezra reached for the call button, ready to tell someone, anyone, that if they didn't get the IV out of him, he'd remove it himself, but answered his phone when it rang instead.

*Rachel.* The one sister who hadn't already been in to see him. The next closest to him and Oliver and Dom in age. One of the few single births Isadora had carried. And the district attorney of Lark's County. Her schedule was intense.

"Hey, little sis, what's up?"

"First, I just wanted to hear for myself that you're as fine as Dom claimed you were."

"Unfortunately, I have to disagree with him there," he said, but he was doing it as much to be contrary as anything. "I'll be fine as soon as someone comes in here and gets this damned tube off my arm so I can go pee in peace. You're the DA—you got any pull here?"

"Yep, you're fine." She chuckled. Asked her version of the same questions he'd been fielding from family members all morning, and then said, "I've already talked to Dom, and will be calling Oliver next, but I wanted to let you know... You remember Clay Houseman?"

"The guy who confessed to the crimes Dad put Ronald Spence away for," Ezra said. He might have kept his distance from the family, but he knew every pertinent detail when it came to what mattered most.

"Yeah."

"What about him?"

"He was killed in a prison fight. Thing is, the guy he was fighting was also killed..."

Ezra's instincts barged full speed ahead. "That's not suspicious," he said with full-on sarcasm. "You think Spence had him killed to stop him from admitting that he paid Houseman to confess and take the fall for him?"

"Some of the others think so. And, yeah, I do, too. At least, I think it's absolutely a possibility that needs to stay on the table."

"This Spence guy. He's close. Right here in town, from what I hear. You be careful, Rach."

"Always."

His sister rang off with her usual "love you" to him,

but this time, when he said it back, he wasn't just spouting words he'd been saying all his life.

He was thinking about what they meant.

He loved his family.

And, whether he liked it or not, he needed them, too. He'd let himself think for years that he didn't. They'd never seemed to require much from him, either.

Or maybe he'd just been a scared ass who'd refused to love so deeply that you could hurt until you wished you'd never been born.

He'd been in town a couple of weeks, and aside from the past few days hunting down Theresa's children, he could have been using his backdoor skills to see what he could find on Spence. He hadn't done so.

But he wasn't going to let his family down again. From what he'd been told by the doctor who'd stopped in to see him earlier, and others, too, it would be eight weeks before he'd be released to go back into the field. That gave him eight weeks to see what he could find on Ronald Spence.

The man had better watch out.

He was soon to have a very determined, very frustrated hunter on his trail.


Theresa took an extra few minutes for herself, stopping for an iced coffee, before heading out to the Gemini to pick up the girls. While she was edgy being away from them, she knew that their path to security and mental health was through her.

She couldn't overprotect them or she'd make them fearful of being out of her sight. The Fitzgeralds hadn't wanted to hurt the twins, not that she'd been to see them or spoken to them since their arrest. But by all accounts, they'd wanted to protect Claire and Neve. And too much of anything could be bad.

But maybe, if they were committed to a psychiatric facility rather than prosecuted and put in jail, they'd get to the point where the girls could visit them. When Claire and Neve were old enough to better understand the nuances of what had happened to them. Hopefully Claire and Neve would then be able to further put to rest the horror of the past few days.

Antsy about leaving them for too long lest they start to lose interest in the horses and start to fret without her, she dumped the rest of her coffee and barely managed to keep her old van down to the speed limit as she headed out to the ranch.

The twins weren't waiting for her. In fact, their faces fell when they saw her and realized it was time to leave. "We were going to have another ride on the horses," Neve said, but the little girl was clinging to Theresa's arm like she never wanted to let her go.

Claire, always the practical one, but also clinging to Theresa, looked up at Isa and asked, "May we have that second ride at a different time, Mrs. Isa?"

"Mrs. Isa?" Theresa glanced at the blonde who was smiling, so clearly enjoying herself that she let the name go.

"Of course," Isa said. "As long as your mom says it's okay?"

"Can we? Can we?" the girls said in unison, and looking into those uplifted little faces—one freckled, one not—reading the happiness in their eyes at the prospect of another trip to the ranch, there was no way Theresa could refuse them.

"Yay!" they both cried out, and then ran to get the

swimsuits they'd brought with them in case the sun came out and they could get in the pool.

Claire carried the bag Theresa had hurriedly packed for the girls earlier. Neve had a big envelope in her hand. Sealed, she showed Theresa when she walked up. "We made it for Ezra," she said, and the second the three of them were belted into the van, both children started begging to stop by the hospital to give Ezra his card before they went home.

"He did save our lives, Mom," Claire said, quite solemnly. "And Mrs. Isa said he gets visitors, 'cept we can't bring Charlie like we do when we visit rooms on Tuesdays."

And, as Claire had so deftly pointed out without actually doing so, her daughters were no strangers to rooms with frail human bodies. They were no strangers to illness, period.

"All right," she told them, partially because she couldn't find the wherewithal to tell them no. And partly, she knew, because it gave her a legitimate opportunity to see Ezra one more time.

Ezra, in sweatpants and that hospital gown, was sitting in the chair by his bed. He was planning his own hospital breakout—seriously, one more night and he was gone—when he heard a bump against his door, followed by whispering.

"Can we come in?" Theresa's voice.

"Hell, yes" turned into "Hellyes—oh" as he saw the two faces peeking around the door at him. When he smiled, they pushed through, practically marching toward him, their mother lagging behind.

Neve carried a card, a get-well wish from their family, he surmised. But when Claire said, "Neve," both stopped a couple of feet in front of him, and Neve gave the envelope to Claire.

"I'm sorry for the intrusion," Theresa said, as Ezra, brows raised, watched the scene unfold. "They insisted…"

He didn't want an apology. Or for her to feel one was even necessary.

"Hey, you two," he said. He kept his face serious as they looked in his direction, recognizing that the rush of emotion he was experiencing was a new kind of love to him. A protective, die-for-you, paternal kind of love. "You know what Purple Hearts are?" he asked, spouting out something he'd thought of earlier.

Theresa stopped halfway into the room, standing a few feet behind her daughters. He saw her, was inordinately pleased to have her back, but mostly was engrossed by the two sets of wide brown eyes as the twins slowly shook their heads.

"It's a medal only the bravest and strongest soldiers earn. And as a sergeant, I decide sometimes who gets one. While I can't give you an army one, because, well, you aren't in the army, I've decided, as sergeant, to give you my very own Colton Purple Hearts for what you did the other day."

The girls looked at each other, and then turned around, in tandem, and looked toward their mother. Her eyes brimmed with tears, but she smiled hugely, too, and they turned back to Ezra.

"What you two did, following my clues when I threw the rocks, and then following my signals and running so fast without stopping…that makes you both the bravest, strongest six-year-olds ever, and I don't ever want you to forget that. That's why, when I get out of here, I'm going to bring you your medals."

He'd get to see them all one more time. Which was great, too.

But… "That way, whenever you remember what happened, and some of the kind of scary stuff, you can always look at your medals and remember what you did and how great that was. You can remember that you're strong and brave and that's why you don't have any reason to be afraid. Deal?"

They nodded. Neve nudged Claire, and Theresa's so-serious daughter took one step forward, handing him the envelope she held.

The envelope she'd insisted that Neve give her.

"It's from both of us." Neve stepped up next to her sister. "We made it."

"Shhh, Neve, don't give it away," Claire told her.

"Open it, Mr. Giant!" Neve said then, shifting from one little tennis-shoed foot to the other. "We were at your ranch today and rode the horses again because Mrs. Isa took us and that's why we had to wear jeans," the girl said.

"And that's where we made the card," Claire added.

He was taking his time with opening the envelope. Making a production out it for their sake, but also because he didn't want to rip it. Didn't matter to him what was inside. The twins had made it for him, so it would be sacred. Would travel with him from land to land, a memento to hang next to his bunk. A lot of guys had them: pictures of families or girlfriends, mostly, sometimes a card.

The twins' card would be his first.

He pulled it out slowly. Also for production. Sort of.

Mostly because when he caught sight of the display inside, the hearts and stars, all traced and colored, surrounding four slightly crooked handwritten words, he had to choke back his own tears.

"It's the Best Second Daddy Award!" Neve blurted, as though he couldn't read what she'd written.

"Because you were like our daddy, coming to save us," Claire said then. And Ezra had no choice but to hold out his arms and catch the kids who hurled themselves against his stitched midsection.

The pain didn't faze him.

The idea of leaving those two girls, of not being some part of their lives, hurt worse than the bullet that had seared his gut.

Theresa needed a hug, too. Ezra knew from the look he glimpsed over her daughters' shoulders. Grabbing the bag of handheld video games Naomi had brought him earlier that day, he gave them to Neve and Claire. And they were soon huddled in a corner of the room, consumed by the sack's contents.

He heard their voices. Heard Neve exclaiming and then asking questions, which Claire patiently answered. But his focus was on Theresa. She'd come to pick up the card her daughters had made. Was studying it with tears in her eyes.

"I take it you hadn't seen it?" he asked as she settled back to the side of his bed.

She shook her head, was still looking at the paper, not at him, and he had to say, "I'll always be there for you and the girls." Even as he heard the words, he knew they weren't right. And weren't enough. "I'll always have their backs," he added. "All you have to do is call."

He'd take leave, do whatever he had to, to help. "I know I'm not the man you all want most, but I've come to realize that being second best is still a win. And it's far better than not placing at all."

Instead of Theresa smiling, thanking him, her chin trembled, and tears dripped down her cheeks. "I loved Mark," she told. "I still love his memory. But I'm no longer the woman he married. I'm no longer his wife. That part of me died with him, and…his illness, his death, raising the girls alone…this past year… It's all made me a new woman. A changed woman. And…" She drew a shuddering breath. Let it out and said, "I know you have to go, Ezra, but please know that, with me, with the woman I am now, you will never come second. Not ever."

He couldn't be sure he was understanding her right. And couldn't blame his confusion on pain meds, because he hadn't had any since early morning. He stared up into her gaze and remembered the way she'd said his name right before she'd shown him that sex was far, far more than mere physical pleasure.

"I might be out of line here, but…what if I didn't have to go?"

He wasn't sure what he was saying. And yet when he voiced the words, they weren't a shock to him.

"Of course you have to go. There's no battle here, no army, no…" She stopped talking. Stared at him.

"I'm thinking that I've been running long enough. Frankly, that I've been running from what I most wanted—the family life I'd believed I had until I was sixteen. A life that's probably always been here. I just cut out when times got tough. But I think I'm done cutting out…"

Dropping to her knees at his feet, taking his hands,

Theresa looked up at him, eyes wide open and serious. "Don't do this for me, Ezra," she said. "Seriously, I'll be here. I'll wait. I'll marry you or not. I'll deal with the fear of you being gone if it means that, when you can, you'll be back. Like you, I don't want to spend my life running from the fear of being hurt."

Ezra knew how to defeat enemies. But he had no idea how to deal with the intense emotions love caused in him, how to let himself just experience or express them.

"I might need a place to stay while I recover." He blurted the best version he could communicate of what he was feeling. "I can always go to Mom's, but…"

He was unprepared for the face that launched up at him, but when his lips were overtaken by Theresa's, he knew exactly what to do.

There were things that had to be worked out. Details to handle. Conversations to have. And adjustments to make.

But he didn't have a single doubt that, with him and Theresa working together as a team, they'd get it all done.

And maybe even, someday, add a set of triplets or two to their own branch of the Colton family.

\* \* \* \* \*

## #2191 COLTON'S SECRET SABOTAGE
*The Coltons of Colorado*
by Deborah Fletcher Mello

Detective Philip Rees is determined to catch the person leaking secrets to the Russian mob. When television producer Naomi Colton wrangles him for her reality TV series, saying no isn't an option. He can't risk blowing his cover, so sliding into the saddle and her heart are his only options.

## #2192 OPERATION PAYBACK
*Cutter's Code* • by Justine Davis

The Foxworth Foundation has stepped in to help Trip Callen before, so when a brutal crime boss targets him, they're willing to step in again. He doesn't know they're helping him because of a past connection to Kayley McSwain, the woman he's beginning to care more for than he ever expected. Will Cutter and the Foxworths be able to keep them both safe?

## #2193 AMBUSH AT HEARTBREAK RIDGE
*Lost Legacy* • by Colleen Thompson

When a family vanishes in the dangerous wilderness, Sheriff Hayden Hale-Walker will stop at nothing to find them before it's too late, even if that means calling Kate McClafferty, the former lover with the search-and-rescue skills he needs—regardless of the long-buried secrets that put their hearts at risk.

## #2194 HER DANGEROUS TRUTH
*Heroes of the Pacific Northwest* • by Beverly Long

Lab scientist Layla Morant is on the run—until a car accident threatens not only her identity but also her life. She can't allow herself to be found, but her injuries need immediate attention. And Dr. Jaime Weathers is determined to help her, not knowing the danger he's putting himself in...

"If it's necessary," he said, undoing Banner's lead rope, "I'll take care of business."

"Maybe I should take that for you, Hayden. Since you're—"

Tossing aside his ruined hat, he gave her a look of disbelief. "Have you lost your ever-loving mind? I'm not handing you my gun. It might be your job to find these people, but I'm sworn to protect them. And you, for that matter."

"I get that, but I don't believe you're currently fit to make a life-and-death call or even to be riding."

Turning away from her, he grabbed a handful of Banner's mane along with the saddle horn and shoved his boot into the stirrup before swinging aboard the gray.

If it were anyone else, she might have missed the way he slightly overbalanced and then hesitated, recovering for a beat or two, giving her time to mount her mule to face him.

"You're clearly dizzy. I can see it," she challenged. "So please, Hayden, you need to—"

The engines' noise abruptly dropped off, but they could still barely make out the low rumble of the motors idling. With the ravine's rocky face amplifying the sound, she knew it was tricky to judge distance. Though the vehicles couldn't be far, they might be just literally around the next bend in the creek or more than half a mile downstream.

Before Kate could regain her train of thought, shouts, followed by an anguished human cry—definitely a woman's—carried from the same direction. The terror in it had Kate's breath catching, her nerve endings standing at attention.

"Call for assistance. *Now!*" Hayden ordered before kicking Banner's side and leaning forward.

*Don't miss*
Ambush at Heartbreak Ridge *by Colleen Thompson,*
*available August 2022 wherever*
*Harlequin Romantic Suspense books and*
*ebooks are sold.*

Harlequin.com

# Get 4 FREE REWARDS!

We'll send you 2 FREE Books plus 2 FREE Mystery Gifts.

FREE
Value Over
$20

Both the **Harlequin Intrigue**® and **Harlequin**® Romantic Suspense series
feature compelling novels filled with heart-racing action-packed romance
that will keep you on the edge of your seat.

---

**YES!** Please send me 2 FREE novels from the Harlequin Intrigue or Harlequin
Romantic Suspense series and my 2 FREE gifts (gifts are worth about $10
retail). After receiving them, if I don't wish to receive any more books, I can
return the shipping statement marked "cancel." If I don't cancel, I will receive
6 brand-new Harlequin Intrigue Larger-Print books every month and be billed
just $5.99 each in the U.S. or $6.49 each in Canada, a savings of at least 14%
off the cover price or 4 brand-new Harlequin Romantic Suspense books every
month and be billed just $4.99 each in the U.S. or $5.74 each in Canada, a
savings of at least 13% off the cover price. It's quite a bargain! Shipping and
handling is just 50¢ per book in the U.S. and $1.25 per book in Canada.*
I understand that accepting the 2 free books and gifts places me under no
obligation to buy anything. I can always return a shipment and cancel at any
time. The free books and gifts are mine to keep no matter what I decide.

Choose one: ☐ **Harlequin Intrigue**          ☐ **Harlequin Romantic Suspense**
        **Larger-Print**              (240/340 HDN GNMZ)
        (199/399 HDN GNXC)

Name (please print)

Address                                                                                    Apt. #

City                          State/Province                          Zip/Postal Code

Email: Please check this box ☐ if you would like to receive newsletters and promotional emails from Harlequin Enterprises ULC and
its affiliates. You can unsubscribe anytime.

### Mail to the **Harlequin Reader Service:**
**IN U.S.A.:** P.O. Box 1341, Buffalo, NY 14240-8531
**IN CANADA:** P.O. Box 603, Fort Érie, Ontario L2A 5X3

Want to try 2 free books from another series! Call 1-800-873-8635 or visit www.ReaderService.com.

---

*Terms and prices subject to change without notice. Prices do not include sales taxes, which will be charged (if applicable) based
on your state or country of residence. Canadian residents will be charged applicable taxes. Offer not valid in Quebec. This offer is
limited to one order per household. Books received may not be as shown. Not valid for current subscribers to the Harlequin Intrigue
or Harlequin Romantic Suspense series. All orders subject to approval. Credit or debit balances in a customer's account(s) may be
offset by any other outstanding balance owed by or to the customer. Please allow 4 to 6 weeks for delivery. Offer available while
quantities last.

**Your Privacy**—Your information is being collected by Harlequin Enterprises ULC, operating as Harlequin Reader Service. For a
complete summary of the information we collect, how we use this information and to whom it is disclosed, please visit our privacy notice
located at corporate.harlequin.com/privacy-notice. From time to time we may also exchange your personal information with reputable
third parties. If you wish to opt out of this sharing of your personal information, please visit readerservice.com/consumerschoice or
call 1-800-873-8635. **Notice to California Residents**—Under California law, you have specific rights to control and access your data.
For more information on these rights and how to exercise them, visit corporate.harlequin.com/california-privacy.

HIHRS22